I
could
see that mist
swirling and
swelling toward
me. I should have got-
ten back into the car and
waited it out...but I've got
a bit of an emotional issue
about being trapped
in a car.

was coming after
me. But I could
outrun it.

I
looked
out of the
window again,
thought of all the
times the rain had kept
me trapped here. The one time
I wanted it to trap me, just for a
while, just so I could sleep for a bit,
the rain was a no-show. A fist against
my window. I see a face; a woman's
face. I have a memory of a time I
was safe in a car and a woman,
already bleeding from the
rain, tried to get in.

I
see my
mom; I
see my mom's
hand reaching out
into the rain, trying
to help someone. My
mom ... my mom
...my mom.

I
am
thou-
sands of
breaths away
from you... Oh
Mom...my mom...
these thousands of
breaths? Every one
of them hurts.

Praise for Virginia Bergin's *H2O*
A *VOYA* Perfect Ten Book of 2014!

"[*H2O*] brings life and humor to an otherwise dark situation. Reminiscent of classic post-apocalyptic and dystopian novels from Michael Crichton to Stephen King to Lois Lowry to Suzanne Collins. A great, high-interest read for contemporary teens."
—*VOYA*

"Creepy and realistic. *H2O* left me thirsting for more."
—Kristen Simmons, author of *Article 5* and *Breaking Point*

"Ruby's candid, addicting narration brought this terrifying and wholly plausible story to life. This is a book you'll devour all at once—from the safety of your umbrella!"
—Jessica Khoury, author of *Origin* and *Vitro*

"It's a gripping concept, and there's something particularly terrifying about the end of the world coming in something as sweet as a misty drizzle. Ruby's narrative voice is exceptional."
—*The Bulletin of the Center for Children's Books*

"Watching Ruby draw strength from her ability to tell her own story is as inspiring as it is harrowing."
—*The Horn Book Magazine*

"Attention to detail, coupled with a very strong main character, will draw readers in and make them think twice about leaving the house—at least not before checking the sky for signs of rain."
—*School Library Journal*

ALSO BY VIRGINIA BERGIN

H2O

THE STORM

VIRGINIA BERGIN

sourcebooks
fire

Published by Sourcebooks Fire, an imprint of Sourcebooks, Inc.
P.O. Box 4410, Naperville, Illinois 60567-4410
(630) 961-3900
Fax: (630) 961-2168
www.sourcebooks.com

Originally published in 2015 in the United Kingdom by Macmillan Children's Books, an
imprint of Macmillan Publishers Limited.

The Library of Congress has cataloged the hardcover edition as follows:

Names: Bergin, Virginia.
Title: The storm / Virginia Bergin.
Description: Naperville, Illinois : Sourcebooks Fire, 2015. | Sequel to: H20.
    | Summary: Fifteen-year-old Ruby's fight for survival continues in a
    post-apocalyptic world where the rain is deadly.
Identifiers: LCCN 2015032242 | (13 : alk. paper)
Subjects: | CYAC: Water--Fiction. | Survival--Fiction. | Bacterial
    diseases--Fiction. | Science fiction.
Classification: LCC PZ7.B452214 St 2015 | DDC [Fic]--dc23 LC record available at
http://lccn.loc.gov/2015032242

Printed and bound in the United States of America.
WOZ 10 9 8 7 6 5 4 3 2 1

For Karen, John, and Sue

'll tell you a weird thing about apocalypses, a thing I didn't even know until I was in one.

They seem pretty bad, don't they?

Well, take it from me…

They can always get worse.

My name is Ruby Morris. I hate rain.

CHAPTER ONE

I was sinking.

That's how it is when you're all alone and there's been a global apocalypse and you're just hoping your dad is going to show up like he said he would but there's no sign of him so what exactly are you going to do if your dad doesn't come and every day you try hard not to think about that because...

Everything's going to be OK

is what you have to keep telling yourself but some part of you or maybe it's all of you thinks it isn't going to be OK so you try not to think at all but you can't stop thinking because pretty much everyone is dead and you've got nowhere to go and no one to go anywhere with and anyway who wants to go anywhere when THE SKY IS RAINING DEATH?

Yes, in an apocalypse-type situation, it's very easy to think bad things. In fact, there's SO much time for thinking, it's really easy to slide way beyond even regular apocalypse-type thinking into TOTAL COMPLETE AND UTTER DOOM THINKING... because there's about a million days when you're stuck inside because it's raining killer rain or it looks like it's going to rain killer rain or you just can't face another day in the library.

Yup, that's how bad things got: I broke into Dartbridge Public Library. Studying up on clouds (I know twenty-four different types!) didn't seem like it was going to be enough to get me through this thing. (Through it and into what? That was a whole other question, one best not asked.) My specialist areas of study were:

1. The self-help section. Oddly, there didn't seem to be that much on feeling a bit gloomy because human life on Earth as we know it has been wiped out—but you could tell people meant well. Ruby usefulness rating: 4/10.
2. Microbiology for people who quit biology at the end of eighth grade, weren't really all that interested in science, and weren't any good at it anyway. It's baffling and creepy. Ruby rating: 1/10.
3. Car maintenance for people who would have dropped that too if they'd tried to teach it to us in school (which they should have done). I would not have chosen to study this, but something happened. I'll explain later. Ruby rating: 10/10.
4. Survival manuals. Frankly, I could have learned most of this stuff when I was in Girl Scouts, but I tended to opt for the cake-making side of things (the benefits seemed more obvious at the time). However, not even the SAS (the Special Air Service = very, very good-at-surviving-stuff British Army crack force), who have handy tips on surviving a nuclear bomb going off right next to you, seem to have been able to have imagined this particular kind of disaster. Or maybe they did, but when people saw the chapter on how the army would abandon anyone they had no use for and we'd all be left to fend for ourselves, they complained that it was an outrage and a lie and the

SAS were forced to take it out. (Even though it was TRUE.) Nevertheless, Ruby rating: 7/10 (because you never know).

5. Oh, and…one particularly sad and lonely day, I had a quick look at cellular telecommunications. There are no phones and no Internet anymore, so I was just curious, I suppose, about how difficult it'd be to build and run a thing like that. (Quite difficult, I think. Judging from the diagrams.) Ruby rating: 0/10.

My cell phone is at the top of a list of all the things there'll be no more of (currently 402 items long with the recent shock addition of chocolate spread; I was scooping the last fingerful out from under the rim of a jar when I realized supplies *will* eventually run out).

There are no people on this list. Their names, the names of the dead, are written on my heart. My small, sad, human heart. Hurt so bad it will never cry again.

Don't get me wrong. I cry. I cry plenty. I howl! But my heart? It is all cried out. It is silent.

I don't do pets anymore either. Apart from the risk that a single sloppy lick from a puddle drinker could kill you, they're nothing but heartbreak and trouble…and they're ganging up. There are probably small, mean teams of guinea pigs and rabbits, but the dogs are certainly hanging out together—I've seen packs of them roaming—and I've even seen *loose affiliations** of cats. Not Ruby,

---

* A very useful term: here's how I learned it:

TEACHER: So, although Molly Stevens is your friend, you're saying you don't know why she's not in PE?

ME: Well…

TEACHER: Just try to answer the question, Ruby.

ME: I wouldn't exactly say we're friends friends…

TEACHER: So… (sighs) despite the fact that I see you in each other's company every single day, you're claiming you're not… (sighs again; does little quote-mark wiggles with exasperated fingertips) "friends" friends, you're saying you're just loosely affiliated?

ME: (Pause) That would be correct?

though—that's Mrs. Wallis's Siamese; she doesn't affiliate herself with anyone. She's still hanging around in a strictly unaffiliated sort of way, and she seems to be doing OK, though I sincerely hope her well-fed appearance has got nothing to do with the disappearance of Mrs. Wallis's shih tzu Mimi (last seen absconding from a car in the school parking lot and running in the direction of home), or indeed with the disappearance of Mrs. Wallis herself.

There is a shorter list of things I'm glad there'll be no more of, currently twelve items long. Exams come top, which I never would— "come top of the class," geddit?—so that's why they are *numero uno*. This list is a lot harder to think of stuff for, so it's brilliant when I do come up with something. The last time I thought of something— "No one can stop me from drinking whatever I like whenever I like!"—I drank to celebrate. I hit my mom's gin.

I remember standing, swaying, at the open front door, watching the rain pour down. I think I was talking to it. I wouldn't have been saying nice things.

When I woke up the next morning, alive, I crossed the drink thing off the list.

The thing about going a little crazy is it's hard to realize that's what's happening.

I stopped going to the library. (What do the SAS know? They're buffoons!) I stopped doing anything much, other than things I absolutely had to do—and even my grip on those got a bit shaky. I'd get up and think, *I must clean my teeth*…and it'd be bedtime before I got around to it—although bedtime itself got a little flexible. Sometimes it happened in the middle of the day; sometimes it happened all day. And sometimes, when it was supposed to be bedtime, because it was the middle of the night, it didn't happen at all.

4

One such night, I shaved my hair off. All of it. It seemed easier to do that than wash it. Easier, even, than trying to find a can of dry shampoo with anything left in it—when in any case, just like chocolate spread, supplies *will* run out eventually, so why not face facts? That's what I imagine I was thinking…when really I don't remember thinking anything much, just picking up my (looted) battery-powered lady shaver…and watching grubby clump-lettes of (dyed) black hair fall.

It should have been the head shaving that alerted me to how serious my situation was. Bit of a clue there. But all I ended up doing was adding the result to one of my other lists: the list of stupid things I've done.

That one's not written down either; it's just burned on my brain. It hurts.

My shaved head looked like a small, fuzzy globe, a planet…inside which strange things happened. Below the spiky surface, dark, wordless thoughts massed, rose, and sunk. Popped up again, doing the backstroke. Giggling. Or hidden deep in the goo of my mind, screaming messages that bubbled up, garbled.

All day, every day, all night, every night, my head simmered with nonsense. Sometimes it boiled. Until finally, there didn't seem to be anything very much left inside my head at all. Boiled dry, I guess. I don't think the thoughts had words anymore. First off, even the sensible, normal ones got texty: "I must clean my teeth" became "clean teeth." Then it was just "teeth." Then, when the words had pretty much stopped altogether, it was probably just "🦷."

I was lost on Planet Ruby, where weeks and days and hours and minutes and seconds (there were some very long seconds) got muddled—and dreams and reality got muddled too. And nightmares, but they were pretty much only about as awful as what was real.

And it might have all gone on and on like that until I really did walk out in the rain (then it would stop), but finally SOMETHING HAPPENED TO ALERT ME TO HOW SERIOUS MY SITUATION WAS...

I crashed a Ferrari. Totaled it.

I was flooring it, coming around a bend (up on Dartmoor, I was about to realize), when I hit a patch of mist, part of which turned out not to be mist but a sheep, so I swerved and—

SCREECH!

KA-BLAM!

BOUFF!

The airbag thing smashed into my face. Only somehow my own hands had gotten involved.

OK, I know how. I like to do this fancy cross-hands thing when I'm turning corners. So, yeah, my own arms got biffed into my face by the airbag.

I sat there. Punched face screaming. Dazed—double dazed, because you want to know a terrible thing? I wasn't even sure about how I'd gotten there. I mean, I must have thought I should get out of the house for a bit—to go on an I-need-something-to-drink mission, most probably. (Supplies always seemed to be running low, but that was probably because time was running weird: one minute I'd have plenty of cola or whatever, and the next minute I'd be draining dregs and panicking.) But since I often thought I should do something and didn't do it or thought something had happened when it hadn't actually happened, I was seriously shocked to realize that this crash thing, apparently, *had* really happened. Though I only knew it for sure because IT HURT. OWWW. ARRRGH. OWWWWW.

WAKE UP, RUBY! WAKE UP!

The car was wrecked; I didn't even have to try to start it again— which I did—to know that. It had made out with a wall. They didn't like each other. Not one bit.

I got out of the car. My eyes were already stinging like something nasty had been flung into them. I put my hand up to my bashed nose and felt blood. I looked at the blood on my fingertips; then I squinted at the thing that would like to eat that blood.

Mist's a funny old thing, isn't it? Basically, it's just a cloud that's hit rock bottom. A cloud (stratus nebulosus, doncha know) that can no longer be bothered to get up into the sky. It drags its sorry self along the ground. Funny? It's hilarious, really: Is it going to kill you, or isn't it? How much of it—*exactly*—would have to settle on your skin before…

I could see that mist swirling and swelling toward me. I should have gotten back into the car and waited it out…but I have an *emotional issue* about being trapped in a car—particularly, in this case, one that had just SMASHED into a wall; probably anyone left alive in Devon would have heard that crash. Some scary someone-anyone could have been on their way to investigate. So—add this to the list of stupid things!—I didn't wait. I ran.

All I could think was: *it* was coming after me. *But I could outrun it.*

I bolted across the moor. I scrambled up—up—up. Up rocks. Up-up-up. Up-up-up. Stupid-stupid-stupid Ruby. Up-up-up.

Until there was no more up.

I knew I was at the top of Hay Tor not because I'm, like, really keen on long, rambling walks in scenic landscapes, but because there was no place higher to go; anyone who lives in Dartbridge knows this place because you can see it for miles around—when it's clear.

I stood on the rocks, where there was no place up—**no** place, no other or farther or higher place—watching the mist rise around me, puffing itself up like it was just remembering it could be a cloud that could get on up into that sky and rain.

I wiped at my throbbing nose, saw blood on the back of my hand. What if it could *smell* it? What if all those little wiggly-legged bacterium ET microblobs could smell my blood? What if they were all now paddling away like mad, waving their little tentacles, letting out little microsqueals of joy at the scent of breakfast?

I didn't know how that would be, having that *thing*, that disgusting little blood-gobbling, world-murdering *thing* get me slowly.

Bad? Very bad? Unimaginably, excruciatingly bad?

And lonely.

I was going to die alone on Hay Tor. My body would be pecked at by crows, nibbled on by sheep bored of grass. Foxes would come and have a good old chew on my bones—maybe drag a few back to the den for the cubs. Someone someday would put my rain-eaten, worm-licked, weather-worn skull on top of the highest stone, and Hay Tor would get a whole new name: Stupid Dead Girl Hill.

I stood. I roared.

No, that's just what I'd like to say I did.

I lost it.

I stood and I whimpered, and in the mist in front of me through stinging, weeping eyes, I saw the shadow of a someone-anyone. Fear crackled through me.

No one moved.

And they'd die if they stayed there, swallowed by the mist—and I felt my arms waving and I heard my own wrecked voice shouting, "COME ON!"

And the shadow-being waved back. She waved back.

And I saw she was me and wasn't real at all.

And I sat down on the rocks, weeping.

And the shadow girl sat too…and melted. She went away. Almost as quickly as she had appeared, she disappeared.

I knew what she was. I'd seen her in the cloud book. A rare thing—called a "brocken specter," when you see your own shadow in a cloud. Enough to spook anyone out. More than enough to spook me.

The mist went with her—the shadow ghost of me—burning off in the sun, until I was just a stupid girl with a punched face, sitting alone on Hay Tor.

Wake up, Ruby Morris.

CHAPTER TWO

I came down off the moor, half-blinded and face hurting and neck hurting and everything hurting, and headed straight for home.

I wound down through country lanes, blinking faster than a strobe light, face scrunching with pain, and trying not to wipe my stinging eyes. Still I fumbled about, opening every field gate I passed. I'd been doing that for weeks: opening gates, opening up chicken coops (you don't want to think how any survived: Attack of the Cannibal Chickens). Sometimes there'd been creatures in the fields—horses, pigs, cows, sheep, llamas (those had been real; the herd of unicorns I thought I'd released probably wasn't)—sometimes not. Still, I opened them.

So I suppose it was probably me that let the sheep out, the one that had nearly killed me.

(See what I did there? I blame it on the sheep.)

First farm I came to, I tried to go in. I wasn't even thinking "🚗." I was thinking "👁👁." They hurt so bad, and they wouldn't stop weeping, and I was scared that if I didn't find something to wash them with immediately, I wouldn't be able to see at all.

A scrawny sheepdog came out into the yard and barked at me.

I know the type; they won't attack you. They're just telling you: this is not your house.

"You good girl," I said—or tried to. Since the picture thoughts had taken over, I didn't even speak to myself out loud anymore, and even though I had just shouted at my own shadow, my voice came out all broken up and ragged and weird.

"Good girl," I tried again, and me and the dog, whose bark also seemed a little strained and peculiar (it could just have been the shock of seeing someone), both stared miserably at each other—except it was getting harder and harder by the second to stare at anything.

"Please…" I begged, but no way was the good girl—who might have been a boy—going to let me in that house.

I drove back home on a tractor. The good girl wasn't too sure about that either, but she gave me the benefit of the doubt. She even followed me, as if she thought it might be time to go to work or something…but that skinny girl, she couldn't keep up. She barked at me to stop and wait for her, but I couldn't. I didn't. I didn't even want to hear that bark.

Dogs, animals…people…they'll break your heart.

I zoomed home on that tractor, so high up on that driver's seat that over the banks and hedgerows, I could make out blurry fields. I didn't feel hemmed in and spooked like I normally do, not knowing what might be around the next bend. Even if we smacked into a wall, the wall would come off worse.

Blind Farmer Ruby, rollin' along. And whatever I might have rolled over, I didn't see it. I just felt the occasional bump. There is some terrible stuff lying about these days.

I made myself dump the tractor at the end of our road because I was worried if I went any farther, it'd get stuck between the lines of cars and I'd lose an exit route. I dumped it and I ran, my eyes so blind, my hands so shaky I could hardly get the key in the lock.

I stepped inside the house and called, "*Dad?!*"
Yeah. That'd be the last time.

I slurped cola and washed my eyes with the tiny bit of water I had left. Couldn't even see anything much in the mirror, just a blurry version of my face that looked like it felt: puffy, red, and busted. I squinted at one particular mark on my cheek. Double circles. Matched my watches. (I wore four: two digital, two wind up—don't ask.) Perfect imprints of one wrist's worth on my cheek. But it was my eyes that looked weirdest.

"Love! You look like Joe Bugner," Grandma Hollis once said to me, at the time when I'd first been told my mom and dad were splitting up and I'd cried so much my eyes puffed up.

I didn't know who Joe Bugner was; I still don't. All I ever knew was that he was a boxer.

Yeah, I looked like I'd been in a fight.

There were decisions to be made. I knew that, but all I wanted to do was go to bed. No idea what the time was, no idea what day it was. No idea what I was going to do. The only thing I did know was that I needed to do something. But first, there would be sleep.

It was a very long, bad, and snore-y sleep. It was snore-y because my nose was full of blood. I couldn't breathe properly, and eventually I worked out this was how come I kept waking myself up— waking myself up but not really waking up—thinking the ghost girl was in the room, speaking some growly shadow language at me. The last time I snored myself awake, I picked out dried blood from my nose (too much information?). It hurt a lot. I guzzled cola and went back to sleep and dreamed the ghost girl in the mist had become a death angel, coming toward me as church bells tolled.

But I wasn't dreaming.

When I woke up, the church bells were close and clanky, and went on and on in a random, awful, dong-clank-dong-dong way— not like the fancy tunes the proper bell ringers used to do. At first I thought I *hadn't* woken up. I'd had plenty of dreams like that— nightmares—when I'd thought I'd woken but I hadn't, and the nightmare would go on and I'd think it was really happening, and then if I did wake up for real, it was no good going back to sleep because the whole thing was lurking in my Planet Ruby head waiting to start over. What you had to do was wake yourself up good and proper and read something or listen to some music (the boom box and the cassette tape of brass band music belonging to my dead neighbor, Mr. Fitch, had been upgraded to a CD player and a vast, jumbled heap of discs and cases) and no matter how much you wanted to go back to sleep, you just couldn't let yourself do it until the nightmare had been battled back into the part of your brain it had snuck out from and could only rattle at the crummy lock on the door.

But those bells, they didn't stop, not even when I got up—WAH! MY BODY HURT! WHOA! I HAD THE MOST MASSIVE DIZZY FIT!—and picked my way around the house slugging cola (I was SO thirsty!), shivering because I felt weirdly, seriously cold and because I was SCARED OUT OF MY MIND.

I must have been asleep all day and all night, because it was day again—middle of, judging from the light, which I had to do because my watches all told different, blurry stories—but at least I could see them. At least I could see. That was the only comfort in the situation because I felt this most incredible panic…a different kind completely to the one I had felt up on the moor, different again to the one I had felt thinking I was going blind and how would I get back home. It was the panic of another human being coming. It was the panic of choice.

14

Those church bells? They'd only clank and dong like that if a person—a real, live, actual person was ringing them.

It was a panic I couldn't even stall by doing something normal, like getting dressed or something, because I was already dressed. Ha! I even had my rubber boots and raincoat on still.

All I could do was stand at the front door, slugging cola and going, "Oh—"

Mom, I can't put any more pretty butterflies where swear words should go. I'll put a new thing: ✸.

It is what killed you. It is the thing in the rain. There is no worse thing. So I will put this thing instead. And I will fill it with hate.

So yeah, I stood at the front door going, "Oh ✸, oh ✸, oh ✸," because I was too scared to go out.

You know that stuff you learned at school and from your parents when you were tiny? That stuff about "stranger danger"? Well, really, right up until the apocalypse, I'd sort of thought, *Yeah, right*, because most people you ever met were OK, really, and some of them were really nice. (And anyway, how would anyone ever meet anyone if everyone was scared of strangers? All you'd ever know was your own family.) But since the apocalypse? Strangers make me really nervous. I've seen all kinds of random freaking out and nastiness. (I've also seen all kinds of weirdness: e.g., opened the door to a discount warehouse near here and saw a butt-naked man lying on a pile of sheepskin rugs singing.) (I closed the door and left.) (Quickly.) If some stranger came now, if someone found out where I was, I couldn't run, could I? How could I go when my dad said he was coming back?

It's that, I think, more than anything, that made my default setting LIE LOW. Anytime I went to a place to check it out for water or food and I even thought for one second that someone had been there, I left. (Quickly.) Even if there was a whole Aladdin's cave of stuff right in front of me and no naked man singing, if I saw something—a spilled thing, crumbs, mold even—that looked fresh or even halfway fresh (know your molds!) or I smelled something recent-ish and human, I'd just leave. (Quickly.) That's how it got. That's how sharp I could be when I wasn't zombied out with misery.

The church bells stopped ringing.

"Oh ✸."

I said it out loud. I think I said it out loud. Seemed to me my own voice boomed out in the silence louder than any bell. It was, perhaps, the most complicated "Oh ✸" there has ever been. On the one hand, relief swept over me—because I could maybe think that it was over, so chillax, Ruby, go back to sleep (as if!)… On the other hand…someone else was in town. Someone who really wanted people to know they were around. A crazy someone-anyone setting a trap—or a desperate someone. Or. Or. Or.

"✸!" I boomed.

I opened the door.

The sky looked OK—for now—some kind of cirrocumulus stratiformis thing going on = basically a high-level mess of clouds that could turn into a whole bunch of nastier ones…but not yet.

I'd run out of all excuses other than fear.

In my family, unless someone was getting married, we went to church once a year—at Christmas, because my mom liked the carols. For me, this was going to be the second time this year, if Salisbury Cathedral counts as a church. That's the apocalypse for you: makes you go places you wouldn't normally go, do things you wouldn't normally do. It's just great that way, isn't it?

I prowled down into the town, the raincoat rustling way too much for my liking. I prowled *cautiously*, listening for every and any sound…but it was difficult to hear any sound that wasn't CLANG DONG CLANG because that CLANG DONG CLANG started up again when I was halfway there.

When the only sound disturbance in your world, for ages, has been yourself or the wind or the ✻ rain, any other sort of noise is REALLY FRIGHTENING. Not that many times but often enough for me to be pretty sure I wasn't dreaming, I'd heard planes. I'd even heard other cars a few times. But this?

It was the loudest thing I'd heard in months (that wasn't coming out of a CD player in a car). Louder even than the WTCH-UH, WTCH-UH thump of my own heart—which was hammering so hard it felt like I could hear it.

I snuck up to the church. I hid behind a grave. The bells stopped. WTCH-UH, WTCH-UH. My body detected nervous sweat pouring from my armpits. WTCH-UH, WTCH-UH, WTCH—HUH?!

Someone came out of the church.

I suppose I did just pop up from behind a gravestone. I suppose it might have been a bit sudden. Anyway, whatever it was, Saskia screamed.

"Saskia?!" my ragged, broken voice squealed out like a strangled thing.

She just stood there, a frozen human explosion of fright. It seemed a little over-the-top if you ask me. (Considering, before the rain fell, we'd seen each other every day at school and every weekend too.)

"*Sask?!*" Erm, so I suppose my voice *was* a bit grunty and cavewoman-like. It definitely sounded pretty weird.

"*Ruby?!*" she whispered, like she really wasn't sure about it when—Hey?! Hello! Of course it was ME. OF COURSE IT WAS ME!

"Oh my ✹!" She gasped. "What HAPPENED to you?!"

I wasn't really listening. I felt this massive…this massive…I want to say it was totally, like, some kind of surge of love and human compassion (even though she looked as annoyingly fresh and perky as the last time I'd seen her, safe inside the army base with all the *useful* people, and—allegedly and apparently—shacked up with Darius "Don't Ever Want to Think about Him" Spratt). The truth is, when I realized it was her, just her and not random, scary someone-anyone other people, I felt this MASSIVE SURGE OF RELIEF…which sort of became this massive surge of…oh, I don't even know what, but before she had time to dodge out of the way, I sort of lunged forward and grabbed her. I hugged her.

She gasped again. "You scared the hell out of me!"

I think I might have tried to grunt something back.

"I didn't know if you'd be here! I didn't know where you lived! I didn't know how to find you!" she cried.

And then there was just this…we hung on to one another, rocking and swaying and trying to hold the world still in the middle of a graveyard. A graveyard full of people who'd died when they should have died—or maybe even tragically, but with people alive to comfort each other, people alive to share the pain and the sweetness of remembering.

We had none of that.

We had only each other.

It took a little while to really get your head around that. It took a lot less time for us both to regret it.

CHAPTER THREE

 ⬛!" Saskia choked, gagging, when I opened the front door.
"✴!" she shouted and made a terrible retching noise.

I was somewhat offended, but also I somewhat got it because I also somewhat knew what she meant. How my family smelled. So I found this pot of menthol rub I had for the times it got to me too (total *CSI* job) and Sask smeared some under her nose and did this oh-so-obvious "bracing myself here" thing, then came inside.

"Oh my ✴," she murmured from behind the hand that was over her mouth.

It took a visitor to make me see the house for what it was. The smell was one thing and could not be helped. Everything else, I realized, seeing it through Saskia's eyes, could, *possibly*, be helped.

Everything else was down to me.

OK, so I hadn't cleaned up much. Household hygiene wasn't a huge priority on Planet Ruby. Also, for convenience, activities that would normally be assigned to designated rooms pretty much all took place in one room. The sitting room—apart from still being my sitting room, where I'd spend hours, um, sitting—was also my dining room, my field kitchen (got me a little camping stove in there), and my bedroom. Also my hair and beauty parlor!

You could just make out a sleeping spot in the corner, littered with empty packets of painkillers and cola cans, but the whole of the rest of the room was…OK, so it was a mess, but there was a way through it, all right? You just had to be careful about not slipping on the treacherous slopes of the CD mountain, but that was preferable to wading through the clothes, books, and makeup swamp because—OK, so there was a lot of food-related debris involved.

But I mean, most of the cans and bottles and jars and stuff were more or less empty and the whole fly situation had gotten a whole lot better just lately. And it was hardly my fault that there was no more electricity, so that waterfalls of wax had cascaded from the candles that stood on every flat surface. The TV actually looked quite pretty, in an arty sort of way, but it remained an *unfinished* work, as I'd eased off on the candle burning after the coffee table fire.

Unfortunately, the sitting room was also my bathroom. Vast flocks of used wet wipes and, um, *tissues* frolicked in the central swamp area. No sanitary napkins, though, being as how I hadn't actually had a period since the rain fell. (I'm assuming that when my body realized the only reproductive opportunity left was Darius Spratt, subnerd of subnerds, it went on strike.)

Ah. Then there were the bathroom buckets. Defensive measure. No use trying to explain to Sask that a full bathroom bucket had once saved my life. Hadn't I chucked one into the face of a someone-anyone scary man? There was a bleach-frothing, half-disintegrated poo floating shamelessly in the closest bathroom bucket. I tried to nudge the bucket out of the way…

"Oh my ✳." She choked, as a fresh waft of stink added itself to…

So my house was a stinking pit, all right?

"Why don't we go through to the kitchen?" I suggested, knowing it wouldn't be any better but that at least no poos lurked there.

At least I thought not; on Planet Ruby anything was possible.

Saskia stumbled her way through.

She looked frightened. I think it was the writing on the walls that did it.

"It's in case my dad comes," I said.

She just looked at me.

"So he knows where I've gone…"

Looking at it through Saskia's eyes, the only place my dad would think I'd gone was Nutsville. Every time I'd left the house, I'd written when I was going (day, date, time), where I was going (or roughly, if I wasn't sure), and when I'd be back. EVERY TIME. But the messages, which had started out all neat and orderly and efficient, had gotten a little vague and scrawly.

First the date went—what did it matter?—then I dropped the days—too much hassle—then the time became approximate. Things like "10:57 a.m." had become "morn." You could see the moment—some time back now—when I'd realized this was happening, which coincided with the whole watch/clock panic.

I haven't really explained that, have I? I am only going to explain it now so you don't join Saskia in thinking I'd lost it. I mean, obviously I *had* lost it, but there had definitely been moments when I hadn't, and the whole clock/watch thing is a perfect example. The very first time I realized I was losing track of time, I had dealt with it. That's when the first digital watch and the wind up (backup) happened. Then I forgot to wind the watch, and the digital one fogged up after a hair-washing session in the camp, so I went into overdrive. Basically, I'd ticked (two wind ups), and the house had ticked (Ruby the clock keeper), although getting all these watches and clocks to agree with each other was exhausting. (I might have given up a bit.) (Though some of them were still hanging on in there, ticking away.)

Anyhow, after the clock/watch panic, the messages on the wall pulled themselves together for a bit before they slumped back into their old bad habits. The most recent stuff on the door (I'd run out of wall and cupboard space)...it didn't really look like human handwriting at all.

"Would you like a cup of tea?" I asked her.

"Ruby...oh my ✹..." she breathed (not heavily). She actually had tears in her eyes. (Though it could have been the menthol rub; it can really make your eyes water.)

Now, see, here's a funny thing. You'd think, wouldn't you, that this could be some kind of lovely moment when I realize that at last a friend has come (well, not a friend, but at least a someone I know), and that she is distressed to see my situation. Let me tell you, it got right on my nerves. Instantly. I felt like she had NO RIGHT to stand in that kitchen dripping with pity. A million times I had felt howling pity for myself, but hers I did not want. Just one look at her was enough to tell you that life on Planet Saskia had been just fine and—

I stopped myself. Though the spirit of yee-haa (saddling up my high horse for a fight!) rose like a dear, stroppy old friend, and though there was something really heartwarming about realizing I could still feel like that, I did stop myself. It wasn't just that Saskia now appeared to be the only real, human "friend" I had in the world; it wasn't even that I wanted to find out what she was doing here; and it certainly wasn't because I wanted to know a single thing about Darius Spratt. (NO INDEED!) It was because...honestly, I didn't know if I was really up to it. My body hurt a lot, but I could feel my mind hurt too.

I felt so tired.

Dog tired. Dead tired.

If Saskia hadn't been there, it would have been one of those moments when I'd just crawl off for a nap—and the urge to sleep right then was so bad I'd have suggested it, but somehow I didn't think Sask would be happy touching anything in the house, much less sleeping in it. (Though there could hardly be worse diseases lurking inside than the one that was outside.)

"Yeah, well…" I muttered. "It's not like I'm going to stay here. I was just going to leave, anyway. Today."

"Where are you going to go?" Saskia blurted, looking scared.

OH NO: THE QUESTION OF QUESTIONS.

That's what it was, and my brain wasn't remotely ready for it, so I came out with the thing I'd been thinking for weeks (months? What date was it anyway?), the thing I'd told myself I'd do, but when it came down to it, I was too scared to go and do it.

"I'm gonna look for my dad," I said, like it was obvious.

I watched her mouth tighten.

No, I thought, *no. You don't get to do that. Don't you do that.*

"Look, he came here," I said, pointing at the wall where he had written.

RUBY—WHERE ARE YOU? That's what the message said. WE ARE GOING TO GET GRANDMA. STAY HERE! BACK SOON! LOVE DAD AND DAN. The smiley face after Dan's name. The trail of kisses.

"That's my stepbrother, see?" I told her, stroking Dan's scrawled name. "That's my stepbrother."

Through Saskia's eyes, I saw the trail of desperation that followed, the hundred and one explanations of where I had gone.

Her mouth—it screwed up tighter.

Yeah, that's right, I thought. *Don't you say that thing. Don't you dare say ANYthing.*

But then her mouth opened a little and I was worried she was going to say it, so I tried to say it for her—or at least the version I could cope with.

"I mean, I know it's…" I trailed off. I couldn't say the words that

23

probably ought to come after that, which would be: VERY, VERY UNLIKELY INDEED THAT MY DAD AND MY BROTHER WILL STILL BE ALIVE. "I'm just going to go and look," I said.

"Where?" said Saskia quietly.

"Loads of places."

On the kitchen table, my mom's address book sat in its own special clear patch. I laid my hand on it. I picked up the piece of paper with the scrawled list I'd worked out weeks (months?) ago.

"These places," I said.

Grandma's, obviously. The aunts and the uncles and the cousins. That lady my mom called "Auntie" but wasn't an aunt at all—my dad had always liked her.

Though I couldn't even think about why my dad wouldn't have come back when he said he would, if he *had* gone anywhere else, these were the places he would have gone to. In my mind's eye, I'd already been to these places and looked. I'd already seen the bodies and the empty houses. But it was all I had.

"Can I come too?" said Sask.

Coils of confusion tangled in my head. See, really, this whole conversation was…OK, it was what you'd call *hypothetical*. Don't get me wrong, part of me would have searched to the very ends of the Earth for my dad, but part of me…kind of hoped that Saskia would know about a place we could go, just for now, from where I could set out on my epic quest…sometime when I wasn't feeling quite so scared and so tired.

"What about the army base?" I blurted—like, surely, whatever had gone on with her and the Spratt (which didn't bear thinking about), her being back here in Dartbridge must mean she'd come to say it was OK and that the army could squeeze me in now, even though I was officially designated as "useless."

"I had to leave."

Huh?! But—

"I'm not going back there." She looked out the window. "I really haven't got anywhere else to go, Ruby," she said.

She glanced at me—then she looked back out of the window. Either that menthol was really kicking in or... Was Saskia Miller...crying?

"Let me come with you," she said. "Please..."

Was Saskia Miller...pleading...WITH ME?

"Yeah, sure, you can come," I said.

During an apocalypse-type situation, it is very rude to say no to any reasonable request, even if it relates to what my grandma would have called a *cockamamy* plan (usually something my dad had suggested), and even if it comes from someone you've recently remembered you're not that keen on.

"Do you want help packing?" Saskia asked. (A little reluctantly, I thought. It would involve touching things.)

WHAT?! ARE WE ACTUALLY, LIKE, GOING TO LEAVE RIGHT NOW?! COULDN'T WE WAIT A FEW DAYS? GET A FEW MORE NAPS IN? shrieked the pain and the tiredness and the fear inside me.

"I don't think I'll bother taking much," I said, grabbing the marker pen and picking my way across the kitchen. I crouched down to make a start on a list on the door for my dad, and my chest hurt so much I gasped, but I carried on. The first stroke of the first letter of the first word came shaking out onto the door like a frightened black snake.

"Why don't I do that?" said Sask, taking the pen out of my hand. "While you...er...freshen up?"

"OK..." I said. Freshen up?! Anything involving makeup felt like it'd be too much of a challenge right now, but I supposed I probably ought to at least put some deodorant on or something. Maybe push the boat out and go for a change of underwear? But that would involve more painful bending… Already my body was saying no.

"Ruby," said Saskia, laying her hand on mine as I clung onto the door to haul myself up. "What *did* happen to you?"

THE SAME THING THAT HAPPENED TO EVERYONE ELSE, the yee-haa spirit in me wanted to point out, but all I said was, "Nothing." I even shrugged. That hurt too.

For the sake of decency, which I had forgotten existed, I grabbed wet wipes and stuff and headed upstairs…to the bathroom, which I avoided going anywhere near because the whole "It's in the taps! It's in the toilet! It's lurking under the plughole!" thing made me freak out.

I dumped my stuff on the floor.

I looked in the mirror.

I did, actually, scream.

"Ruby?! Ruby, are you OK?!" Saskia shouted.

I heard her blundering in panic across the treacherous margins of the swamp.

"I'm OK! Sorry! Just got a fright!… Spider!" I added.

It was the only normal scary thing I could think of.

I heard Sask tread her way more carefully back to the kitchen through the swamp of me.

And I stared at myself in the mirror.

Oh my word. Oh my ✳ word.

Filthy hands with chewed, chocolate-spread encrusted nails pawed at my reflection. I had two black eyes. Two black eyes under a stubble of black-tipped shaved hair.

I looked like a panda. I looked like a lovely, cute…endangered species. With a root regrowth problem.

The panda started crying.

"Stop it," I told it. "You're lucky to be alive."

Still it sniveled.

"You need to remember that," I told it. "You need to remain positive, just like the SAS told you."

The panda forced a grin.

OH MY ✹!

I was missing a tooth. How could I not notice a TOOTH FALLING OUT? I did this crazy thing, scanning the sink, the floor, patting down my clothes, to find it… And like, what if I actually found it? Was I going to put it back?!

I pulled up my lip; yup, my braces sailed over the space where a tooth should be. What the ✹…

The gappy-toothed panda stared back at me, forlorn.

"You crashed a Ferrari," I reminded it. "Not every panda can say that."

I did what I needed to. I cleaned myself. I put on less stinky clothes. I popped the last of the painkillers I had and swallowed them with cola, then cleaned my teeth with the rest of it.

I spat brown spearmint gunk into the sink, watched it slip down the plughole.

"Enjoy, you ✹," I whispered at *it*, at the thing down the drain.

"Are you ready, Ruby?" Sask was yelling.

"Yeah! Nearly! Yeah!" I shouted.

"The sky's looking bad," she yelled.

I glanced out of the window. "Nah, it's OK," I shouted.

It *was* OK—just the same messy stratiformis thing working out what to do.

I heard her stagger, tripping on ✹ knows what, to get to the bottom of the stairs.

"But I think we should just get going," she shouted.

Hello?! You are not my parent, I thought, peering at my panda self in the mirror and wondering if there was even a cover-stick product in the universe that could do anything about the black-eye situation. *We are not late for school.*

"Ruby, really!" she shouted. "We should get going!"

I heard her take a step up onto the stairs.

I realized a couple of things pretty quickly:

1. I did not want Saskia coming any farther up the stairs. Because I felt:
2. I did not want her anywhere near the family tomb…my mom's bedroom, where she and my stepdad, Simon, and my babiest brother-brat still lay. My babiest brother-brat, darlingest beloved: Henry, boy sweetest. One year old.

The family tomb—door sealed with masking tape and kisses.

I did not want comments or questions about that. That was private.

"Just coming!" I bellowed to keep Saskia at bay.

And I realized a third thing: Sask wouldn't come any farther up those stairs because she was grossed out by the smell and—I realized a fourth thing: Saskia was scared.

I tried a concealer stick on one of my eyes—it slid on a tear and the pressure caused instant pain. Nothing to be done about it then. Nothing to do but go.

I looked out the window again, thought of all the times the rain had kept me trapped here. The one time I wanted it to trap me, just for a while, just so I could sleep for a bit, the rain was a no-show.

So also, number five, I realized Saskia knew nothing about clouds. And that there was going to be no time for a proper good-bye.

Mom, Simon…Henry…babiest brother-brat beloved. I went to

your door. I felt so bad about the dried-out flowers sitting there in a dried-out vase. I kissed your door. Taped up because this girl wanted to stop the smell of your deadness. Not taped up because I wanted to stop remembering you. I will never stop remembering you.

And then I walked away from them. Ruby Morris: alive.

Still breathing, Mom. Still breathing.

CHAPTER FOUR

O K?" Sask asked as I crunched into the kitchen.

I knew how I looked to her now, and believe me, it was NOT as bad as I looked to myself.

"Yeah," I said.

But, honestly, it was pretty obvious neither of us were OK.

"I wrote it all down," she said.

And so she had.

On the door, in her incredibly neat handwriting, there was my list.

Only it wasn't my list.

"I sort of reorganized it a little."

My panda eyes gazed at her.

"It makes better sense this way," she said.

My panda eyes studied the door.

"It's more geographical?" she said.

My panda eyes flicked back at Sask.

"If I were your dad, this is the route I would have taken."

The panda, who had very little knowledge of geography, nodded.

One more thing puzzled it, though: the date Saskia had written.

"It's September…" I said.

That's what it said on the door: Sept. 3rd.

"Yeah?" said Saskia.

It wasn't so much the fact that I had been there, waiting, for more than three months; it was the fact that I was pretty sure… That is to say, I was vaguely sure… That is to say—look, I think it was August when the car crash happened.

"Ruby?" she said, anxious to go.

"You know, I think I might have been in some kind of coma," I wanted to tell her, but I didn't. I just took the pen off her, bent down—it hurt—and scrawled kisses.

Then we left the house. I took nothing with me, only the list of addresses—*my* list, in *my* order—shoved in my pocket.

The next part of this story—*my* story—is one I can only stretch out so far. And that is an outrageous shame because it is really fairly, utterly, completely, and totally brilliant. So it is the *worst kind* of crying shame indeed that I cannot make this stretch out further.

READ YOU THIS:

From my SAS days, I had a bunch of cars parked, waiting and ready, supplies stacked in trunks. These were my getaway cars, which I'd acquired weeks (months?) ago in a state of paranoia about what I'd do if someone-anyone who wasn't my dad turned up at the house.

Anyway, none of them would start, except the one that had hardly any gas in it because I might have used it for other activities— looting expeditions and the like.

Ha HA! Luckily this had happened to me before, cars mysteriously not starting, and it was what had forced me to study car maintenance. Apparently, like phones, cars have batteries; apparently, like phones, car batteries run down.

"Are you sure about this?" Saskia asked as I popped hoods.

HA HA HA! Sure I was sure!

I jump-started the car.

That's it. That's my moment of triumph.

Once you've jump-started, you do not stop. You need to charge up the battery of the car you're in, so you need to keep going.

There is no point crying about whether you're doing the right thing. Or just plain crying for what you're leaving behind. You just have to go.

I cranked up that motor and speed-wove out of Dartbridge, but I could feel my head and my heart were still at home. Sask was also quiet, and it made me think of something.

"Hey, do you need to go and get stuff from your place?" I asked her.

"What's the point?" she said.

I got what she meant—or at least I thought I did. I felt like… it was just too sad and awful having anything that reminded you of the past when your head was already stuffed full of it. There was this silence for a few minutes.

"I just feel like…like it's *contaminated* or something," she said.

Huh? I thought and glanced at her, worried she might not be as un-crazy as she looked and that this would pile even more pressure on me to pull myself together.

"My house. Some ✳ broke in," she said. "Can you believe that?! Some ✳ broke in."

For the benefit of those of you who have not come across my first journal, which is placed in a prominent position on the "THIS MONTH'S HOT READS" shelves in Dartbridge Public Library (in fact, after I did some rearranging, it is now the *only* item on the "THIS MONTH'S HOT READS" shelves of Dartbridge Public Library), I should tell you that the ✳ in question was me. I broke into her house and stole her mom's dog.

It was a bit of an awkward moment. Until—*Hold on a minute,*

I thought. *And what ✳ left sweet little Darling the Chihuahua locked inside?*

"Maybe they were trying to get your dog out," I blurted.

"*What?*" said Saskia.

"Your dog...you had a dog, didn't you? I mean, maybe someone saw it and—"

"That's ridiculous," said Saskia. "Who in their right mind would have bothered about a dog?!"

"Well..." Me. I bothered. I bothered a lot about a lot of dogs.

"...the cat flap," Saskia was saying.

"Sorry, what?"

"The cat flap. It's in the wall, like, right next to the kitchen door? I mean, if the dog was even still there, they could have just opened that up and coaxed her out, but no... Ruby, someone *smashed in* through the patio doors."

I could feel this nervous, guilty sweat between my palms and the steering wheel.

"They went into the house. They *touched* stuff. *My* stuff. I never want to go back there," she said. "Never."

I tried to shift up a gear and went down one instead.

"Do you want me to drive?" she said. "I'm useless, but I will if you want."

"It's OK," I said.

I definitely felt like I needed to be doing something because it seemed to me that this was going to be a very, very long journey indeed. Every which way the conversation could go, something unpleasant lurked. It was the sitting-room swamp of conversations—and you know what? It had barely started.

"Sorry," she said.

I couldn't particularly think what she might be sorry about. That was OK. I just left it there. No need for details.

She gave details.

"I wasn't, like, criticizing you or anything. You're a really good driver."

"Thanks."

"Dar said you were good."

DAR?! EXCUSE ME: *DAR?!* SINCE WHEN DID YOU CALL—

Oh ✳. This was it, wasn't it? We were here already, at a treacherous fork on the treacherous path through the treacherous swamp— with both possible routes ending in yet more treacherousness, I had no doubt.

I s'pose sooner or later, this sort of had to come up. I s'pose I had been thinking about Darius Spratt from the second I saw her. I s'pose I wanted to know, and I didn't want to know—about how he was. About what had happened with him and Saskia, about how come she'd managed to get in with him at the army base, and about whether they'd... Ah, ✳ it. Might as well head straight into the alligator's mouth. I cleared my throat:

"So how is...?"

Something in my brain short-circuited. I wanted to say "*Dar*" but in a scathing way. Only it wouldn't come out. Nor would "Darius Spratt," or just "the Spratt," or anything else—not even "he."

It had been so very long since I had spoken to someone, any sort of chitchat was going to be tough, but this?

I could feel Saskia staring at me. I would not go red. I would not get flustered. I would not blurt stuff. I would not—

"I don't exactly know," said Saskia.

Oh my ✳. Was he dead?! What had happened to him?!

"I mean, he kind of seems just about OK."

I breathed.

35

"Though it's hard to tell for sure," said Sask, settling back into her seat.

Why? Because why? Why? WHY?! IS HE IN A COMA TOO?!

"Oh yeah? Why?" I asked squeakily.

Saskia turned back around. "I mean, he doesn't exactly speak much, does he?" she said.

Another breath. The Spratt I knew would not shut up.

"Hn," I said.

"That's it!" she shrieked. "That's what he says ALL the time."

Hn.

"Like—what DOES that mean?" She laughed. She actually laughed. I knew exactly what it meant. It meant: "I am thinking."

"HN!" she shouted.

He'd never shout that. It was a quiet thing.

"It's, like, 'Darius! There's a fire!'—'Hn.'"

I forced a panda smile. It hurt.

"Oh, Ruby! I'm so sorry!" blurted Saskia.

About what now?

"I could see—you know… It seemed like you must have quite liked him…"

I gripped the steering wheel.

"He likes you, that's for sure!"

I swallowed spitelessly. "Yeah?" I said, supercool and not bothered. Casual interest only.

"And I wouldn't blame you if you did like him," she blundered on. "I mean, he's no Caspar, that's for sure, but…"

I didn't much listen to the next part, as Sask listed all the ways in which Darius was OK in an apocalypse-type situation, but that, really—wow—Caspar had been amazing and…

"You got lucky there, all right…" Saskia said.

◆

SEE, YOU HAVE TO KNOW—RIGHT HERE, RIGHT NOW—THAT CASPAR MCCLOUD WAS THE HOTTEST GUY IN THE UNIVERSE AND I HAD—FINALLY—BEEN KISSING HIM ON THE NIGHT THE RAIN FELL AND THAT THE FACT IT EVER EVEN HAPPENED WAS NO THANKS AT ALL TO SASKIA, WHO OH SO TRANSPARENTLY (A BIT LIKE HER UNDERWEAR) HAD THE HOTS FOR HIM AND BASICALLY TRIED TO STEAL HIM RIGHT FROM UNDER MY NOSE AND THEN...AND THEN...OH! OH! THIS GIRL! HOW DOES SHE DO IT?! AFTER CASPAR DIED, HORRIBLY, SHE NABBED THE ONLY BOY LEFT IN THE WORLD, DARIUS SPRATT, WHOM NEITHER OF US WOULD HAVE EVER LOOKED AT PRIOR TO THE GLOBAL MEGADISASTER AND NOW SHE HAS THE GALL TO CALL ME LUCKY WHEN—

"Caspar was in love with me," I said.

"He was in love with your dad," she said.

"*Excuse me?*"

"Your dad? Old Caz just wanted a record deal, didn't he?"

I drove. A little faster.

"That's ridiculous."

"That's what we told him! We said your dad was basically a nobody."

I felt air suck through the gap where my tooth had been.

"In the music industry, I mean. You said it yourself!"

I had—but I had been trying to make it sound like the opposite must have been true. (FAIL.)

"Come on! You knew what Caspar was after! You knew!"

I did not know.

Saskia reached out and touched my arm.

Get off me, I thought. Get. Off. Me.

"You must have known," she said more gently—but not gently enough. "Everyone knew…"

Not Leonie. My best friend wouldn't have known a thing like that and not told me.

"…Zak, Molly, Ronnie…"

No. No. Don't.

"…Leonie."

My best friend knew a thing like that and didn't tell me?

"Ah, Ruby, you're kidding me!"

"I didn't know," I muttered.

"✱," said Saskia. "Sorry."

There was this pause, and then…

"Darius does really like you, though, you know. I even think he's a little in love with you. Hey, he said he wanted to come and look for you, but—"

I snapped. In a controlled way.

"I don't want to talk about him."

"Yes, but—"

"I said I don't want to talk about him."

Eurch! Did my voice just go REALLY squeaky or what?

"No, but, Ruby—"

"Look! Sask! It was a horrible time, OK? A lot of horrible things happened, and Darius…was one of them."

I don't mean that, I thought. *I don't mean that, and I shouldn't say that, not even to make this stop. And I wish, oh how I wish, that the Spratt were here now going "Hn" about this whole "I'm going to find my dad" plan, because I know, oh how I know, that this is a stupid plan, and I just need someone to have the guts to say that—because I haven't, not even to myself. And then we could have a massive argument and come up with a better plan. But Darius Spratt is not here.*

"What I mean is..." (We were just loosely affiliated? It meant nothing?) "...I just really don't want to talk about him, OK?"

"OK," said Saskia.

It didn't feel OK, but she went quiet for a bit anyway; well, fairly quiet. I could see her cringing at the sights on and around the road; sometimes she'd mutter, "Oh ✹," and cover her mouth as she looked away.

Finally, "It's dreadful, isn't it?" she said.

"Yeah," I said.

Like, really, that was another thing I didn't want to talk about: the stuff you see.

"I mean, they're just everywhere you look," she pointed out.

"Mm-hmm."

"Yesterday," she told me solemnly, "I saw one that was *practically a skeleton*."

Honestly, I almost laughed. It came out like this horrible kind of sniggering snort.

"✹, Ruby!" she said. "That's *so* not funny."

I stopped the car. I had to. I stopped it in the middle of the road, and I turned to her and—what I wanted to do was just shout at her. Shout that I did so obviously KNOW that it wasn't funny, but that, HEY! I'd been looking at stuff like that—AND WORSE—for months (apparently—apart from during the suspected coma, obviously) and that, yes, it was awful, but going on about it being awful wasn't going to make it any less awful and would, in fact, ONLY MAKE IT WORSE.

But when I turned around...all I saw was how frightened and horrified she was. All I saw was...myself, I suppose. How I imagined I might have been if I hadn't had to look at all this stuff day in, day out for months (apart from during the coma).

"I know it's not," I said—very ✤ gently, considering. "Try not to look, and try not to think about it."

I wanted to add, "AND JUST BASICALLY DON'T TALK ABOUT IT," but I didn't have the heart.

She nodded, like it was the most sensible thing anyone had ever said.

And—maybe there is a God?—she also stopped talking about it. She stopped talking altogether. BECAUSE SHE FELL ASLEEP.

I can't tell you how much I resented that. I can't tell you how much I wanted to sleep myself…but I don't like being stuck in a car when the rain is coming… And the rain? It was coming.

So I carried on driving, trying to outrun it yet again.

And I heard Sask mumbling scared mumblings in her sleep.

And I thought maybe surviving an apocalypse is not a competition. Maybe no one has had a worse time than anyone else. People have just had…the time that they had.

That's what I thought.

She woke up as we came into Bristol over the suspension bridge.

I took that route because it was a route I knew, but I suppose I took a risk going that way because if some other genius like me had tried it, the bridge could have been completely blocked now, and I really would have had to try to reverse, and although I am now a brilliant driver (*"Dar said you were good"*) the very thought of that height—of that drop below—scared me just even thinking about it.

As did the sky. The cirrocumulus stratiformus had got depressed about the lack of action and had sunk and massed and was now cooking up trouble at a much lower level. Not great.

Sask woke up. "Ruby! What are you doing?" she asked—at

almost exactly the same spot on the bridge where the Spratt had freaked out. I bumped coolly over the remains.

"We need to get another car," I told her.

She leaned over me to look at the gas gauge.

"No!" she said. "Let's just keep going!"

I glared at her then. I did. "That'd be a stupid thing to do," I told her.

Be kind, Ruby, I thought. *Try to be kind. She doesn't know.*

"Trust me," I said. "It's better if we look for another car now. It's better not to wait."

She wanted to say stuff, but I said more first. "You would *not* like it if we ran out of gas on the highway."

Well, I definitely wouldn't like it. I've got a bit of an *emotional issue* about it, etc.

"It's better to be safe than sorry," I said. Ha! Priceless! Vintage stepdad speak!

Saskia didn't like it one bit, I could tell, but at least she shut up, and I could concentrate.

What you want, when you're car hunting, is a street packed with them or a lovely—but not too spaciously arranged—housing development. Otherwise, you're going to waste a lot of time walking and waste emergency reserves of adrenaline getting stressed out. (You never know when you are going to need that adrenaline to RUN.) Annoyingly, the way I decided to drive, it all started looking a little hopeless—the houses getting bigger and bigger, with fewer and fewer cars.

"This doesn't look great, Ruby," said Saskia, like she knew—or like she'd worked out fast what I'd learned through scary, horrible experience.

"I can see that," I said.

I did a U-ey. Midturn, I saw a pink thing. Bright ❀ pink.

CHAPTER FIVE

It's hard to miss a pink stretch limo.

It was outside a mansion. A house so big you'd have to call it that. Like, really, you could have stuck it in the country, and in the time before the rain, people would have paid to go and see it.

I remembered a girl pointing—when Darius Spratt and I had been here in Bristol thirsty (so thirsty!) for water—and even more vaguely remembered the direction she was pointing in.

Where we were now, that's where she had pointed.

"Ruby?" Saskia said, freaking as I drove up to the house.

I idled in the road for a moment, looking at it. That's how good my driving is now: I can "idle," foot just resting on that accelerator, hand still clutched on that gear stick, ready at any second to take off.

"I know these people," I said, ignoring her freaking. I turned off the engine.

"Ru," breathed Saskia.

I could hardly hear her. I could hear music! Thumping music! Someone was having a party.

A grin—a small but hopeful grin—crept onto my face.

"We could just say hi," I said. "Just see what's happening… Trust me…these people are cool. They're really, really cool."

Trust me? How could I even trust myself? I didn't really know those people at all.

A kid dressed as a pink fairy ran past the front of the house, chased by another kid in a dinosaur getup, spiny tail dragging.

"They've got kids here..." said Saskia as if that was a wondrous thing.

"Yeah," I said. I'd seen that before too—how these cool people had been kind enough to take in stray kids.

The track that was playing quieted—for a second or two, you could hear the noise of a generator—and then—OH! A track we knew came on! I grinned bigger. It hurt...but any place where kids are messing about having fun, that's got to be all right, doesn't it? Any place where people like the same music as you... Those people have got to be all right, don't they?

"S'pose we could just see," said Saskia.

We piled out of the car. Couldn't have cared less about the sky. Excited, that's what we were—nervous, obviously, but *excited*. We crunched up the gravel of that drive, the both of us high-pitched whisper-singing the chorus right up until we got to that great big front door. Then we went quiet. Nerves.

We did knock, but I don't suppose anyone would have heard over the racket. The front door was open anyway, so we went in.

We stood in the darkness of a grand entrance hall. There was this huge staircase right in front of us. Around the banisters, Christmas lights were wrapped: twinkling, disappearing into the blackness at the top of the stairs. There were portraits—old oil painting–type portraits—hanging on the stairwell. I didn't suppose they'd had glasses and mustaches like that originally. Certainly not the ladies. I also didn't suppose their clothes had been spray-painted in rainbows of neon paint. And I know for a fact that none of them would have had speech bubbles coming out of their mouths saying—

44

"Hi!" shouted another kid, this one dressed in one of those crazy, padded muscleman Superman outfits as he chased the fairy and the dinosaur through the hall.

They whacked open the door to the room where the music was coming from—a blast of sound and smoke and weed and alcohol-y drink fumes escaped—and ran in, the door slamming behind them.

Two seconds later, Superman flung the door open again and shouted "Bye!" at us, then disappeared again.

"Sask?" I said.

That was pretty much the last thing I remember saying to her that night. A new track started up—superb mixing!—we burst into singing and—hey!

She shrugged and grinned. She walked toward the door, singing. I followed, singing. Did a little shimmy. (It hurt.)

Sask poked the door open:

PARTY CENTRAL!!!!!

If you need that explained to you, your life has been even more unfortunate than mine. But I judge not, so here's a summary:

MUSIC FRENZY! DANCE FRENZY! FUN FRENZY! CHAMPAGNE FRENZY! (CLASSY!) AND MOST HILARIOUS AND BRILLIANT OF ALL: FANTASY COSTUME FRENZY!

Ha! Every single fabulous person in that place was in a costume. Every kind of beautiful and fantastic creature was there, from masked and gowned ladies to aliens from outer space to a very convincing beady-eyed fox in a hunter's jacket, and a gold-painted guy who actually appeared to be naked. Hard to tell with everyone dressed up, but it seemed like there might have been a lot of new people because I didn't seem to recognize anyone much…apart from the one who had to be as old as my grandma: Granny Lycra—last seen wearing a leopard-print catsuit and now rocking a white meringue of a wedding dress.

Sask and I, we looked at each other, eyes wide… If there's one thing a Dartbridge girl loves, even during an apocalypse—maybe especially during an apocalypse—it's a kicking, crazy party. (Even— and also maybe especially—when that Dartbridge girl has been scared stupid and scraped rock-bottom low and has no clue about what kind of a future there might be.) (*Bring it on!* If I thought any- thing, that's what I thought: *Bring it on!*)

In the blockbuster film of *my* blockbuster story, the next thing that happens will be a *tzzzzzzzzzp!* as the DJ rips the needle off the vinyl and the whole room goes silent.

What really happened was the music got turned down a little, and out of the crowd, the only other person (apart from us) who wasn't dressed up approached: Xar.

I'd met him before, what seemed like years ago but was only a few months: a six-foot-something, impressively gorgeous, blond, dread-head, tree-hugging crustie—only not really a crustie. More manicured. More deliberate. More composed. Naked from the jeans up, his chest shone with dance sweat. And I got that impres- sion again, the one I'd first had, that he was somehow their king, because everyone made way to let His Royal Hotness through.

"Lay-deez," he said, pulling on a white cotton shirt as he strolled through the madness toward us.

The music got turned down a little more, and everyone quieted down with it, looking our way. That's how mesmerizing he was: you tuned in to his voice automatically.

"And what can we do for you?" Xar asked.

"Hi," I said, a bit too shoutily. "I'm Ruby?"

"If your name's not on the list, you're not coming in," hooted Granny Lycra, pulling not a bride's veil but a widow's veil of black over her face. It looked weird and horrible and scary—but I ignored her. I ignored them all and spoke only to Xar.

"Ruby from Dartbridge? We met? Before…"

"Did we," he said. It wasn't a question.

"And this is Saskia," I shouted.

"Any chance of a drink?" she asked, and before Xar could answer, she was elbowing her way across the room.

That's Sask for you; she just does stuff, doesn't she? And she gets what she wants. She wasn't going to wait to be invited, so she invited herself. Xar didn't look too pleased.

"She's just come from the army base," I said, hoping that would explain Sask's party-jeopardizing behavior.

"Oh, has she," he said—again, no question—and he laughed—a quick and quiet ha-ha of a laugh—and waved his hand in the air in a very royal way, which was apparently the command for the music to be turned back up, because that's what happened.

The music got cranked back up, everyone carried on partying, and King Xar wandered off after Saskia.

For a moment I just stood there, like a panda/idiot—then I spied… Oooh! There was a table piled high with food. Not the kind of trash I'd been eating, but properly made stuff. Stuff that looked deliciously good. I felt my stomach growl louder than the music.

Come to Momma! my head whispered at it.

I barged toward it.

"Hi!" shouted this girl who was already at the table. Her costume was hilarious: a walrus in a furry brown onesie, her plate piled high with items that she stuffed into her mouth between the two enormous papier-mâché tusks on either side of her jaws.

47

"You look brilliant," I shouted, giving her huge belly a friendly poke. It was seriously hard and seriously…real.

"I'm so sorry!" I shouted.

It wasn't just an apology for the pregnant belly poke; it was a sorry for…uh. Dressed up or not dressed up, I could see immediately that she couldn't have been much older than me. Nah—it was worse than that. She was younger.

"You *do* look brilliant though," I told her.

"You look awful," she shouted but in a kind way. In the din, in the madness, I heard that kindness.

"I feel awful!" I shouted.

I did feel awful. I mean, it all looked great and stuff—the party, the food—but… Oh, my body! It hurt! And my head, which so often seemed to have a separate life from my body, it hurt too. It hurt a lot.

"I think I might have been in a coma," I shouted.

And Grace—that's what I was just about to find out her name was—said, "Oh my ✳!" and stared at me, oozing big walrus sympathy.

I could have cried right there and then, because that sympathy felt so gorgeous. I put down the plate I'd grabbed.

I want to warn you about this. I want to warn you that if you know you should be hungry because you can't remember the last time you ate but you no longer feel hungry—for whatever reason—YOU SHOULD STILL EAT. Just something. Eat something. Same way with drinking (water!). YOU SHOULD JUST DRINK. Just take some stuff in, so your body and your brain will at least stand a chance of making some sensible decisions about things.

I gave neither of them a chance.

"Do you wanna dress up?" she yelled. "We could get you an outfit and stuff."

"Yeah! Yeah, sure!"

I mean…why not, eh? Why not?

That's how I ended up in a room with Grace, the party blasting on downstairs. In a plush, wood-paneled bedroom of the sort you'd normally have to stand behind a red "Keep back, you visitor" rope to look at—me and Grace and a bottle of champagne.

"I know I shouldn't drink," she said, rubbing her walrus belly as she glugged a glass of bubbly, "but it's hard not to. You know, *under the circumstances.*"

"When's it due?" I asked her. But "it" sounded so harsh. "The baby," I said.

That's what people ask pregnant people, isn't it? That's what they're supposed to ask.

"The seventh of October," said Grace. She rubbed her tummy. "But they do say a first baby usually comes early. Up to two weeks, the midwife said…"

Guess that had been said to her in the time before the rain. Guess that had been said to her when there were still midwives, when there were still people around to help and there was no reason—or at least a lot fewer reasons—to be scared. Guess there was now.

This girl, Grace, I felt so sorry for her. She ditched her glass and rummaged through the pile of costumes on the (four-poster) bed.

I tried on stuff—because she was so happy, playing dress-up like that. I mean, most people like dressing up, don't they? But Grace? Ah, she was loving it!

"See?" said Grace as I looked at myself in the mirror.

The costume…I guess you could call it Evil Fairy. Like, it had the puffy skirt and the glitter and the wings and stuff, but it was jet-black.

I did, really, just want to go then—like, just dance myself stupid and forget about the whole thing—but she pulled the panda card on me.

"I could do your face," she said.

"Could you?" I asked. I so just wanted to go. "Like how?"

"Like," she said, "just wait there!"

I sat on the bed. In the moments that she was gone I did briefly think, *What* am *I doing here?* But then she came back, bubbling with excitement, and dumped out the world's most massive makeup bag.

And I smiled so hard it hurt. She had A LOT of products. A LOT of products.

Grace rolled up her sleeves—her arms were covered in tattoos—and worked at my face so lightly I could hardly even feel it. And as she worked, we chatted—and drank!—and she told me all about how she'd gotten expelled from school (she hit a teacher who had said that she shouldn't have hit a boy for calling her a slut) and had to lie to her mom about the whole thing because her mom didn't know about the pregnancy, but Grace was going to tell her when...

That's the problem with any conversation these days, isn't it? Sooner or later it blunders into the unbearable. She didn't have to say it for me to know it: her mom had died when the rain fell.

"She wouldn't have been cross with you for long," I told Grace. It seemed like the right thing to say.

"She wouldn't have been cross at all. She'd have gone ballistic."

I smiled. I couldn't help myself. Grace grinned. "Seriously, she would have gone ✳ crazy," she said.

"I guess my mom would too," I said. Actually, I could only picture my mom crying. "She'd have gotten over it," I said. "She'd just be glad you're OK."

"Yeah..."

"Hey!" I said softly. "You're gonna be OK now, aren't you?"

"I guess…"

"I mean, it seems pretty cool here," I said, changing the subject for her, for both of us. Or at least, I thought I was.

"It is pretty cool," she said pretty coolly.

What I noticed even then was how she didn't exactly seem as wowed by it all as I was. "It's a great house," I said. That definitely *had* to be a change of subject, didn't it?

"Yeah—it's Xar's."

"He owns this?!"

"It belonged to his parents, so…I guess it's his now."

"Wow…"

I thought about our little house in Dartbridge. Guess I owned that now.

"But anyone can own anything now, can't they?" she said.

"S'pose…"

"I could claim Buckingham Palace…"

"We should do that!" I said. I was drunk. I'll admit that. But still, I could just see it: me and Grace and the baby out on a balcony waving to…no one in particular, a few random dead people where a crowd should be, angry packs of dogs yapping at us.

"He's on a power trip, if you ask me," she said, suddenly ultra-serious.

"Who? What—Xar?"

She nodded.

I snapped out of my drunken daydream. "How d'you mean?"

"You'll see."

"Grace?"

"He sort of controls everyone a bit. A lot. I mean, people go along with what he wants because…" She stopped what she was doing and rubbed her belly. "There's nowhere else to go, is there?"

51

This felt like another treacherous swamp.

"Is he horrible to you?" I asked.

She hesitated. "It's...more complicated than that. He...he thinks the rain is a good thing."

That's what she said, and she stared at me. As if she was expecting an answer. Maybe some kind of answer other than—

"*What?!*" I almost laughed.

I almost did. HOW COULD ANYONE IN THEIR RIGHT MIND THINK THAT?!

She didn't even smile. "You know, because of the environment and stuff," she said. "He's very environmental."

"Grace?!"

"He really loves the Earth," she said.

Massive stuff crowded up in my head—about polar bears and tigers and rain forests...but still. "That's not environmental. That's just...*mental,*" I said.

It was not meant to be a joke. It was... Ah, the people I had seen die. The hurt. Ah ✳. The hurt. We are all hurting. There can be no one alive who does not hurt.

"I don't think it's that he hates people exactly. He just thinks the planet would be better off without them here," said Grace, interrupting herself. She held up a little compact mirror.

I caught a glimpse of something weird and terrifying, more shocking than the thing Grace had just said. I gasped. I stood up. Dizzy stars buzzed.

I checked *it* in the big mirror.

The thing Grace had done with my eyes? She'd delicately drawn in a mask. A black-and-gold, twirly, vine-like, complicated mask that made my panda eyes look like a thing of witchy beauty. Meet Evil Witch Fairy Ruby: the shadow girl from the mist.

The only thing that let me down was my hair. It just looked so peculiar. A head full of long spikes that started in mousy brown and ended in tips of black. I ran my hand through it.

"We could bleach it?" offered Grace.

I shook my head. Stars spinning. "Not now," I said. "It doesn't matter."

I caught the look on Grace's face: disappointment.

"This is incredible though," I said, tracing a finger over a winding curl of black.

"Don't touch! You'll smudge it!" she cried, but she was so, so pleased. "I was training to be a tattoo artist," she said. "Well, unofficially. Just at this salon, it belonged to…a bloke I knew. You know, after I got kicked out of school."

I'm guessing the bloke was *her* bloke. Or that she had feelings for him. Who knows? All gone. It's all gone. "You would have been amazing," I told her.

Then I thought about how terrible that sounded. "You ARE amazing," I said.

"I could do the outline in ink if you really like it," she offered.

Ha! Know what?! A part of me felt like saying, "Oh, OK then."

"My mom would go ballistic," I said.

Grace laughed and I…HA! I smiled so hard it was almost a laugh. And I thought that neither of our moms would have gone ballistic in the least. About any of this.

They would—they really would—have just been glad—so glad—we were alive.

And that's how it was for the rest of that night. I smiled so hard I almost laughed. And it was just such a shame I couldn't laugh because, basically, it was the most brilliant party I had ever been to…or ever will, I suspect.

I forgot to eat. I forgot to drink anything that wasn't champagne.

And everything stopped hurting, so I danced. I just danced.

Partly because, after Saskia had finished having her intimate tête-à-tête with Xar (which was still going on when Grace and I trooped/waddled back down stairs), Sask kept trying to grab me, going "Ruby, I really need to talk to you" (in an increasingly slurred voice), and the only way I could shake her off was to just keep on dancing—because I tell you, I did not want to talk about ANYTHING.

So I danced. I just danced.

Like it was the end of the world.

CHAPTER SIX

A nd then I woke up.

Ha! You are NOT going to believe how many times I wish I could say this in this story—MY story. The story of what happened to ME. I want this to be like the kind of story I would have written as a kid, when a ton of really awful, scary stuff happens—but then you go:

AND THEN I WOKE UP.

And everything's OK.

Anyway, I woke up.

We hadn't just danced till dawn. We had danced till… Uh, I don't even know what time it had been, but it had been bright and sunny and warm, which is what the weather usually does in September. It realizes the holidays are over and turns lovely, but you can't go and join it because you're locked up in a classroom all day. Ah, the joyous start to a whole new school year.

Only there was no more school, was there?

It was late on a sunny afternoon; the veranda doors were open, fancy sheer curtains spray-painted a rainbow of colors, billowing in a gentle breeze. They looked kind of tacky in the light…but maybe that was just because the whole of the rest of the room looked trashed and sad.

But that's how a place is supposed to look after a really good party, isn't it?

Grace had gone. Everyone had gone…except me and a bunch of kids.

I sat up. Dizzy. Very dizzy.

The dinosaur kid—just a little girl—was sitting alone in a chair, making two plastic ponies fight.

"I want my mommy and my daddy," she said.

I guess she was talking to me. She didn't look at me; she just made the ponies fight.

"I do too," I whispered.

My head hurt. I felt too hot. The room felt too hot. The log fire from last night was still smoldering. Two little kids I didn't even remember seeing before (a ghost and a zombie) were right in front of it, playing "Let's Chop Wood" with a massive ax.

Whoa. NO.

I got up—a ka-trillion dizzy stars spinning—and descended upon those kids.

"You DO NOT play with that," I said, removing the ax from hands that were too small to argue.

I put it out of reach on the great stone mantelpiece.

"And you DO NOT play in front of a fire," I told them, even though the fire was hardly blazing… But, like, really? Hello?! Small children?! Fire?!

The kids stared up at me. Uh. I remembered something. I wasn't a friendly panda. I looked like a witch, didn't I?

"I'm a nice witch," I told them.

That zombie kid? Know what she did? She went, "Pah!"

56

Those kids weren't scared of me; they were angry about being told off.

Too bad, I thought.

I shook my head at them and at the room, and at… Above the fancy fireplace, shoved in front of a smashed gold-framed mirror, there was this massive TV screen on which all kinds of pretty pictures had been played at the party. Now there was a horrible—really horrible—film on, playing silently. Some wildlife thing, but an X-rated version: a baby wildebeest staggered around with its guts hanging out, while lions—young lions, just babies too, really—tried to snatch up a jaw full.

I pawed at that screen. I jabbed and speed-swiped at the bottom of it in shocked, angry disgust until I got it to go off.

"Hey," said a lazy voice. "I was watching that."

Xar, whom I had not seen, sat lounging in an armchair behind me.

That's when the first gunshot happened.

KA-POW!

I dropped to the floor, searching for a hiding place. Sounded like the gunshot came from upstairs, from right above our heads.

"GET DOWN!" I screeched at the kids.

"I said," Xar sighed, "I was watching that."

He flicked the TV back on with the remote.

KA-POW!

"For ✹'s sake," he said. He leaned out of the chair and grabbed the ghost kid by the arm. "Go and tell them to use the gun with the ✹ silencer."

And the ghost kid, who wasn't scared of Evil Witch Fairy Ruby, nodded in a scared-kid way at Xar and went running off.

Little feet tread around me. I grabbed an ankle. The kid bent down to me.

"They're shooting the dogs," the kid said…like that explained it all, like that was normal.

In front of my eyes, another set of little feet padded up.

"The dogs hurt my sister," the other one said.

I crawled to the garden doors; I parted the sheer curtains. Looked out. Saw: a huge garden that must have once been very fancy, the lawn still beautifully mown. An ice-cream van parked on the edge of it. And a long, ornamental pond—nearly as big as the Dartbridge swimming pool, water lilies flowering in it.

Eyes flick back to the lawn. On things in the middle of it. Bloody ribs of a butchered something. Dead dog—pit bull?—next to it. Dead—shot dead?—pit bull dog, lying there.

Eyes flick to back of garden. Eyes see movement in bushes. Eyes see—

No. No. No. NO.

Whitby.

Sweet puppy! The dead-person's-arm-munching, big, goofy dummy of a dog I liberated from the neighbors' house—then was forced to ditch for his puddle-drinking activities. Whitby! Last seen howling, abandoned, on a highway in this very city! Huggable hound! Sweet puppy of my heart!

That big, goofy, dummy of a dog blundering out of the bushes, ready to snatch the tasty ribs of the butchered something.

Brain screeches: *He'll get shot!*

Heart acts. Big, goofy dummy of a girl races out.

"Whitby! Whitby! Whi—"

THUNK!

◆

Silent bullet bites earth.

Big, goofy dummy of a dog—he stops; he doesn't quite get it, but he doesn't like it.

"Whitby!" cries girl.

Big, goofy dummy of a dog sees girl running at him. Big, goofy dog snarls.

"Whitby!" cries girl.

It hurts, the confusion in his brain. Girl stops. Dog snarls; humans bad.

"Whitby!" cries girl.

Big, goofy dog remembers that is him. Smells girl he likes. Forgets his pack-food-guns-scary, forgets all that stuff: GIRL-I-LIKE!

"Ruby!" someone shouts.

Girl looks up at balcony. King Xar's Court gazing down. Who shouted?

Saskia! Saskia—pointing—

Big, goofy dog launches himself, lickily, at girl.

At last second, girl realizes she HAS TO STOP HIM. Puddle drinker. Lick of death.

"NO!" she roars.

"NO!" with more power and force than she has ever spoken to another creature in all her life.

Big, goofy dog hesitates. GIRL-I-LIKE?

"NO!" she screams. She has to scream it. It is killing her to scream at him; all she wants to do is hug him, but—

"*NO!*" She has to make him stop.

Big, goofy dog sinks down. He isn't sure what he has done wrong, but he is so very pleased to see Girl-I-Like, he will do anything.

See how pleased? He is lying down, but his tail is sweeping around, mad with joy! *Oh pet me, pet me, pet me, I like you, I like you, I like you, I like you lots! See how good I am?! Hey, Girl-I-Like, hey girl, hey girl—*

"STAY! Good boy! STAY!"

"Ruby!"

Other-Girl saying that. Girl-I-Like looks round.

Other-Girl running at Girl-I-Like. Dog called Whitby doesn't like it. Thinks Girl-I-Like is being attacked. Other-Girl flings her arms around Girl-I-Like. Whitby charges—

"*NO!*" Girl-I-Like screams.

He crouches. He cringes. He does So-Sorry Good Dog.

He is a good dog. He didn't know.

He didn't know.

It is too late. The Other-Girl…she backed off so far…she stood on the edge of the lily pond. She lost her balance.

But Saskia was a gymnast; Saskia gets her balance back.

Only her toe had dipped into that cool, dark water.

THUNK!

I'd never heard a dog scream like that. My heart screamed for him. He never, ever would have meant this to happen. I screamed back at him. "*GO! GO ON! GO!*"

I never, ever, for as long as I live, want to scream like that at another living creature. I never ever want to do that again.

Whitby, shot, yelping—with no thought now but *HURTS*—is already going. Dumb dog makes smart decision: Girl-I-Like or Pain and Fear. He is already limping as fast as he can away from this terrible place.

Saskia is going nowhere.

She had sat down; the tiny patch of damp on her left Converse spreading.

"✸!" she cried, clutching her leg. "CUT IT OFF!"

I just stood there. Weird, awful, half-forgotten memories of stuff I thought she'd tried to say last night banged around my head. I just… You can't do that, can you? You can't just say, "Oh, OK then," and chop a person's foot off, can you?

Everyone piled outside, watching Saskia pleading with me, for—it felt like hours. It wasn't even minutes. She crawled at me and grabbed my leg. "CUT IT OFF! YOU HAVE TO CUT MY FOOT OFF. IT'S THE ONLY WAY. I'VE SEEN IT! I TOLD YOU! THAT'S WHAT YOU HAVE TO DO. DO IT. CUT IT OFF! IT'S THE ONLY WAY! CUT IT—"

Her scream was louder than the sound the ax made. It took another blow for Xar to chop Saskia's foot off completely—so hard a blow the ax rang as it bit into the stone at the edge of the pond. Then he batted the foot away with the ax, like it was a ball and the ax was a hockey stick. It *splopped* into the lily pond.

Saskia had passed out on the first chop; she didn't see fish nibbling at her sneakered foot. I did. I couldn't look anywhere else: not at Saskia and the bleeding; not at the Court of King Xar, who'd all gone "Urrr!" like they were watching something awful on YouTube and not something awful that was happening for real, right in front of them.

"Help her, someone help her, someone help her," I heard my own voice saying…because there was nothing—nothing I could do, nothing I knew to do. That chapter in the SAS book about first aid? It had scared me just thinking about it, so I'd skipped it—and in any case, even if I had known what to do, would I have done it? What if Saskia's blood was infected?

People started to drift away, back to their hangovers and a lazy day.

"We can't help her," muttered Grace, crying and hugging the baby inside her. "Come away, Ruby. Just come away."

I shook my head at her; unable to stand it, she turned and waddled back into the house, sobbing. That just left me and Xar.

He was staring at Saskia—observing, I guess...to see if it was true, what she had said, that the only way to save her was to cut off her foot.

"She'll bleed to death," I whined at him. "She'll die anyway."

"Yes," he said.

And then I got it; no one was coming to the rescue here. There was only me.

CHAPTER SEVEN

At this point in time, there are a number of things I don't really get. But these are only the things I know I don't get, and not the things I don't know I don't get, which are, unfortunately, to be revealed.

I dragged Saskia into that ice-cream van myself. No one helped. No one tried to stop me. Crying, dog tired (don't think about dogs)—no, dead tired (don't think about death)—*very* (that's OK) tired, very hungover, very ill, and very aching-all-over, I drove that stupid ✹ ice-cream van toward the army base. It was the only place I could think of where there would be medical help, and I took the only route I knew to get to it: highway, turn right at Swindon.

I was on the same highway I'd once driven along with the Spratt, when we sang and played silly games—as you do when you're trying to take your mind off an apocalypse-type situation. And I realized a dreadful thing. That journey? It was the last time I'd laughed. I *had* smiled since. I had smiled pretty hard last night. Grinned witchy grins. But that journey? It was the last time I had laughed.

In an attempt to block out thoughts about the disappearance of my own laugh, I tried to find other things to think about—but I didn't much want to think about a single thing. Except…why had Saskia even turned up looking for me in the first place? Why would she—why would anyone?—leave the Camp of the Useful: the army camp where you'd be protected and taken care of? Where everything was surely…*tickety-boo*, as my grandma would have said.

It was the one thing I probably should have asked her about, and now I couldn't ask her about it, and no explanation I could come up with seemed remotely plausible:

EXPLANATION #1: Saskia is a kindhearted girl who really likes me and was so worried about whether I was OK she left the army camp.
Comments:

EXPLANATION #2: Saskia had ditched the Spratt, and she had come to beg my forgiveness.
Comments:

EXPLANATION #3: The Spratt had ditched Saskia, and she had nowhere else to go.
Comments:

EXPLANATION #4: Ruby, she kept trying to tell you something and maybe you wouldn't have to be dreaming up explanations if you'd listened.
Comments:

There are no comments because I have nothing to say about any of my own explanations. It was almost enough to make me want to stop the ice-cream ambulance and go and shake Saskia back to consciousness for just long enough to get the truth out of her, but only a monster would do such a thing—and I am not a monster.

Thinking bad thoughts is not the same as doing bad things, and plenty of people who think they think GOOD thoughts do TERRIBLE things. (They used to call it "politics" or "religion" or "teaching mathematics.") All I do is drive an ice-cream van.

When we finally arrive at the gates to the army base, there is a camp of useless people, like me. There are cars; there are caravans—fires burning, people sitting out under tarps…people wrapped in blankets and duvets that tumble from their shoulders as they rise to their feet, laughing and…hooting, jeering, and cheering.

I remember that I am a witch-fairy driving an ice-cream van.

Ahead of me, at the gates, electric lights in the dusk burn so brightly, I am blinded, and I stop long before I have to, blinking, dazzled. My head hurts.

I am getting into this base. I am getting Saskia into this base.

THUMP!

A fist against my window. I see a face—a woman's face. I have a memory of a time I was safe in a car and a woman, already bleeding from the rain, tried to get in. Like I said, I have *emotional issues* about being trapped in cars.

"Make mine a King Cone!" she shouts through the glass, laughing.

"I'd rather have a Popsicle!" someone shouts.

I see others crowd up.

"There's someone in there!" another voice shouts.

"It's a kid! She's got a kid!"

"She's bleeding. Kid's bleeding!"

Saskia—maybe responding to this new sound, maybe responding to us having stopped—groans loudly. People back off at a million miles an hour.

"She's hurt! She's just hurt!" I scream to anyone who'll listen, not even thinking to roll down my window.

Hello, silence. Know you well. You make me feel like I am dreaming. But I am not. Oh! My brain wants to tell me this is not really happening. *Go back to sleep*, it is trying to say.

This *is* really happening.

"She's not sick!" I scream. "She's hurt! It's her foot!"

Some brave someone comes back up to the van, flashlight in hand, and peers inside.

"Kid's hurt," she shouts.

That's what it takes—an adult to say what I have said.

"Kid's hurt!" someone echoes.

"They're just kids!" a someone yells at the gates. That means "go," right? That means it's OK? I press on the accelerator. I see wire—too late: I bump the gates. In the blinding light, stick figures of soldiers form in front of me.

"Get back! Get back!" I hear them shouting, stick guns get cocked.

No, I think. *No.* I do not know what else to do. I hammer on the horn. I flick switches, and the jingle comes blaring out.

All I hear is a crackling racket of tuneless bells. I can't hear what anyone is shouting anymore.

THUMP!

The King Cone lady bashes my window.

"Back up so they can let you in!" she shouts.

I smash gears to find reverse—the shadows of wire against light swing open ahead of me.

"Come on!" bellows a stick soldier.

Forward, then?

I accelerate and—thump!—hit another set of gates.

I didn't even see the wire. The light—it is dazzling.

In my side mirrors, I see gates shut behind me. Shadows of soldiers step away from the closed gate; the useless people crowd up, clutching wire…waiting to see what will happen.

I am trapped between gates. A flashlight gets shined into my face—very unnecessarily, I might add. It's not as though it's the middle of the night.

THUMP!

"Stop the engine!" a soldier yells at the glass.

Just in case I didn't get that, he points this big gun at me. There is glass between me and that gun, but I don't suppose ice-cream vans come with bulletproof glass, or at least they probably wouldn't have in Dartbridge.

I've seen films. I turn the engine off, and I raise my hands.

"And turn that off!" he yells.

I kill the jolly tune. Raise my hands again.

"Get out!" he yells.

I get out. Raise my hands *again.*

This sniggering murmur goes through the crowd; even the soldiers look like they're trying not to laugh. Hilarious, no? A witch-fairy driving an ice-cream van. Hilarious? NO.

I see soldiers prowl around the van—and behind them, there's a whole crowd watching, fingers hooked into wire for this evening's entertainment. The back door of the van gets yanked open. Guns and torches get waved into the back of the ice-cream van…where Saskia lies, pale and sweating. Her blood filling the floor where a jolly person once stood asking, "Sauce? Sprinkles?"

"She needs help!" I shriek.

The crowd at the gate falls silent.

67

My brain kicks up a desperate gear, and I realize what the soldiers must be thinking.

"She's not *sick!*" I gibber. "She's not *sick* sick!"

Yeah, Ruby, P-R-O-B-A-B-L-Y?

Ignoring all those films I've seen, I start to shout.

"She had her foot chopped off! It happened hours ago! She's going to bleed to death! SHE'S NOT RAIN SICK! SHE NEEDS HELP!"

"SHUT UP," says a soldier on a walkie-talkie.

When he says what he has to say to the person on the other end of the line, any normal, kind person would just say, "Oh my goodness! Those poor girls! Let them in immediately!" ("The driver must obviously be a brave hero," etc.), but the person at the other end of the line… Oh, I can SO tell—they do NOT want to be bothered by this drama.

Know what it reminds me of? When you overhear parents talking to other parents about some kind of situation and TOTALLY FAILING TO APPRECIATE the seriousness of it.

"We're kind of busy here," I hear the person at the other end of the line say. "It's a one-oh-one."

In the silence, the crowd at the gate register that.

A terrible booing and hooting and hissing starts up. I do not know what a 101 is, but they obviously do. I'm guessing it's NOT GOOD.

"One-oh-one!" the walkie-talkie soldier shouts over the din.

The soldiers, guns at the ready, step up to the gate I just came through—the booing crowd quiets and backs off, snarling. You don't have to be Einstein—and I guess you know by now that I'm not—to realize—

"We cannot assist you. You must leave," the gun wielder tells me.

I FLIP OUT.

"NO! SHE'LL DIE! YOU HAVE TO HELP HER! HER FOOT

WENT IN THE POND AND…AND"—I see fish, nibbling—"HER FOOT WENT IN THE POND AND WE HAD TO CHOP IT OFF!"

I see my mom; I see my mom's hand reaching out into the rain, trying to help someone.

My mom…my mom…my mom.

I am thousands of breaths away from you.

I cannot…I cannot think…if we had known to chop off your kind hand, would you have lived? Oh, Mom…my mom… These thousands of breaths? Every one of them hurts.

I am not so lost in this terrible thought that I am not mad with myself for thinking it right now. I am Ruby. I VOW I WILL NOT CRY! I am strong. I am fierce. I am—

"SHUT UP," the walkie-talkie soldier tells me. Realizing I'm not going to, and that the crowd is starting to join in, he walks away from the racket so he can discuss whatever he wants to discuss—probably whether there's any chance of a cup of tea after all this—in private.

A cheer rises up from the crowd of the useless as the second set of gates is opened.

"Get in and shift over," a soldier tells me, scowling because his mates are laughing at him.

"Got any choc-ices?" one of them shouts at him.

I snarl a witchy snarl at the shouter. This isn't funny. It is also, in my opinion, very unprofessional behavior. And from the British Army.

As they wheel Sask into the hospital section, she wakes up and starts screaming all over again. It's all a little garbled, but the gist of it is, "No, no, no. NO! Oh my ✳, NO!"

I mean, I know hospitals can be scary places, but honestly. There's gratitude for you, eh?

Mercifully, they knock her out with an injection of something and I sink down onto a chair, wondering if there's any chance of a bed for the night because I tell you, I am DONE IN. But it won't matter if there is no bed, because even the floor is suddenly looking extremely comfy. Through eyes rolling shut from exhaustion, I detect a nurse approaching, and before I can even inquire about their B&B facilities, she dumps some random, ugly coat onto my lap and tells me, "You can go now."

She is smiling kindly, beaming nurse-y kindness.

I am speechless. (Ha! But you know me—only for a second!)

"Is my friend OK?" I ask her.

"She'll be fine. You need to go," I get told.

"Go...where?" I say.

"It's a dry night. You'll be OK," she says cheerfully. "Stay with the people outside the gates tonight, then get out of here."

Lady, you cannot be serious, I think, staring at her, shaking my head, my ~~dog dead~~ very tired jaw lolling open in weary disbelief.

I see her eyes do this microscopic flick thing, a thing that has to be universally understood by anyone who ever had the misfortune to go to school. It is the teen equivalent of that white flash on a rabbit's bum—only exquisitely more subtle, obviously. It means DANGER, which usually means a teacher is watching (or worse, approaching). I get it instantly. I turn, and (tragically forgetting the intricate eyeliner work all over my face) I do a brilliant faux mascara-rub move on my sore eye sockets, swiveling my eyes about to locate the danger...which turns out to be a surveillance camera above the nurses' desk. Sneaks.

"You have to go," she says.

HEY! my brain shouts. *HEY! I THINK THIS LADY IS TRYING TO HELP YOU!*

I get it! I suppose staying in any place with security cameras isn't a good idea, in case some bored bloke in front of a bank of screens decides to investigate the witch-fairy. If they work out who I am, I'm out of here—because I am officially useless, doncha know?

"Thanks," I tell her, studying her face for some sort of sign about the secret tip-off she's just given me, but she has a flawless smile mask painted on her face (unlike my face, which, though I don't realize it, is now a total smudgy mess). I am deeply impressed by her self-control. (Although I suppose nurses get trained for that sort of thing. "This won't hurt a bit," etc. They are brilliant at remaining cheery during hideous and difficult situations of all kinds.)

I stand, pull on the coat she's just handed me because it would seem rude not to, and look for some sort of sign about where exactly I should go, because all I see is a maze of doors. On one I see it: a label. One word:

Sunnyside

That's what it says—in cute, kiddie-friendly letters. Clowns cavort with balloons on either side of it. A most un-cute, un-kiddie-friendly memory of something Saskia tried to say the night before goes shuddering through my brain—

"Over there," the nurse is saying, pointing at another door.

"Thanks," I say again, nodding significantly at her.

"Just go," she hisses at me through a cheesy smile.

Honestly, there's no need to get nasty about it, some part of me starts up, but I am too ~~dog-dead~~ tired and depressed to pursue it. There's no point even asking if I can have my ice-cream van back; the last I saw of it, it was being invaded by people in biosuits, and in any case, I doubt there'd even be enough gas left to get me to the gate…so I just plod to the door and go.

CHAPTER EIGHT

A s soon as I get outside, I realize I don't even know how to get back to the gate. The door has shut behind me. My fist goes to hammer on the door so I can demand directions, but maybe that's not the best idea…not least because I can feel a small flame of anger licking round my heart. I'm in a sort of hub of army polytunnels—walkways between buildings. These people, they don't even have to worry about what the sky is doing. These people are *safe*.

I stand there for a moment, feeling the small flame crackle, trying to figure out which way to go. I pick the longest tunnel—I can hardly see the door at the other end—and trudge down it.

Some woman marches straight past me and gets to the door ahead of me.

"Excuse me—" is as far as I get with asking where I should go to throw myself out of here, because when she bats that door open, I am struck speechless.

It's the army play park. An undercover oasis. They've got themselves a gigantic polytunnel stadium thing, trees in it and everything. Swings and stuff for kids, places to sit and chitchat about the apocalypse… This is probably why they let the ice-cream van in. Cleaned up, it will make a nice addition. People—normal people, not just soldiers and medical types—are sauntering about or standing, gossiping. A bunch of blokes are playing basketball. Some fool is even going for a jog.

I sure wish I had hair left to fiddle with, because I need something comforting to do right now…while I stand, watching, feeling the flame burn brighter and harder. I notice someone noticing me, so I glare at them ("Yeah? What's it to you, *safe* person?") and start walking.

It is an OUTRAGE.

But le cherry on le icing on le great big fat army cupcake is:

Outside one of the many doorways leading in and out of this place, I see a chalkboard sign with a dinner menu on it. It's written in French so fancy it is way beyond even my superb grasp of the language. ("*Je m'appelle Ruby. J'habite en Dartbridge. J'ai quinze ans.*") Fancy French for a fancy menu: it's *à la* this, and *au sauce* that, and *avec* and *et*. Yes, there's a lot of *avec*s and *et*s. Then, scribbled at the bottom, it says:

IRISH STEW
EGGS, HAM, CHIPS, + BEANS

I used to be a vegetarian, but anything—anything—on that menu would do for me right now. With all the *avec*s and *et*s you can eat. The mystery of where they'd be getting all that food is of no concern at all to me. I am reading my own thought menu:

Quelle brilliantness!
I am going in!
What's the worst that they can do?
The worst they can do is kick
me out—et I was going to kick myself
out anyway!

74

HA! HA! AVEC HA! HA!

I go in. My stomach couldn't care less, but my brain is pleased to note that this canteen place just looks and feels like any normal kind of canteen—which is just as well, because I'm really not going to have enough time to do any kind of thorough reconnaissance before I drown in a pool of drool. My two principal observations are: there's nobody much in there and—

Noooooooo! THEY'RE CLEARING THE REMAINS OF THE FOOD AWAY!

Oh, honestly, really, I am probably going to be thrown out of this place any second now, so I might as well…

I grab me a tray and a plate and rush at the counter.

"Could I just get some of that?" I say, gripping the edge of the metal tray of leftovers this cook type in chef's whites is about to remove.

He looks at me in a startled way (for reasons—to do with my face— that I will understand shortly) and for a micro-nanosecond I am fairly somewhat startled by him too, because he really does look like that French chef bloke off the TV, the one my grandma really liked, but there is no time to dwell on that because I am already shoveling *le* contents of the tray onto my plate. I scrape it clean. He gives me the sort of disgusted-chef look that makes me think he really might be that bloke off the TV, but I do not have time to dwell on that either because—

AARGH! They're clearing away the desserts!

By the time I've finished, my tray is so heavy, my arms are questioning how long they can hold it as I turn and… So the whole place is pretty much empty, right? There are a few people left, lingering over *le* top nosh, but I want to sit away from people. I want to stuff my face in peace, then find a place to sleep—in this canteen if I have to. I look to the far end of the room; it is darker there, the

75

lights down at that end off already, chairs stacked on tables. Only one person sitting there, alone.

I must be really, really, really hungry, because I suddenly feel all shaky and my stomach does this funny flip.

As I get closer, I see that he has a book open in front of him... but he isn't trying to read in the darkness; he is just staring out of the window—into space, I presume, because you can't see into the stadium from here and the view's not all that, just more boring buildings. But at least he can see the view; he's got new glasses.

D-A-R-I-U-S S-P-R-A-T-T

I wish I knew how terrible I look, but maybe I don't look terrible at all. This is not because I care about what Darius Spratt thinks, you understand. This is for the sake of my own dignity. There's quite a lot of black makeup gloop on my hands, but it can't really be smudged all over my face, can it? (Oh yes, it can!) On my tray, the tiny upside-down reflection of me in the spoon (for quicker stew shoveling) gives no real clue—because the light is so bad, I suppose. I'd rustle up some inner dignity, but I won't be able to hold the tray for long enough to get that done. I take a deep breath and a long, shaky walk across that room.

I spill my water putting the tray on the table. It goes all over my food.

The Spratt, startled, looks around and—

"Ruby!" he gushes.

This makes a change from what he usually says to me, which is, "What have you done to your hair?" That will be coming, I am sure. For now, the gushy voice is the least of it—he actually surges to his feet and opens his arms and—

I dump myself down as elegantly as I dumped the tray. There will be no hugging here, I can assure you.

"Hi," I say—as *curtly* and as crisply as I can manage.

The Spratt gawks at me with joy and—oh no! You're kidding me! Glistening tears well in his eyes. (TEARS OF GUILT. Should be.) The effect on me is horrific; I have had a very traumatic time and very little sleep and so, in my weakened state, I feel a surge of emotion at the sight of his familiar, nerdy face. (See how dreadful apocalypses are?)

"*Siddown!*" I hiss.

The Spratt sits back down—but he can hardly stay in his seat; he leans across the table at me, and I see his hand creeping across it toward my hand, which is just lying there, ~~dog dead~~ exhausted by all the goings-on. I grab my spoon and shovel stew into my face. It is hard to swallow. I am starving, and the *irksome* presence of the Spratt is putting me off my food.

"You're alive…" he breathes at me.

Yup. He is definitely one of the smart, useful people. I nod at him in a mean sort of way, eyes narrowed; if my mouth wasn't crammed full of unswallowable cold stew mush, I'd tell him straight out what my look is intended to convey: "NO THANKS TO YOU."

"Did you find your dad?" he blurts.

How did he do that? How did he just manage to pick the one question that stabs me straight in the heart? I have been back in the Spratt's company for approximately ten nanoseconds and already I am wigging out. Right. I've got to shut him up. I need to swallow so I can talk. I grab his mug of—cocoa? He's drinking *cocoa*?!—swig, and force that stew mush down.

"Oh, Ruby," he whispers softly, like he already knows the answer. So softly and kindly and sweetly, I feel myself choking up—which is even more annoying than wigging out.

I shove my plate of food away, mainly so the spoon is out of reach. Otherwise, I would be tempted to find out if you can stab with one. Instead, I stab with words.

"Did you find your mom?"

The Spratt is adopted. He now basically has a snowflake's chance in hell of finding her.

He glances around, and I think he's about to yell at me, which I already know in a way—but only in a certain sort of way—I would deserve for asking such a cruel question—but no: "I did," he whispers, his eyes wide with the marvelousness of the thing.

The seething troll monster of my own feelings bristles. I'd slap it, but it is covered, all over, in razor-sharp spines. It has a heart though; somewhere in the *gargantuan* raging mass of its troll body, a small, sad, human heart beats.

"Really?" I say.

"Kind of," he says. He glances around again. "I looked it up," he whispers—so I'm guessing he wasn't supposed to or something. "I know who she was—her name and where she lived. I just don't know what happened to her, you know…"

I do know. I know exactly. And I know exactly what that feels like. And I also remember the too-many times (twice) the Spratt dared to point out to me that my dad was probably dead, and the troll monster wants to say this now, to him, about his mom, and see him hurt, but I just can't stand it. I can't stand any of this. I get up, shoving my chair backward.

I don't know where I think I am going. I have nowhere to go.

I burst into tears.

"Ruby!" says Darius.

His arms are around me. His arms do not feel the spines. The troll monster shudders and judders with tears.

Ah-hoo, ah-wah, ah-wooh, blubs the troll.

But you will notice that it was the troll that was crying and not the small, sad human heart.

CHAPTER NINE

The Spratt led me to another block and into what was basically a cell. As I have actually seen a cell—in Dartbridge Police Station—I would in fact say that it was smaller than a cell. There was one tiny single bed in there, one chair, one minute desk, a tiny TV screen stuck high on the wall, and a closet. Not exactly five star, but maybe those people in the camp were so gorged out on scarfing delicious food all day that they just needed somewhere to flop in between.

I had not scarfed delicious food, but I did need to flop—so I flopped on the bed. Darius hesitated, then took the chair—keeping his distance from my body, but not—unfortunately—from my mind.

"Ruby…" he started up.

"What?" I muttered. It felt like there was this slow-motion thought whirlpool in my head—like probably there were things to be said, but all those things were mixed up, bobbing in and out of sight as they swirled around and around and around, spiraling into sleep. Fat chance.

"I'm so glad you're here," he says. "I was going to come and look for you."

"Yeah, Saskia said," I mumble, my eyes drifting shut.

"You've seen Sask?!"

"Yes, *Dar*, I've seen *Sask*." I sigh. "She's in the hospital." I haul a thing out of the whirlpool; it is Saskia's foot. "Well, most of her is. Her foot went in some water and someone had to, you know, *remove* it."

"Oh my ✳."

"With an ax."

I feel so sick. I think I'm going to be—my eyes snap open, and I edge myself up. The Spratt is staring at me with a horrified look on his face.

"It was what she wanted," I tell him. I hear Sask begging: *Cut it off, cut it off!* "And then I brought her here myself, in an ice-cream van. Have you got something to drink?"

The Spratt seems to take a moment to process this simple request. He gets up and rummages in the cupboard and hands me a can of something. The crack and hiss of the ring pull is loud as a bomb.

"Is she OK?" he asks.

"I don't know," I say. "They said she'd be fine. I don't think the rain thing got her, but she lost a lot of blood."

I glug the fizzy drink, something disgusting I don't even like.

"And a foot, obviously," I add. "I think I'm going to be sick…"

I lurch off the bed looking for something, anything, to throw up into—there is only a trash can, so I throw up into that, the Spratt rubbing my back and me too weak to resist.

"Sorry about that," I tell him, wiping spew drool from my mouth. I feel disgusting, inside and out. And I'm dehydrated, aren't I? You'd think I'd know the signs by now, but, hey, no one's perfect. (*Not even me*, booms the troll.)

I sip at the drink in the can. At least it's a fluid. My stomach grudgingly accepts it.

"She said she didn't want to come back here, not ever."

"Yeah, well," says the Spratt.

"She was screaming her head off about it."

"Look, Ru," says Darius. "Saskia…she got a little spooked."

I am too weak to tell him not to call me Ru. I try to lie down—the whirlpool starts up and my head spins with it. I sit back up. If I think about how I feel, I really will spew again—not that there's anything left in me to spew out, so I might as well attempt to continue with this hideous conversation.

"What about?" I ask the Spratt.

I cannot imagine what's coming next. There are plenty of things to be spooked about in an apocalypse—being forced to share a room with Darius Spratt, for example. Sask can't have liked that unless…

"Well," says the Spratt, "she kind of got it into her head that…"

He tails off, looks doubtfully at me.

"What?!"

"Oh, it's such a horrible thing, Ruby. Maybe now isn't the best time."

"Believe me," I tell him, "there is NOTHING you could tell me that's any more horrible than the stuff I've *actually seen*."

The troll within me is stirring. I've been in this place for, like, five seconds and I already know that whatever counts as a trauma in this place—for example, they've run out of caviar to put on their cornflakes—does not count as a trauma in the real world—of the useless—where I have been forced to live.

"It's just a rumor," he says.

Ha! It's not even a REAL thing!

"And this place is full of rumors. People say all kinds of crazy stuff."

Yeah, and outside here, they DO it. (That would include me too, of course.)

"Someone told Saskia they're experimenting on people," Darius says.

81

Huh…

"You know, trying to find a cure?"

I nod. That's what experimenting is, isn't it? Trying to find stuff out. I mean, actually, when you think about it, it would even make sense—in a way, I mean. If this thing doesn't harm animals, what else would you test a cure on?

People, obviously.

WHAT?!

"It's nonsense, of course—Sask even thought so herself…to begin with. But then this girl she worked with disappeared, and Saskia was convinced that… Well, I think she thought…people were being done away with. You know? *Experimented* on?"

Darius, you made it sound crazy. And it seemed crazy. But.

"Sunnyside," I whisper. It comes back to me again like a thing from a dream, a thing Saskia was trying to tell me—the only word I remember.

"Yeah," says Darius. "She said that to you too?"

I nod.

"She got spooked, Ru. She snooped around…and she thought it was a thing that got put on people's records when…they'd gone to be *experimented* on."

That's what she said, wasn't it? I see Saskia, drunk, hanging on to me, going "Sunnyside, Ruby, *Sunnyside*. They're killing people. *Sunnyside…*" and me shaking her off, so I could dance. I just wanted to dance.

"She thought it might be her next," Darius is saying. "She was doing an admin job—but it was an easy one, not exactly that skilled. I think she thought she might be *expendable*."

I am staring at him.

"Ru! It's OK! It's just stupid nonsense! Honestly! People come and go from here all the time!"

82

"Saskia ran away…"

"Yeah, I guessed that's what she did."

"…and I brought her back."

"Ruby…"

"I thought it was the right thing to do."

"Of course it was the right thing. Of course it was!"

"Darius, you didn't hear her *screaming*."

He leaves his chair and crouches down in front of me, puts his hands on my sparkly witch-fairy knees, and stares up into my face.

"None of it is true, Ruby. None of it. People are just scared, that's all. Scared people say crazy things, and other scared people believe them."

I nod slowly. I want to believe this. I've heard crazy stuff myself: "I got told the government knew the rain was coming. That they knew and they didn't warn us."

Darius looks down at my knees. I want him to tell me it isn't so.

"Yeah," he says. "That part might be true, Ruby."

He looks up at me. No, I don't want to believe this. I don't want to believe this.

"I don't know. It's what a lot of people are saying."

"Darius…"

His family, his family's friends, his neighbors—they all died too.

"They seemed *prepared* here, that's all," he says. "I mean—not brilliantly prepared or anything. There's stuff that's taken months to sort out…just like maybe they had a head start."

We stare at each other. I know we're both thinking of our families…and though it's not exactly appropriate right now, "head start" makes me think of school and of games and of watching delighted teachers watch the fast kids, while the likes of me and Darius Spratt huffed and puffed at the back, losing.

"It's done now," Darius says. "It's done."

I stare bleakly at him.

"And Saskia was wrong," he says. "All that's happening here right now is there are people trying to find a cure."

I am nodding this calming information into my brain—where it sits, very unhappily, alongside that memory of Saskia—calm, cool, superpoised, supersmart Saskia—screaming her head off.

"Really," says Darius. "*All* that is happening in this place is that there are a lot of people working twenty-four/seven to try to work this thing out. Day and night, Ru, that's all we're doing."

"We? Is that what *you're* doing?"

"Yeah! Course! I've got a job here too. Everyone has. Know what I do all day? I crunch numbers."

What numbers, Darius Spratt? That's what I should have asked him. But I drank up every calming word he spoke.

"You can't imagine how boring it is," he says.

Crunching numbers? Oh, I think I can.

"But we've just got to get on with it. *I've* just got to get on with it. That's the only way we're going to be able to sort this thing out."

I nodded. I felt reassured. I did. I believed Spratt the Sensible. I believed him because he believed himself. And, in a way, everything he said *was* true…because he didn't know any better.

"I'll go see Sask tomorrow," says Darius. "See how she is."

I nod a bit more.

"Look, I kept all your stuff," he says.

From under the bed he pulls out bag after bag of my looted goodies. (Although I see instantly that they are not how I left them. Things have been *folded*. That's pretty freaky in itself, but it also means that someone has been through it all. It is possible that Darius Spratt has touched my ten thousand pairs of looted knickers, the only slightly sensible thing I packed when I first went looking for my dad.)

"Well, most of it. We couldn't fit it all in here, so we had to dump some of it. Sorry."

I'm not really listening because... Come to Momma, pretty baby, come to Momma... I've just found ♥*my phone*♥. I'd kiss it, but the Spratt is watching—and in the next second, I discover even my beloved cell phone has been *touched*. Not only is it charged...

"*It's unlocked!*" I shriek.

"I... It...it's not what it looks like!" the Spratt stammers, flustered.

Know what? It IS what it looks like. He's gone bright red. He has SO looked on my phone.

"You ✹! How DARE you!"

"Whoa! No! Ruby! OK, I did look, but just to see whether anyone had called or anything—"

"Have they?!" I'm jabbing away at my phone now, checking everything: messages, call logs. My fingers claw and scrape at the screen; all by themselves, they remember what to do.

"No," says Darius.

I cradle my phone to my heart. I am as cross as cross can be, but I feel a troll-ish *ah-hoo, ah-wah, ah-wooh* trembling on my lips.

"We decided to do it—"

"*We?!*"

"Me and Sask."

Uh. My mind spins somewhere way out of the known universe thinking what's on that phone, what they've both seen. Some particularly nasty comments about Saskia come flashing back like incoming texts in my memory.

"We were just worried about you, Ru. They keep saying they're going to get the cellular networks back," Darius blunders on, "so we thought we should keep the phones charged up—you know, in case anyone called. There's this guy I work with who cracks them in exchange for water. He likes taking baths. Got a tub in his room, I heard. Oh, Ruby, I…"

More private incoming messages pop up in my head, and I can't help myself: I groan out loud.

"We really thought it was the best thing to do," says Darius quietly.

I gulp and nod. I get it—just about. I still feel *violated*…and guilty. Some of those things I said about Saskia? They really were truly dreadful.

"Can I get you something, Ru?"

"I'd quite like to have my old life back."

(Yeah—and with a phone that's safely locked.)

"But then I wouldn't be in it."

I can't help it: some kind of cough that could almost be a laugh comes spluttering out. The Spratt grins.

"What would make you feel better?" he asks. "You want a shower or something?"

"That's not funny," I tell him.

CHAPTER TEN

Indeed it is not. These ✸ have showers. Apparently they only get one swipe-card-monitored, time-limited shower a week because—oh the poor lambs!—there's only so much FILTERED water available.

"*You can FILTER it?!*" I whisper-screech.

"Shh!" says the Spratt. "Sure."

We are standing in the corridor outside the aforementioned swipe-card-monitored, time-limited showering facility.

"*You can FILTER it?!*" I do believe I just whisper-screeched even louder.

"*Yesss*," hisses the Spratt, "but not like through a sieve or something. The bacterium is too tiny. It's like *0.1 micrometers in diameter*," he says, like that explains it.

I don't have to tell you that I have no idea how big a micrometer is, let alone 0.1 of one, and only a hazy recollection of which part of a circle a diameter is—however, this does not seem to me to be the point.

"*But you can—*"

"*It's a complicated process. Trust me, it's really complicated.*"

I open my mouth to tell Darius just how simple I think it is when someone opens their door. Darius shoves me into the aforementioned swipe-card-monitored, time-limited showering facility.

"*Can we just discuss this later?*" he hisses, pushing towels and clothes and toiletries into my arms. "You've got three minutes."

"*What?*" It's going to take me that long to get undressed.

"From when the shower goes on. Three minutes," the Spratt hisses and shuts the door on me.

Whoa! My stepdad, Simon, if he were still alive, would have loved this. He moaned at me so, so, so, so, so many times about the amount of time I took in the shower—which was only partially my fault because, as I pointed out to him so, so, so, so, so many times, if the shower were a decent one, I wouldn't have to do that. I smile, just remembering that—and then the smile dies on my face.

Why can't the dead come back alive? Why not? Why shouldn't it be possible? What difference would it make to God—if there is a God (which I doubt—and if there is, it/she/he/the Supreme Panda is in BIG TROUBLE with me)—or what difference even would it make to the general *micrometer* mathematics of the universe if just one of them did? Henry! Could I not just be given back Henry, dearest babiest brat beloved? Surely the universe could give back just this one, small, baby life?

Don't go there, I tell myself. *Don't think those things*.

I tear off my witch-fairy frock, still thinking those things, and I storm at the mirror to give myself a pep talk and I...

Ooooooooh, gosh. In spite of everything, I almost want to laugh...I look SO bad. Grace's pretty design has been wrecked. It is nothing but a great band of smudgy black and gold across my face. You can think, right here, if you want to: so why didn't the Spratt tell me? Hah! Only a nerd would fail to mention such a crucial thing.

I get stuff ready. Three minutes, huh? I need to make them count. Since the rain fell, ignoring the time I had jumped into a swimming pool to escape death (then jumped right back out again for the same reason—don't ask me about that, and don't ask me what happened after, which involved Darius Spratt and kissing)—I'd had ONE bath. No showers, obviously. ONE bath. On a crazy, mad day when I'd scored six—count 'em!—six great big plastic bottles of water from a gym. I'd left five outside in the summer sun, heating up to a glorious lukewarm, then poured them into the bath. I'd got new batteries for Mr. Fitch's boom-box ghetto blaster especially for the occasion. I lit candles. I had prime beauty products lined up. Super-prime looted beauty products. I slicked my crackly, under-nourished hair with a super-prime looted moisturizing treatment and slathered on a face mask. I pressed play on Mr. Fitch's brass-band music tape, though it was getting kind of wobbly and worn, and I got into the bath.

For approximately ten seconds, it was delicious.

I sighed into it. I laid back. Clouds of bubbles frothed around me.

In the candlelight, from the showerhead, which had not been used in weeks and weeks and weeks…I saw a single drop of water fall. It landed in the bathwater.

splip!

Drip, drip, drop, dead.

I jumped out of that bath like there were piranhas in it. I hugged towels around me, scratched and scraped them all over my body. No, oh no, oh no, oh no, oh no. Oh no. OH NO.

All that water wasted. All that water wasted. Wasted.

But I was alive. I was still alive.

I told Simon to fix that shower.

Three minutes? This is going to be a luxury. I will not miss a second of it. Pre-shower gelled loofah at the ready (I'm surprised the Spratt takes skin care so seriously; it might be Saskia's influence—certainly I suspect there must be something other than *le* fine French cuisine to account for the improvement in his skin), I stand under the showerhead.

I stare up at it. It is one of those big, fat daisy-head showers. Is it going to come out cold? Do I care? I care enough to crank the setting thing up to hot. Am I really ready for this? Oh yes. I am so ready. I press the lever—nothing happens. I have that moment of frustrated confusion you have in any new shower—OH! Maybe it's like—I lift the lever.

The daisy head bursts into life, water pours—pours—down—but HOT! SO HOT! I have to scrabble around immediately to work out how to cool it down.

And I work it out.

And I shower, scrubbing frantically…but I tell you: that—those three minutes—was the best, the most appreciated shower I swear I will ever have in my life.

I swung open the door, clean and serene, in a pair of the Spratt's pj's.

Darius, waiting outside, took one look at me and said, "Oh my ✳."

He hustled me back into the room.

"*What happened to you?!*" he hissed—even though there was now obviously no need to hiss at all.

I knew why he'd be asking that. *Sans* Grace's makeup, I had reverted to…pure Panda Ruby, I suppose. You can't scrub away major bruising.

"I…" I said, flopping onto the bed and trying to work out what I did want to say about it…but I was too ~~dog dead~~ just plain tired. "Let's not talk about this now," I murmured.

"OK," said Darius, leaning across me.

90

My eyes snapped open in panic. He was staring at me in—ah—
um—a *tender manner*.

WERE WE GOING TO KISS?!

"I need to get the other mattress, Ru."

"What?"

"It's underneath you. Can you get up, just for a sec?"

"Yeah, course," I said, flustered.

I got to my feet and stood by the closet as Darius sorted out beds.
A sticky fug of embarrassment filled the room. And I reckoned it
wasn't just me either.

I climbed into bed and pulled the covers up to my chin.

Darius started taking his shirt off.

"Hn. Um, maybe I'll just…" He pointed at the light switch.

"Yes!" I squeaked—and I turned over anyway, trying not to think
that maybe it might be a nice thing to do right now to curl up in
bed with the Spratt.

"Night, Ru," whispered Darius.

"Night," I squeaked back.

"I think you're really brave, you know."

I grunted squeakily.

"You really are. Even the shower. Most people around here are
too scared to use them." He yawned.

Sometime in the night, I woke up. I was hot, and I kicked off the
duvet. And I lay. I just lay. The Spratt was reading—with a flashlight—on a bed on the floor, down beside me. And I knew he knew
I'd woken up, but neither of us spoke.

In the light from his flashlight on the wall, he did a shadow
thing. He waved. Waggling fingers that looked way too much like
the wiggly space bug thing-in-the-rain for my liking shook shadow-
ishly about.

When the Spratt knew I was watching, he spoke.

"You do know nothing...you know, *happened* between me and Sask, don't you?" he whispers.

"Hn."

Oh my ✳, did I just say "Hn"?!

"She was just there, on her own, so we teamed up—but not, you know, like *that*."

"Whatever," I say. And the second it comes out of my mouth, I feel a bit bad about saying it and I feel cross with myself that I feel bad.

"I was going to come and look for you, Ru," he whispers.

"But you didn't, did you?"

"I couldn't see," he says—and for one beautiful, weird moment I think he means that he must have kind of lost sight of my exquisite beauty or something. "I had to wait an age for new glasses."

Those glasses. Those ✳ glasses. I do not want to talk. I just want to sleep, but my eyes, staring at the wall in front of me, refuse to shut.

"I crashed a Ferrari," I tell the Spratt. "That's how come...you know. My eyes."

"You crashed a Ferrari?" he says.

"Yeah. Totaled it."

I smile in the dark.

"You TOTALED a Ferrari?" he says. His voice is about ready to burst with laughter.

Ah! How *can* this be happening? "Yeah," I tell him, with something that feels like a giggle rising in my throat.

I hear the Spratt spit laughter into the dark—and oh, oh, oh, oh. What is this? I laugh too.

The flashlight beam on the wall shakes—and HA!—a dog-head shadow puppet, formed by the Spratt's own hand, appears in it.

"What's that supposed to be?" I laugh, even though I know perfectly well. Didn't Simon play that game with me when I was little, making shadow puppets with his hands, trying to win a smile?

That thought could almost make me stop laughing, but—ha!—the Spratt shadow dog tips back its head, opens its jaw, and HOWLS.

"I missed you," he says.

CHAPTER ELEVEN

In the morning, the Spratt wakes me up with breakfast. I'd have been pretty grumpy about that because I was sound asleep, but he brought a spectacular selection of items. I couldn't have stacked up that tray better myself: as well as *Les Pastries Française* there's *Le Full English Breakfast:* fried everything and a pile of baked beans.

He sits and watches me cramming food into my face like a cavewoman. Part of me wants to ask about where, precisely, all this stuff comes from, but mainly I just feel like I don't want to hear it—haven't I seen enough already to know that while I have suffered Apocalypse Max, these people have been living in Apocalypse Lite?

I was wrong; survival is a competition, and these people are winning—which reminds me, about twelve hours later than a nicer (nice?) person would have thought of it:

"Hey, what happened to the Princess?" I manage to ask between glorious great mouthfuls of eggs and bacon.

I may need to remind you that the Princess was this mute kid the Spratt found—or rather she found him—after the rain fell. An Asian kid, maybe Indian, I'd guessed. Age unknown, name unknown. Tiny, beautiful, heart-woundingly sad. Mute with fright (we reckoned), but never silent…least of all on the subject of me.

The Princess didn't like me, not one bit. I tried to be kind; I did try. I just shouted a lot. It was a stressful time.

"That Welsh family took her. They had to. What do I know about looking after a kid?"

"You did OK," I say, cramming in fried bread. And then I think the thought that goes with that thought. "What happened to my dog?" I ask, stabbing a sausage. I mean Saskia's dog, the Darling Chihuahua.

"They don't let animals in here, Ru," says Darius.

There is this awful silence during which I can no longer face eating that sausage. Not that I think Darling got turned into one. These people are spoiled, but they are surely not monsters. Just coldhearted abandoners of small, innocent dogs and…

"Or people like me."

"Ru…" says Darius.

I amaze myself that I am the one to say it, but the thought comes to me, cutting through the snuggly hug of food and sleepiness as sharp as a surgeon's knife: "I'm not going to be able to stay here, am I?"

"We can talk about that later," he says.

While seeming not to be an answer to my question, that is an answer. It isn't a very specific one though, because it's not clear to me who's going to kick me out first: the British Army, the Spratt—or me. Am I capable of doing that? Am I capable of trying to walk out of this place with bravery and dignity? (Once I have finished breakfast, obviously.) (Or maybe tomorrow, if I lie low and the Spratt doesn't get too pushy.)

"I think, if you leave—" says Darius.

"When. It's 'when,' isn't it? Not 'if.'"

"I want to come too. I mean—if that's OK with you."

I do sort of feel I could faint or something, so massive is the storm of conflicting *stuff* in my head. This is a conversation I never ever thought I'd be having in a place I never ever thought I'd be— physically, emotionally, mentally, you-name-it-ly. (Have I told you before how much I hate apocalypses?) There is only one way to deal with this, and that is to push it all back onto the Spratt.

I amaze myself for a second time—and I haven't even finished breakfast.

"Yeah," I say, "and what about your job, Darius? What about working twenty-four/seven to save the planet?"

He's quiet for a moment, then, "Maybe they can manage without me?" he says.

Uh. I shake my head. The truth is harsh. "It's me they can manage without."

"But maybe I can't, Ru," he says.

I feel like I want to cry. "Yeah, you can," I tell him. "Just pretend we're back at school."

I get that in quick—so quick. To him, I was a clueless snob. To me, he was the subnerd of subnerds. If the rain hadn't fallen, I don't suppose we would ever have even spoken.

It'd be very wrong if you thought I was in any way being noble at this point. I am saying what I am saying, but my heart is running about like a headless chicken. And what solution there is to this, I do not know. I don't even know what to say next. Nor, it seems, does the Spratt.

"I'd better go to work," he says.

I stare up at him, blinking. I don't want him to go. But I can't say it.

"Will you be OK?" he asks.

"Sure," I say, taking a slurp of tea. "Happy number crunching."

"I'll see if I can check on Saskia at lunchtime," he says. "Then I'll come back here. You sure you'll be OK?"

"Sure I'm sure."

"Well, there's always the TV if you get bored."

Oh yes, they've got TV.

I'd pull myself together enough to be enraged about that too, but I've got other things on my mind. The second the Spratt shoves off, I spring into action. The temptation of all my friends' unlocked phones, which has been quietly gnawing away at the weaker parts of my brain all night, instantly gets the better of me, and then the consequences of the temptation of the unlocked phones gets the better of me too.

Much gasping and weeping takes place. I find out a number of unpleasant and alarming things (e.g., just how many people knew Andrew Difford had gone around saying I was a lousy kisser). (Seriously, if I ever have the misfortune to clap eyes on him again, he's gonna wish the rain had got him first.) Most hideous and heart-breaking of all, I find out that it could, incredibly, be possible that Saskia was right about Caspar. On my friends' phones I find texts from him and about him that are not exactly reassuring. But it cannot be true. To console myself, I press the beautiful earphones that had once been pressed into his beautiful ears (ears that I had nibbled, and not like a hamster would) into my own ears and crank up Caspar's MP3. I don't stop to question why anyone would have bothered to keep it charged.

My misery is complete. That moron Spratt has deleted my true love's achingly gorgeous acoustic demo tracks (surely written for me and surely all about me) and has replaced them with a ghastly medley of eighties hits from the car journey we had taken together, when we'd laughed.

I am not laughing now.

In despair, I am forced to turn to the TV. It is actually fairly totally excellent—they've even got more channels than we ever had at home, so I pass a jolly/miserable morning scarfing down pastries and channel hopping and feeling sorry for myself—when I remember to. TV is so distracting, right? You don't even have to skip commercials anymore because there aren't any. This isn't live TV I realize, just streamed reruns of every kind of program...and that would have been OK by me for the rest of the day, but I stumbled across *that* talent show.

I watch again, jaw wobbling, as that poor girl loses. That poor girl who was actually very talented indeed, but just not *as* talented—and certainly not as *boringly gorgeous*—as that other girl, the one that *won* (even though I'd voted for Miss Loser with all my might and have a colossal phone bill to prove it hidden under my bed at home).

It makes me thoroughly depressed. Because...basically...I *am* Miss Loser, aren't I? The kind of girl who'd lose even with a head start.

I don't want to feel like I am useless like the army/government has said...but maybe—URGH! IT HURTS MY HEAD TO EVEN THINK IT!—maybe I am. I never meant to be useless. I only ever meant to be me. And it's not fair—it's SO not fair—that I never got to find out who that "me" was. I was just getting around to it, don't you see? I was going to be fantastic. My life was going to be fantastic.

I feel that room and the hypnotically animally scent of boy-pong that fills it closing around me. As my own looted packing was useless (OK, so those super-skinny jeans? I only need to look at them to know it's a no), and I couldn't squeeze into Saskia's stuff even if I wanted to, I put some of the Spratt's clothes on. I go to find the bathroom. What's inside the toilet is already fizzing with bleach—and

I discover why: in a most un-luxury way, the toilet doesn't flush. Maybe you need a swipe-card for that too? Swipe and wipe?

This ✳ apocalypse. It's really getting on my nerves. It's REALLY getting on my nerves.

I come out of the bathroom. I walk to the end of the corridor. I look out of the window in the door. My recollection of the night before is so hazy and jumbled, I wouldn't have known I was even looking at "the hospital," but I see the ice-cream van parked outside, under a canopy, alongside an ambulance.

I think about Saskia.

I block out the hideous memory of her screaming.

I feel pretty sorry for myself right now, but the stuff that's in my head is a mess of ugly choices that exist in reality—and not in fear. Sask has not had the benefit of a calming anti-freak-out chat from the Spratt. As far as I know, no one is offering to go anywhere with her—and if, before the rain fell, my life was *surely* going to be fantastic (I was convinced it was heading that way), Sask's already was.

When you look at it like that, taking dead families out of the equation, she's lost things she actually had (including, specifically, a foot). I've lost things I never had (a hot boyfriend, a life).

So maybe that means I can't have lost them?

Hn.

It just feels like it.

It also feels like…the least I can do is to go and see her. Maybe, if she hasn't started screaming again, I'll be able to give her a calming anti-freak-out chat. And I'll just see if there's anything she wants. Like flowers and fruit! That's what people take people who are in the hospital, isn't it? Flowers and fruit! Ha! And if there is any fresh fruit to be had anywhere, Monsieur le Chef would have it. And I'll ask Sask about him too—whether he really is that guy off the TV.

Yes. I'll go see Sask.

I step out of the building.

From the door I leave by, there is no polytunnel walkway; there is just open space—and clear sky. Clear September sky. A school sky: clear and blue and warm—only the odd dunce of a congestus cloud skulking about. They are my weak point, those clouds: cumulus mediocris, cumulus congestus. One rains, one doesn't. In my opinion, no one but a total nerd could tell them apart.

In any case, I am not worried—not in the least. The sky above me, the only sky that counts, is blue as blue can be, which explains why there are kids out. I catch a glimpse of one wandering up to the ice-cream-van ambulance. Makes me smile, seeing that; he's studying the menu of delights—poor thing. Half an arm missing, bandaged.

You're probably thinking things already. I wasn't. I just saw a hurt kid.

And as I get closer, I hear other kids—laughing, shouting…one crying…and I…I detour, around the back of the building, figuring, if I am thinking anything at all, that this might be an easier way in. No tricky nurse station/desk/explanation/camera situation. Just slip in, right?

I round the corner.

Kids out playing in the yard. Emergency exit door to ward open.

I don't really think about what this is. I don't think about it until I walk into the ward.

I don't want them to make a film out of this story anymore. I do not want this picture—ever—to be seen in another person's mind.

Except…maybe you should know it. Maybe you should know.

The ward. What would I say, Darius Spratt? How much time, really, does it take to understand what you are seeing if you look? In 0.1 MICROMETERS OF A SECOND I get it:

The ward is full of kids—KIDS. Some are out of their beds, walking or limping about…kids with hands and arms and feet and legs chopped off. And fingers. I'm guessing those are the lucky ones in the ward. The ward of bandaged stumps.

They look with wide eyes at me, at the scary crazy lady—yeah, I guess that's what I am to them, even though I am only fifteen years old. Shaved head, black eyes, wearing a boy's clothes, tooth missing in a mouth that is open in a silent scream.

I can hardly breathe.

A nurse strides past me to tell the kids off, to shut the door and come inside. Then she comes bustling up to me. "There is no public access here," she says.

"I've come to see my friend," I tell her.

There is no feeling in my voice. I breathe—I try to breathe.

"There is no public access." She takes hold of my elbow and leads me out of that place.

She shuts the door. I see that ward name again:

Sunnyside

So we're back where I was last night. At the nurses' station, in a corridor, surrounded by a maze of doors. The nurse behind the desk—who is not the same one who was there last night—does this WT✹?! thing at the sight of me and looks in panic at the other one.

If there's one thing I learned in school it's that in potentially traumatic and difficult situations ("Did you copy this homework from someone, Ruby?") it is best, at least to begin with, to show no emotion whatsoever. That is OK, because I am not aware of feeling any emotion. It is also best, at least to begin with, to stick to your story ("No, I did not copy this homework"). Words! Oh, words! You come back to me now!

"I've just come to see my friend," I tell them. "Her name is Saskia Miller. I brought her in. Last night. Someone chopped her foot off."

"No visitors are allowed here."

No. I expect not, eh? I expect not.

"I will be five minutes," I tell them. "And then I will go."

THEY—ARE—STILL—FREAKING.

"**I'LL GO**. I promise you *I'll just go*."

"I'm sorry," the desk nurse says. "Your friend died."

I. FEEL. SICK.

"No! She was OK! She was going to be OK! They said she'd be fine!"

They won't look at me.

"Did you *kill* her?"

Obviously, the ideal answer to this question is no…but that's not what they say. In fact, they don't say anything.

"Oh my ✳. It's true, isn't it? It *is* true! You're killing people!"

"You need to leave," I get told.

Too right, I do. I blunder back into the Sunnyside ward of kids.

"You gotta come with me," I tell them.

I grab at them, the loose kids. They are terrified of me.

"Just go—please go!" the nurse says.

"Not without them," I tell her. I get hold of the nearest kid, who—smart kid—smart, dumb, lovely, hurt, doomed kid—twists out of my grasp and squeals, "But we don't wanna go with her!" Which sets the rest of them off, crying and whining about how they don't want to go with me.

"Just GO," the nurse yells at me.

And I turn and I run for the door. The fire door, the emergency exit that is now shut.

I shove it open. Before she can scream, I run out.

All those times I've gone outside and forgotten to look up at the sky?

I look up at the sky.

CHAPTER TWELVE

O h," I whisper.

Hiya, Ruby! yells the rain. It is falling on my face.

It is pouring down. Where'd that come from?

It is pouring down. I feel each drop—I swear, EACH DROP—land on me.

I am going to die.

I AM GOING TO DIE.

"Sorry," I say to myself, to my life…to the nurse, who's standing—looking utterly horrified—at the door.

But I don't want to die! ✹ this! ✹! **No. NO.**

I'm coming back in—right, Nurse? And you're gonna cure me.

I don't want to die. I do not want to die.

That nurse sees me coming, and she'd love to shut the door, but she can't because she'd have to reach out into the rain—but her face—her face. The terror on it!

Too bad, lady—comin' in… She looks down; I look down. I see small kids coming up, clustering around her. I see the terror on their faces and—

"Hey," I say.

I stop where I am…right in front of them all, getting rained on.

I'm great with kids, me.

I try to smile at them. "Hey."

My own stupidity pours down on my head harder than the rain itself.

What did I think they'd be able to do for me anyway? Cut my head off?

I am ✸.

✸.

I'm ✸.

I feel…how I suppose Simon, my stepdad, must have felt…how a ton of other people must have felt…like I just wanna go home. To die. Only I will never make it home.

I'm never going to make it home.

I sit down. I do not fall to my knees. I just sit. And it rains on me.

Hiya, Ruby! shrieks the rain.

"✸," I hear the nurse swear, calling on a God I can't seriously believe she believes in anymore. She pulls kids away from the door. "✸," she says.

I am not offended. I am not *emotionally* hurt in the slightest. I'm going to die. That's all.

I get it.

Who would want to see this?

Those kids shouldn't have to see another person die.

I stare into the face of the sky. To every side of me, I can see scraps of blue sky, clouds that have yet to decide to become killers.

But—hey!—hello you, cloud that is raining on me.

Cumulus congestus. I get the difference between congestus and mediocris now. Yeah, I get it.

I stumble, roaring—finally roaring!—through the rain…and around the corner…

"RUBY!" I hear this shout so muffled it seems to come from somewhere inside my own head. "*RUBY!*"

I turn. I look. I see this wibbly-wobbly shadow person, hands pressed against the plastic of an army polytunnel walkway.

D-A-R-I-U-S S-P-R-A-T-T

Wibbly-wobbly shadow Spratt.

"DARIUS!" I run at him—

His hands and mine, they press together through the plastic, palm to palm.

"You were right," he is shouting. "Saskia was right. I checked. They're killing people. They're killing kids. The numbers I was crunching, they're doses. Bacteria doses, survival rates—oh, Ruby, I…"

I'm doomed. It's going to hurt a lot.

I wipe my hand across the plastic so, for one last moment, I can see his face more clearly. He has no words left, so I must find some for us both.

"Get out of here," I tell him.

The rain pours down between us.

"JUST GO! PLEASE, DARIUS! JUST GO!"

I close my eyes. I do not want to see this…but I feel it anyway. My heart lurches at the change of pressure. The gentle warmth under my palms is lost. He has gone.

I open my eyes.

Gone.

I saw a film once, where a guy who was going to die saw his life flash before him—and it made him smile, because he knew that although his family had annoyed him, it had been good. And he could feel like that because the people he cared about were still alive.

I can only hope Dar lives.

The rest of the people I care about are all dead. Most of them.

My dad. I'm never going to find my dad.

I wasn't going to find him anyway. Not him—not the Dan brother-brat.

I cannot die happy picturing people in the future feeling sad because I am not there (obviously).

I've got nothing. I've got nothing left.

I just wonder how bad it's going to hurt.

I sit down.

I am not even crying.

Hey, rain! Look! I am not even crying.

Who cares? laughs the rain, tumbling down my cheeks.

Yeah, well—whatever. *WHATEVER.*

I hit the rain with THE GRIN OF INDIFFERENCE, a smile known to teens all over the world as it is often our last defense against some appalling outrage. Of course, it is fairly completely and utterly useless as a form of defense, since it is generally likely to provoke intense anger in the recipient and make things a whole lot worse… But it's what you do, isn't it? When there's nothing else you can do.

There *is* nothing else I can do.

The rain couldn't care less.

So I think of a thing I can think about. My one last thought. I think of the plants and the creatures and the planet, and about how all that…about how all those things will go on.

(Apart from Whitby, almost certainly possibly…but he was just limping, wasn't he? Wasn't he?! He could still be OK, couldn't he? And apart from Darling the Chihuahua… Can't bear to think about that… And apart from the guinea pigs Gimli and Prince Charming—whom Ruby the Cat may have eaten… And apart from Fluffysnuggles the hamster whom I left in a mint-chocolate-chip ice-cream carton in an abandoned car. He WILL make it home.)

It's a pretty desperate image, snatched out of the dripping, glinting, sharp-toothed jaws of death, but it is all I have right now. That's it. That's all I have: the planet is going to go on. Like a lonely merry-go-round in the middle of space, but with not enough people left to enjoy the ride.

I lie down on the tarmac.

You **are** *a stupid, stupid girl!* laughs the rain, pouring down on me.

I start to get cold.

In fact, I am freezing cold and really wishing the whole hideous, painful death thing would just hurry up and get on with it when a bunch of people in biosuits stomp out and pull me up off the tarmac and drag me into the building.

CHAPTER THIRTEEN

I'm a freak.

I SEE MY HANDS ON LEAKING POTTERY.
I held a vase that had had space-bug water in it, but—
I SEE SAP OOZE.
I picked a flower to give to the fairies so as they'd not forget my dead mom, but—
I SEE THE CRAZY TERRIER LICK MY HAND.
I touched dogs…that had munched on dead people, had probably been out in the rain, had probably drunk from puddles, but—
I SEE GRASS STAINS ON NAKED FEET, SCRATCHES ON MY ARMS AND FACE.
I ran in flip-flops, through grass, getting cut by brambles, but—
I SEE A DAMP PATCH ON MY OWN BOTTOM.
I sat on Primrose Hill…on the stones, at night, at Stonehenge, but—
I SEE A SINGLE DROP OF WATER FALL.
Splip! Into a bathtub, where I was lying.
I SEE A KISS.
I kissed Caspar when he'd been out in the rain, and I thought his lips were dry, but—

I am alive. I touch my lips. I feel my panicky breath, sucking and puffing in and out through them. I am alive.

I am a freak. I'm a freak. I'm a freak. I'm a freak. I'm a **FREAK**.

It goes on and on like that in my head; if it looks strange and nuts on paper, that's too bad. It was a lot worse in my head. It was like some nightmare thought-GIF that just looped over and over, getting faster and faster and… Nah, worse than that: it cut and recut itself as it looped, so it was just this high-speed jumbled mess that kind of looked the same as the last high-speed jumbled mess, but in a different order, and before any idea in it made sense, it'd start over.

That is what it is like inside my head.

To the outside world, I am an object of fear and wonder and dread. A medical miracle. That's what I tell myself. To make myself feel special. Because I do not feel special; I just feel like a thing.

I am a thing that is kept in a plastic tent. They feed me well. I am not hungry—or cold or thirsty. I even get to watch TV—through plastic. I'm just not allowed to leave, is all. It is worse than a cage. A cage only has bars. Through bars, air is free to pass. My plastic cage is completely sealed; it has its own artificial air. Even what comes in—food and drink—and what goes out—half-eaten plates of food and half-drunk cups of tea…and my poo and my pee…are exchanged through hatches. My poo and pee are treated especially carefully; they are vacuum-packed before being removed.

Somehow I don't suppose they just go and throw them in the trash.

They like removing things from me. They push their gloved hands into even bigger gloves that let them reach through the plastic to take stuff from me. They take my blood. Lots of times. And lots of it. They take my spit. They take samples of everything that comes out of my body. I obediently wipe cotton swabs around every nook and cranny of my poor freak body and they stash them—even the snot, but the snot supply is limited because I don't cry much anymore.

It's not like no one speaks to me. They come with plastic helmets and gowns and boots and gloves and all kinds of garb on, like I'm some kind of leper, but still they're like, "Hello, Ruby, and how are you today?" And I'm, like, "I'm fine, thank you."

"I'm fine, thank you."

Why wouldn't I be? Is there something they're not telling me? I'm not sick, am I? I'm just…different. I am a FREAK.

I am terrified of myself. I am terrified of what I am, of how come I am like this.

But, of course, I want them to be able to make some kind of cure. I am just worried about *how* they're going to make it and what that might involve doing to *me*.

Yes, having seen what these people are capable of doing, having seen that ward of kids, I am also terrified of them.

So I am being polite. I am polite and I am very cooperative.

If I understand what they are trying to do with their big blue rubber hands, I offer to do it for them. I have one of those gowns that shows your bottom to the world. In this case, it is a bottom clad in (BIG, BAGGY, FLOWERY) hospital-issue underwear—but really, there is no point in wearing either the gown or the underwear because there is no part of me these people have not seen.

Except my mind. Except my heart. Except…me.

But even that they…prod. They will not leave me alone.

After that, after "I'm fine, thank you," there shouldn't exactly be much to say, should there? And there isn't, not with the regular nurses or doctors or scientists or whatever these people are. Except… there is this one woman, whom I suppose is a doctor, who comes and talks to me a lot. And I do mean a lot: day and night.

They got my medical records from Dartbridge—and my mom's and Simon's and even dear babiest brother-brat beloved Henry's—but it is mainly mine we talk about. We go over and over and over every illness, every injury I ever had: What do I remember about it? Not much. Sometimes nothing at all. This is not deliberate. I just can't remember.

What I can remember (but lie about) is who I've seen, who I've been with. I do not understand why she would be asking all this stuff, but I have such a bad feeling about it, I don't even ask *why*. There's a whole web of people I could drag into this. Everyone is best left out of it. No one else must be brought to this place where they chop bits off kids to find things out. They've got me. What more do they need. Period—no question mark.

With this stuff, I will not cooperate. I don't tell them anything… and I don't ask anything—and I don't ask about *anyone*. Not even Darius Spratt.

All I ever say to them is, "I don't know."

It is very easy to lie when you're shut in a plastic prison. I discover that. They know I'm lying, but there's not a thing they can do about it.

Unless they start torturing me, I suppose. That'd be tricky, maybe, through the plastic. They'd be like, "So, Ruby, could you just beat yourself up a little?" And I'd say, "No?"

But if they found a way, I wonder if I'd even care. I'd be, like, "Ow."

I am just kidding. I'd scream the place down, of course I would. But I wouldn't blab. I'd try not to.

I tell the doctor who may not be a doctor I have been alone since the rain fell. I know she knows this is almost certainly a *colossal* fib, but she doesn't push it.

What she does push is... She asks, again and again and again, about my dad. She asks it in a whole load of different ways, but really it might as well be:

"Where's your dad?"

"I don't know."

Every single time.

And every single time, it hurts.

CHAPTER FOURTEEN

And then a thing happens.

All that time I am being poked and prodded and injected and sampled, I don't pay much attention to whatever they're going on about. What they go on about is science-y stuff, so you can imagine how well I can follow that, but after about a week of this poking and prodding and injecting and sampling—and I tell you IT'S A LONG WEEK, it goes on for about SIX MONTHS (or equivalent: one double math lesson)—I notice that they're getting a bit testy. Not with me—I am a model patient—but with each other. They start having little science scraps between themselves.

Sometimes the scraps turn into full-blown science hissy fits, and I am forced to turn up the TV (mercifully, I have been allowed the remote) to block them out, and it's on one such morning when I am thinking I might actually need to be not quite such a model patient and tell them to put a sock in it because I really am trying to concentrate very hard on watching an ancient episode of *Scooby-Doo*, when—the nerve of it!—they tell me to put a sock in it first.

"Ruby!" one of them practically shouts. (See? Testy!) "Could you please turn that down?"

"Trying to work here," one of them has the gall to snarl.

Trying to exist here, I think. For one tiny second, I turn the volume up instead of down, but then I remember that I am a model patient, and so I do turn it down with my spare hand. My other arm is about to be involved in one of their experiments.

"Thank you so much," one of them mutters.

"You're welcome," the old me would have said in a voice dripping with sarcasm, but model patient me just goes back to trying to concentrate even harder on what Velma is saying to Shaggy. They do not make it easy for me, but I don't listen to a word of it, of what they're going on about, until I hear the one word that makes me listen.

"…mother."

"Yes, but—"

"I told you. I did tell you."

"No, you didn't. You said it was unlikely."

"Only after the sequencing on the brother."

"Half brother. *Half* brother, that's my point. HALF."

"Half, schmalf. It isn't genetic."

"You *can-not poss-ib-ly* KNOW that."

"We need a paternal sample. Simple as."

"We're not going to *get* a paternal sample."

"Yeah. Well. This is still a COMPLETE waste of time."

"It ISN'T genetic."

"Look, shut up and let's just do this."

"Waste of time," growls the snarler. "We need Daddy's DNA."

They are, I realize, talking about my family. I mute Velma.

"Excuse me?" I ask.

"Yeah, can you just hold still a moment?"

"Please," sighs the mutterer—but not to me. Not really. None of them are even looking at me. They are all totally focused on whatever thing it is they are doing now.

My arm is outstretched. There are three of them messing about with it. They really must be getting desperate because it looks like the least science-y thing they've done so far: one is poised over my arm with a syringe full of something clear; one holds a dish under my arm; one has an empty syringe at the ready.

"This is so stupid," goes the snarler, through gritted teeth.

"But what—" I start.

"In a sec!" says shouter.

I withdraw my arm from this particular experiment.

"✹," swears the snarly one. The snarly one has the full syringe. Nervous, isn't she?

"No…look. I'm sorry, but what is it you're saying?" I ask them.

"It's just water," says the shouter, who's holding the container under my arm. "We're just going to run some water over your arm, and then collect it."

"Which won't hurt you," growls the snarler. "And also won't show A THING," she adds—but for the benefit of the other two. "Because it's genetic," she sings at them and reaches out and gets hold of my arm.

"No, it's not," the mutterer sings back quietly.

"What are you saying about—" I start again but am silenced as the snarly one counts in:

"Three…two…one…"

I flinch as cold water runs over my arm. I can't help it. I know what kind of water this will be. I might have sat with it pouring down on me, but I swear I still don't want it anywhere near me.

"What…um were you saying about genetics and that? About my family and stuff?"

I watch the water running off my arm into the container. Drip, drip, drop.

"We got a negative result on that," says the shouter.

Like me, they are all just watching: drip, drip, drop.

"A negative result on…?" I ask. I hated biology in school. I know nothing about biology, but still—drip, drip, drop—there is some information somewhere in my head. Like why would they know about my mother's genes? Why would they know…

"DNA samples," mutters the mutterer.

Drip, drip, drop.

"Yeah, how would you get those?" I ask.

"I'm a go on this," mutters the mutterer.

"It's a go," agrees the shouter, and the mutterer draws up a syringe full of what has run off my arm.

It is NOT a go. I grab his wrist. It is immediately very, very obvious to me that these people are terrified. I have been a problem to be solved—suddenly I am a very scary and real problem. I am an *interactive* problem.

"How," I ask them, "did you get D-N-A?"

I say each letter very, very slowly in the hope that I will make it clear to them that I get what they are going on about, even though I don't. I just know DNA is the stuff inside every living being, the stuff that makes you you and me me.

The shouter is easing her hands out of the plastic cage, slow as a scared thing.

"How?" I ask the mutterer. He's the one I have ahold of, the one with the syringe full of arm water.

"Ask her," he mutters—meaning the snarler, whose hands are escaping too.

I guess the shouter has hit some kind of panic button or something, because a whole bunch of other people come storming in, including the one who asks me the questions, notebook in hand.

"Ruby, what seems to be going on here?" she says, super-calmly but with an edge of parenty-type irritation. The sound of her voice throws me a little because I've talked to her more than I've talked to any of these other people—because up until just now, what did we have to say to each other, me and the people with the needles and swabs?

"I just… I'm asking a question, that's all."

"Well, Ruby, if you can just let Professor Beardsall go, we'll be happy to answer that question."

That sounds so reasonable, doesn't it? And I feel kind of cruel, but you know what? "Well, I'll be happy to let Professor…"

The stress of the thing makes my brain cut out—either that or I've got so used to saying I can't remember names that I've actually damaged the part of my brain that's supposed to remember stuff like that.

"Beardsall," mutters the mutterer. "The name's Beardsall."

"He's the best microbiologist we've got…" says Dr. Questions.

"Tchuh!" scoffs the snarler, loud enough for everyone to hear.

"…and he's very, very important to us. As are you, Ruby."

"As is this sample," mutters Professor Beardy.

That gets me back on track. "So all I'm asking," I say, directing my attention to him, "is where did you get the *other* samples? Where did you get the D-N-A?"

"The thing is, Ruby," says Dr. Questions, coming closer—which is bothersome, because she's blocking out my view of what the rest of them are up to—and they are up to something; there's someone creeping around the back of my plastic cage. "What you are doing here, helping us, it's a really wonderful thing. And what you've got to think is that, really, you're helping people just like your mom…"

Oh, don't you do that.

"And your stepdad…"

I hate her so much for having to glance down at my notes to check his name.

"Simon," I tell her, before she can read it out loud.

"Or your brother, Henry," she says.

"HALF brother," I say.

Babiest brother-brat beloved, forgive me. This never meant a thing to me, dearest. Not a thing. It's just that I cannot stand to have this creature act like she knows things she really knows nothing about. All she knows is bits of paper. I knew a little baby boy.

"You touched them?"

"We needed samples."

"Did you cut them? Did you cut… *Henry*?"

"We took tissue samples."

I lose it. *Yee-haa* would not go even close to covering this. I lose it, and I charge at her, at Dr. Questions, at Dr. The-Very-Sight-Of-You-Makes-Me-Sick. That's what I am going to call her. Sick to the very core of my being. Dr. TVSOYMMSTTVCOMB.

Only I can't charge anywhere, can I? There is a wall of plastic in my way. About a million hands dive into every available glove space, grabbing at me, grabbing at needles, grabbing—and, oh, but someone screams. The muttering professor screams.

"Sharp! Sharp! Sharp!" he shouts, pulling his hands out of my plastic cage so the syringe that's stuck in his hand falls onto my bed.

"Sharp injury!" that's what everyone is saying—but no one goes to help. No one will go anywhere near him.

The professor stops shouting. He wrenches off the anti-Ruby biosuit helmet on his head. He backs away from everyone, backs into the corner of the room. The man is crying, clutching his own wrist, holding his gloved hand in the air.

"Someone get Thurley," shouts the shouter.

"He's in surgery," someone shouts back.

But this isn't regular angry shouting; it's stress shouting. I know it very well. I do it a lot.

122

"There is no point," says the weeping professor, but someone goes to get Thurley anyway.

"We need the rest of that sample," he keeps saying, louder and louder, over and over—the stress shouting of a weeping man.

The snarler, I note, says nothing. I do note that. So this awful thing has just happened and I can't be sure about anything, it all happened so fast, but didn't I see—did I see?—did the snarler stab the needle into that guy? It wasn't me. I know that. It wasn't me.

Dr. TVSOYMMSTTVCOMB comes back toward my cage.

"Ruby, can you please give us that syringe?"

"It wasn't my fault!" I gibber, dumping the syringe into one of the sliding boxes they use to get stuff out of my plastic cage.

"This is a ✹ disaster," spits the shouter, taking the syringe and examining it. "Two mil left."

As she leaves, there's nearly another *sharp injury* because the one I'm guessing is Thurley, the surgeon (bloodstains down the front of his bio-garb), comes in with a SAW in his hand (I feel like I'm going to faint)—and the two of them collide at the door.

"✹," says Thurley, and they edge around each other. "How much?" Thurley asks.

"Eight mils," says the professor, shaking his head.

"Anything we can do for you?" asks Thurley.

"Find a cure?" says the professor. He laughs a bitter laugh and peels off his glove.

"It's *in* him, for ✹'s sake," someone says. "You can't just chop off his hand."

"Aware of that," says Thurley. "Go and get some ✹ morphine."

The someone stomps out of the room at high speed.

Everyone else just stands around, looking at Beardy's hand.

I'm too far away to see properly, but I swear there's hardly a scratch on it. It's not as though he's bleeding to death in front of us or something…but the room falls completely silent.

It must be clawing its wiggly-tentacled way through his veins, through his arteries. Gorging on what it wants—the food of red blood cells—that's what everyone got told when the rain first fell. The too-late Emergency Public Service Broadcast told us: it eats human blood cells. It wants the iron. Inside Professor Beardy, it is already replicating, replicating, replicating—smacking its greedy bacteria lips, spurting out living selfies, and chowing down for more.

He has a first-class ticket to death. They are just waiting for the professor to die.

I cannot stand it. I cannot stand a single thing about any of this thing. I go back to watching *Scooby-Doo*.

After a short while, the professor speaks…in a most un-professorly way:

"It's a 🌑 phage," he says. "I 🌑 told you. I told you it 🌑 could be. I 🌑 told you, I 🌑 bet you 🌑 anything it's a 🌑 phage. 🌑."

Phage. That's not a word I've heard before, but I'm guessing other people have. They just don't seem to believe him. In the silence, people are pulling these scrunched-up don't-know-about-that faces—apart from the snarler, who looks totally, seriously 🌑 off.

Apparently, Beardy is not dying. Not at all. He punches the air—with his needle-stabbed hand.

"It's a 🌑 phage!"

CHAPTER FIFTEEN

I get left alone for most of the rest of that day. This in itself is fairly shocking and weird because I haven't actually been left alone since I got picked up off the tarmac and dragged in here. There has always—always—been someone in the room. Being alone there feels strange enough to be frightening. I don't like it. They check on me ("How are you doing, Ruby?" "I'm fine, thank you.") and they come to give me food, but I don't want anything to eat.

"Is that guy OK?" I manage to ask them.

"Oh, yes," one of the nurses says, like she's sick of the whole thing already.

"Well, did he—is there a cure now and stuff? He seemed kind of excited."

"Didn't he just."

I'm guessing it's no to a cure, then, or else surely everyone would be jumping for joy—and even more surely SOMEONE WOULD HAVE TOLD ME. But maybe, under the circumstances (apocalypse), it's better to check, not guess.

"Well, is there?" I ask.

The nurse shrugs. "He's a little *away with the fairies*, that one," she says.

I know she means she thinks he's crazy, but that makes me smile in a sad way, because it makes me think about my mom, who whispered on about fairies to me so much I believed in them with all my heart. Where are they now? Sipping nectar from acorn teacups as they discuss science with Professor Beardy?

I put the TV on and watch it with the sound turned right up. I want the noise to blast every thought from my head. I don't want to think—about anything at all, fairies included. And most especially not about my family, because even the very edge of a thought about them being *sampled* makes me white-hot sick with angry disgust.

I concentrate on feeling numb. Numb's OK.

The next morning, when the nurses come, they're dressed how nurses normally dress. All the scary bio-garb stuff…it has gone.

No one told me this was going to happen, no one explains why it is happening, and it has quite a peculiar effect on me. I could sort of detach myself from the hideousness of it all until I got to see their faces…because, their faces? They're not just NORMAL; they're actually pretty cheerful. I had thought the attempts at the happy "And how are we?" voices were just that—attempts to make the being poked around marginally less completely dreadful…but no. These people have gone back to how they seemed when I first arrived. They are actually fairly ✳ chirpy.

This, instantly, ✳ me right off.

"Excuse me?" I start up, as they start taking my cage apart around me. "What's going on?"

"We don't know," says a nurse.

Yeah, right. Did you catch that 0.1 micrometers of a second delay before she said that?

Something is up and I don't like it. What I also don't like is… seeing all these people looking normal, carrying on like normal. I realize all over again how not normal I am. And I realize how *angry* I am about it. And how sick I am of being treated like a moron/child (these are the same thing to these people).

I am a freak with *attitude*.

It starts with a huffy sigh or two and ends with me refusing breakfast. I now haven't eaten for twenty-four hours. This doesn't seem to cause any great alarm, which annoys me even more.

Don't get annoyed, I beg myself.

✳ *off*, myself swears back.

This is a state I have never quite been in before. I mean, I've talked to myself plenty. I've tried to make myself think positive thoughts a billion times—and when that failed, I learned to unthink the negative ones. And when that failed, I wallowed…but I have never been like this: swearing, angrily, at myself. My head feels…like a hurricane, gathering itself, gathering everything around it. Getting ready to just—

"Don't get annoyed," I beg myself out loud.

When Dr. TVSOYMMSTTVCOMB—who is also about the only one who doesn't seem particularly cheerful—arrives, she notices the hurricane. Big time.

Sans spacesuit, she's the only one not doing the whole white coat/uniform thing. It doesn't make me like her more. She wears a different kind of suit: dull, but business-y, like she's going to work in a bank or something. And her nails and her makeup and her hair—all of it—while not exactly glamorous, are super-perfect.

I feel angry at the sight of her. I feel like a total "UG!" cavewoman scruffbag. I'm still wearing the stupid gown that shows my butt (in BIG, BAGGY, FLOWERY hospital-issue underwear) to everyone.

"Is there something wrong, Ruby?" she asks about ten nanoseconds after she's walked into the room—which has been enough time for me to think all those things about her, but not enough time to think what scathing words I might wish to speak upon the subject.

"Nope."

"Are you still upset about what happened yesterday?"

"Nope."

"Would you like to talk about it anyway, Ruby?"

"Nope."

"Is there something else you'd like to talk about?"

"Nope."

"I expect you're wondering where everyone is…"

I can't "Nope" this, because I am.

"What you need to know is that we are working very hard indeed to find a cure here, Ruby. And you are such an important part of that. You are *the* most important part. We are *so* grateful to you, Ruby. So grateful! Everyone thinks you are *brilliant.*"

Ha! It takes me a few moments to get my head around what's going on, because, basically, no one has ever spoken to me like this in my entire life. And man! She's good at it! I could almost believe it myself. I mean, obviously it's true in all sorts of ways but—HA!—I realize a thing. I realize that Dr. TVSOYMMSTTVCOMB thinks I'm going to snap out of it if she keeps this up. I don't blame her for thinking that—apart from yesterday's outburst of rage, she has only seen a silent, sniveling shadow of a girl. The sort of girl who'd suck this stuff up and then ask politely for a spoon to scrape the bowl with.

"…because what you have to understand is that you are really, really special to us. You are really special and important and…"

I am tempted to let this go on. This is the apocalypse. Everyone could do with a bit of praise—take what you can where you can get it, huh?—but I have the most hideous feeling this particular praise is being laid on too thick. It is being laid on with a knife. I am being buttered up. For what? I don't know and I don't care.

"…yes, everyone—*everyone*—here wants what you want."

I doubt that. I mean, obviously, I'm not some total loon like Xar. Obviously, I would be delighted if there was a cure. How could I not be? But, also obviously, what I want, really, is to have my life back. ("And then I woke up.") Obviously that is not a possibility. So, failing that, I'd just like…to get out of here. That would be good. To at least get *some kind* of a life again. I hate this place. A whole lot less obviously I…

"I want to know what's going on," I tell her.

For the first time in my life, I really, really want to understand something. I don't want to be palmed off. I want to know.

"I want to know why I'm a freak."

"Oh, Ruby, we would never call you that! That's not what you are!" Dr. TVSOYMMSTTVCOMB coos.

"I want to know what a *phage* is," I tell her.

She pauses. I see her brain behind her eyes. I see it calculating stuff. I step it up:

"That's what I've got, isn't it? A *phage*. What is that?"

The calculation is complex for her, I can tell.

"I think I've got a right to know," I say.

I am immediately scared I have blown it. Teenager + rights = NO.

I try to fix it: "I just want to understand," I say softly.

"We would too," she says, calculating.

She arrives at her answer.

THE RUBY MORRIS GUIDE TO THE ROCKETY THING

B asically, I wish I'd never asked.

This is *The Ruby Morris Guide to the Rockety Thing (Phage)*, and, trust me, if you want to skip it, you can. Knowing all this, which is what I was told at the time, plus what I had taken in during my library studies, plus a *tiny* bit of stuff I learned later, won't make a single bit of difference. It won't change the situation, and it certainly wouldn't have changed what happened next.

But still, for the *keen* types, here we go…

About my person, there was some other hideous kind of bacterium. Not the one that came in the rain, but another one. Specifically, Prof Beardy suspected it had been lurking up my nose.

That in itself is fairly disgusting, but before you go "Euuuw!" and stop reading, let me tell you that you and *your* nose, like everything else on this planet, are also SWARMING with bacteria—every single bit of you, inside and out: SWARMING. And astonishingly, no one, not even Prof Beardy, has the slightest clue about what most of them do, or whether they're even friends and help each other out, or whether they hate each other and fight.

It's a little like people, really—only there's a whole lot more of them. If your body were a planet—which I guess it is, to the bacteria that live on you (Ha! Planet Ruby!)—people would be saying that it was seriously overcrowded. But somehow, most of the time, all the bacteria just muddle along. Some get along, some don't; some do good things, some don't, but it's so complicated and so mysterious, how they work—let alone how they all work together—that it is quite possible for a "bad" bacterium to end up doing good (because it'll make other bacteria pull themselves together and do the right thing). That's how complicated and mysterious the whole thing is.

The bacterium I had…it wasn't bad. It wasn't good. It wasn't particularly anything. How it even came to be on me is a complete, total, and utter mystery. It was just there, sitting around (up my nose), minding its own business. Until I stepped out into the rain.

(Or possibly before. All those things I thought of? All those risks I took? Maybe no one is that lucky.)

The point is, *my* bacterium…it *knew* the bacterium in the rain.

Or rather, it *remembered* it.

It has a very long memory.

This planet has been thumped and bashed and smashed into by stuff—meteorites—from outer space since way before people were here to worry about it. There is no telling when *my* bacterium got here. It just smacked into the Earth on a meteorite and then sat around somewhere dark and damp (most recently, a nose), waiting.

The *keen* types, headed by Prof Beardy, will no doubt be quick to point out that bacteria don't "know" anything, don't "remember," and most certainly don't "wait," but this is how I think of it—and it may as well be true. *My* bacterium had met the rain bacterium before. And it knew how to take it out. Destroy it. Annihilate it.

It had a phage. A phage is a virus inside a bacterium.

Forget your regular antibiotics, made in a factory. This is a target-specific killing machine. Secret weapon job.

It looks like this:

I promise you, this really is what it looks like.

My bacterium used to casually fire off a few of these rockety things, but they had nothing to do. Just fizzled away, like crummy fireworks.

When I stepped out into the rain, *my* bacterium went crazy. It went to battle stations. Think microbiological *Star Wars*.

Small, slow things might look like they stand no chance, but let me tell you, they do… It's the tortoise and the hare, isn't it? The tortoise, *my* bacterium, and the hare, the one that came in the rain, raced.

My bacterium, dear tortoise, had waited patiently, peacefully, but now it released stacks and stacks and stacks and stacks and stacks and stacks of phage. I am covered in a coat of furious bacteria and protected by an invisible force field of microbiological phage rage.

BLAM! BLAM! BLAM! BLAM!

KILL! KILL! KILL! KILL!
WAY TO GO! TORTOISE! KILL! KILL! KILL! KILL!

The phage is tinier than tiny. Smaller than a nothing. But it is a nuclear missile.

This tinier than tiny rockety thing, this phage—it is "night-night, baby" for the wiggly-legged space-✱ in the rain.

There, that's pretty much all you need to know…according to

Professor Ruby. I think I'll give myself another A+—but wait! A conclusion, we need a conclusion!

CONCLUSION

People don't tend to look at the small things. They also do not like slow things. People tend to look at the big, fast stuff.

In my opinion, this may not always be the smartest thing to do.

CHAPTER FIFTEEN
(PART TWO)

W hat would really help us," Dr. TVSOYMMSTTVCOMB says, "what would really help *everyone*, is if you could just think hard about how you might have *acquired* the phage."

I would quite like to know the answer to that myself.

"I would quite like to know that myself," I tell her.

"Great!" She smiles and shoves a pen and a pad of paper at me.

"So now you need to think, Ruby, don't you?"

Right at that second, I notice a thing: she uses my name A LOT. (Like during the spacesuit phase, I suppose it was OK, because it reminded me I had a name and that she was remembering there was a person at the end of whatever needle was poking into me, but right now I feel like I don't need reminding, thank you very much. I know who I am.) (I am a FREAK.)

"We just want you to think hard—very hard—about that. About a time you…came into contact with *something* the rest of your family wouldn't have come into contact with. A place you went where they didn't go, for example. Anything you did that was *unusual* in any way."

That's mad that is. I shrug. I look bewildered. I know I do. I *feel* bewildered.

She smiles, picks up the pen, hands it to me. "Just try, Ruby."

(See? See what I mean about the name thing?)

She smiles at me. She has good teeth. My teeth are train tracked. One has deserted me. And I stink, and my hair's in a state, and… and…I feel like I am being *patronized*. The Rage-O-Meter tips into red. I put down the pen.

"But *why* do you want to know that stuff?" I ask.

Uh. I have just done the worst thing any teen anywhere can do. I have just *questioned an adult in a position of authority*. Now is not a good time for that, I can tell—instantly—by the look on her face. But I cannot pretend I have not just said what I just said; I'm going to have to stand by it. I am going to have to stand by *myself*.

"Just asking," I say—oh so lightly.

"It might turn out to be important," she says.

Uh—it's worse than I thought: I am going to have to *think*. (That sounds stupid of me, doesn't it? I think about a lot of stuff… What I mean is, I am going to have to think what on Earth it is *they* are thinking—about which, I have no clue. It must be BIG, FAST stuff, I suppose—stuff that is way bigger and faster than me.)

"But if you've got the phage thing, why would you even be bothered? Doesn't that mean there's a cure now?"

It seems like a reasonable question, it seems like—

THWACK!

Dr. TVSOYMMSTTVCOMB slaps me across the face.

It is, in fact, the first time in my life that another human being has hit me.

I gasp in shock—and pain. Clutch my face.

"You need to think, Ruby," she says. "You need to think."

"I don't know! How would I know?! I can't remember!"

"You're going to have to try harder."

I swear…I see every second of every minute of every hour of

136

every day since the rain first fell flash before my eyes. "You want…
me…to try *harder?*"

"Yes."

It upsets me so much that I feel tears roll from my eyes. They
creep between my fingers to soothe my stinging cheek.

"I just want to go home," I whisper.

CHAPTER SIXTEEN

They come in the night.

I am awake when it happens. I am awake because there is some kind of argument going on. It didn't start out as a fight, it started out sounding like a party—the dull kind that mature types have, with not enough music and too much chat and hoo-hoo, har-har (oh-gosh-darling-you're-such-a-hoot!). That kind of thing. This would not have kept me awake (I would hardly feel like I was missing out on anything, would I?), but when it started getting nasty…I hate that SO much, the sound of a fight. And I hate it even more when it's muffled. (Not that I want to hear it clearly, just that it reminds me of parents fighting. *My* parents fighting.)

So, yeah, I am awake, doodling on that stupid pad and trying not to listen to the distant sounds of an argument I couldn't even hear properly if I tried. I have drawn all sorts of things—raindrops and skulls and rockety things—but I have yet to scribble anything that looks like a word. I got a slap just for asking why they wanted to know this stuff; I feel sick inside thinking what will happen if I don't do what I am told… But still…my hand has refused to write a single letter. My brain has tried to reason with it, but it is being very stubborn.

VIRGINIA BERGIN

YAP! GRRR! YAP! NO! GRRR! snarls the argument as the door opens.

KZZZZ! The overhead lights are dazzling as a nurse snaps them on.

That's what the argument might as well sound like. In reality I hear: "**OUTRAGEOUS!**" (that sounds like Beardy)—followed by the grrr of a low, cold voice (Dr. TVSOYMMSTTVCOMB?) speaking words I still cannot make out—followed by "… **DISGUSTING!**" (that's someone else) and "**NO!**" (someone else again)…and then the low, cold grrr again before the door closes.

"I was just gonna do it," I gibber at the nurse, waving the pad at him, squinting and blinking in the dazzling light. "It's not my fault! It's them!"—I jerk my head at the argument noise—"I can't concentrate!"

"Ya gotta go, Ruby," he tells me, chucking a biosuit down on the bed next to me.

"What?! Why?! Where?!"

"Shh! Sweetie! It's OK! No one's going to hurt you."

But someone already did. I shake my head at him, terrified. "That woman slapped me."

"Who slapped you?"

"That woman—the doctor that asks all the questions."

He frowns. "She's not a doctor," he says.

I feel an exhausted tear crawl down my cheek.

"I just want to go home," I tell him. In fact, anywhere but here would do. I hate this place. I hate these people. I trust no one… and I have the eeriest feeling everyone is LYING TO ME AND TREATING ME LIKE AN IDIOT.

"We all do." He sighs. "Come on, let's put this on," he says, and he helps me put the biosuit on over my gown. "Sorry about this," he says, "but we're all out of jeans."

I am being dressed for the first time since I was little. And I feel little. I feel little…and scared.

"We're all out of sneakers too," he says, holding up a pair of ghastly white bio–rain boots.

"Sit down, sweetie."

I sit on the bed. Trollish shudders of misery pass through my body.

He crouches to put the bio–rain boots on my feet. He does it very, very slowly, and as he does it, he speaks to me very, very quietly.

"Ruby…there's a treatment. There is a *cure* now, thanks to you. There is a cure."

That's fairly stunning news, isn't it? That can only be good, right? I'm going to be some kind of national hero or something. No! *International!* Probably there'll have to be a new public holiday— maybe on my birthday. That'd be nice…

You will notice that this story is not over.

"Really?!"

"Truly. Beardsall's cracked it," he says. "He's stewed up a whole tankful of *your* phage. You've done it, sweetie! You've saved the planet!"

"I have?"

"Sure! I mean, Beardsall's trying to grab all the glory, but everyone knows you're the real star."

"They do?"

"Absolutely."

He pats my successfully rain-booted foot, lets it go, then takes hold of the other foot.

"So…*how come I can't go home?*"

I jerk my foot away.

"*Why can't I just go?*"

He hesitates.

"Hey! I'm not a kid, you know. I'm not some stupid kid."

And then it comes to me… I've seen what they've been doing to kids, haven't I?

"Oh my ✱…. It's because I know too much, isn't it?"

"Um. No. To be honest with you, Ruby, I think there are plenty of people who know quite a bit more than you."

"Just tell me the truth. Please, just tell me the truth. Am I sick? Am I going to die? Am I infectious? I'm infectious, aren't I? That's why I've got to wear this thing, isn't it? Please just tell me. I swear—I promise—I swear I won't tell anyone. *Please…*"

He reaches to take hold of my foot, and I let him.

"Oh my ✱. I'm going to die, aren't I? Or… Oh my ✱! Are… are they going to kill me?"

He shoves the other boot on and then stares up at me.

"No one is going to hurt you," he says. "You are way too precious for that."

Precious. I have never felt less precious in my life.

"They're just trying to scare you. Even this," he says, plucking at the biosuit, "there is no need for it. It is a 'precaution'; that's what they said. It is not necessary."

My mouth thinks about opening. My brain tells it to shut up.

"Listen to me, sweetie," he says. "The people who are currently in charge of this country want to keep this whole thing a secret."

My mouth opens. Words fail to come out. My brain freezes.

"I know. It's appalling. That's what the fight is about. Beardsall told…too many people. They want to keep the cure a secret…and that means you too."

That's the thing about precious things, isn't it? People don't want to let them go…

"You're being moved to the high-security lab," he says. "There's no need to panic."

Yeah, right. I am totally freaking out.

"It's just a temporary move to a more secure place."

I stare at him, open jawed; ice from the brain freeze creeping into every cell of my body.

"Sweetie?"

Though my vision is fear blurred, I see the name on his badge. I do a thing my stepdad used to do when he wanted to win people over.

"Right. Thank you, Ibrahim," I tell him.

"Don't mention it," he says, getting to his feet. He puts his hands on my shoulders...and squeezes. I think he's going to start shaking me, but, "Really," he says, eyeballing me, "*do not mention it.*"

I swallow—no spit to swallow because my mouth is so dry—and I nod.

"That's what they're worried about. Do you understand? They do not want this to get out."

I nod harder.

His pager goes off; he reads it. "✹!" he swears—and he laughs, but in a shocked, dead kind of way.

"Honestly, you really are best off out of this one," he says. "Beardsall's on a bender," he whispers. "*Drunk!* This is going to get ugly."

He picks up the helmety-thing and holds it in front of me.

"I won't tell anyone," I say.

"Good girl," he says, and shoves the helmet on. "Everything is going to be OK," he tells me again through the plastic, shoving gloves onto my hands. Then he offers me his hand. "C'mon, sweetie."

My gloved hand takes his gloved hand and, in that too-big plasticky-rubbery suit, I squeak and sblob out into the corridor.

Even though the helmet muffles sound a little, I detect instantly

that the fight has heated up…but I really don't care to listen to the
YAP! GRRR! YAP! NO! GRRR! of it. Behind the desk, a nurse is on
the phone. It is not the nurse who tried to help me get out of here. I
have never seen her again. It is some other nurse who is all composed
until she puts down the phone; then she looks a little freaked out.

"They need you back at the *party*," she tells Ibrahim. "Beardsall's
gone coco-loco."

"I know!" he says, and laughs that shocked, dead—frightened?!—
laugh, glancing at me.

"Yeah, well," she tells him, "I think you might have missed the
fun part."

"Typical! Sweetie, I'm going to come with you in the ambulance,
so just you wait there," he says and goes running off.

I plunk my plasticky-rubbery behind down onto the seats where
I sat the night I brought Saskia in. I want to go. I just want to go. I
don't like this place. I don't like these people.

I try to look around me. Doing anything in the suit is hard.

"All right?" the desk nurse says.

I nod. Lying is super-easy inside this suit.

"You must be feeling pretty pleased with yourself," she says—not
in a nasty way, in a nice way.

"I guess."

Her phone rings again. She listens, with a superb eyeball roll
of exasperation for my benefit, to the shouty voice on the end of
the line.

"He *is* in surgery," she says.

She holds the phone away from her head as the shouty voice
shouts louder. I swear, that's ~~Dr.~~ Ms. TVSOYMMSTTVCOMB
losing it, and the thought of that makes me shudder and smile all at
the same time. Maybe someone will need to slap her.

"OK. I'll get him. I—WILL—GET—HIM," says the nurse,

slamming down the phone. "✹, since when did Thurley become the voice of reason?" she says—to me, I suppose, being as how I'm the only other person there. "I mean, whose side is he on anyway?"

I shrug under the ten tons of rubbery plastic, but really, I've got other things on my mind.

She picks up the phone, jabs one digit. I'm guessing no one picks up, because she slams the phone down. "He's such an *asshole,*" she says.

Sorry, Mom, I know I promised. I know you'd say even this "asshole" word counts. You hated swearing—no, just *me* swearing. And up until now, I've laid off it, because I wanted everything I had to tell to be…for you, really. To show you that I will never, ever forget you. But, Mom, I am about to have my heart ripped out.

Again, Mom, again.

And you, whoever you are, reading this, would you please read very carefully, and would you please…please just think what you would have done. Because I had sixty seconds to decide. I feel very precise about this, because I swear I felt every beat of my heart. But as that was already cranked up from the start and ended up totally hammer-hammer-hammering in my chest, we'll just stick to seconds, shall we?

Sixty seconds.

1–2

"Right, back in a min," says the nurse, getting up.

3–6

She stomps—just a few steps—to the nearest door. It is labeled "Prep 1."

7

As the nurse bats open the door labeled "Prep 1" to call for Thurley, I get to my feet.

8

In Prep 1, I glimpse the Princess, sitting on a gurney. Some kind of sign around her neck. I feel I've been slapped across the face all over again.

9–10

Too shocked to stand, I sit back down.

11

The nurse comes back out, looking flustered.

12–20

"Are they still experimenting on kids?" I ask in a dead voice.

"Yes," she snaps. "But it WILL be stopping soon."

21–22

"Or not," she says as the door at the end of the corridor bursts open and a blast of cool Earth night rushes in—cool but not raining. Outside, under the canopy, there's an ambulance and a dark-windowed scary car (the kind drug-dealing gangsters in movies drive). A bunch of male versions of Ms. TVSOYMMSTTVCOMB are piling out of it, but these ones have guns. I'm guessing these must be the "Oh No, the Scientists Are Having a Fight Police" (plain-clothes division).

23

The nurse swears.

24

I swear. (Out loud.)

25

Thurley (the asshole) comes out of Prep 1, his blue gown splattered with blood.

26

Before that door swings shut behind him, I see the Princess again.

27–29

"No one leaves," the last suit barks at the nurse as he and Thurley the bloodstained child butcher (asshole) barrel off down the corridor after the others.

30

The nurse swears again.

31

I swear.

32

The nurse sits down.

33–40

"This is not ✳ right," she says, taking off after them all.

41–55

I sit alone in that corridor in a state of terror.

56

I decide.

57

I get up.

58

I sit back down.

59

I get up.

60

I do it.

I speed-splop through that Prep 1 door and grab the Princess by the arm; she cowers in fear. "It's me," I tell her. Not got time for this. "Darius said," I shout at her, pulling her off the gurney, dragging her down the corridor.

I open the back door of the ambulance; a soldier is sitting there. "All set?" he asks me.

My guts lurch, but I am NOT about to let this spoil our escape. I shove the Princess in.

"Yup," I shout in the deepest voice I can manage—I have to; otherwise, I can feel for a fact that my voice would just be a frightened squeak.

I slam the door shut and go around to the front of the ambulance, the driver's door.

Unfortunately, there is already a driver—having a ciggy that he flicks out of his open window at the sight of me.

My guts lurch, but I am NOT about to let this spoil the escape either. I must stay *on mission*. I go around to the passenger side. I get in.

"All right?" says the driver, rolling up his window.

"Yup," I shout.

"Oo! Wait up!" he says, watching his rearview mirror.

I check the one on my side; Prof Beardy is being dragged toward us by suits.

"Oh dear, oh dearie me," says the driver, tutting.

Beardy and the suits disappear from sight.

"Had too much of the hard stuff, hasn't he?" says the driver, grinning.

The back door of the ambulance slams shut. There is a thump on this little window behind us that makes me jump—the driver shoves it open and our heads nearly bump as we both look: just the soldier, the Princess, and Beardy (who looks like he's about ready to fall off his seat) in there.

I look back around. *OK. OK. No suits. That's good.* Well, you know, not "good" good, but better than it might have been.

"This isn't a cab, you know," the driver informs the soldier, and shuts the window.

"Might as well be," he laughs to me.

He starts up, puts the headlights on, and we roll away from that place.

"I used to drive one," he tells me as we head off into the night, "and let me tell you, it's true what they say—"

I don't get where we are going; we are driving away from the buildings.

"—you really do get some funny people in cabs."

We are driving away from where I think the main gate should be. Could possibly be.

"Not *him* though," says the driver. "Had *him* in here before."

I do a token micro-glance at him, to act like I'm listening when really I wish he'd just shut up.

"That soldier? Sense of humor? Must've been surgically removed."

We are driving away from everything.

"Surgically, geddit?"

We are driving into the night.

"Thought you'd like that," he says. "You know 'surgery'?!"

I cannot figure this thing out…but a move will have to be made, sooner or later, and I will have to make it.

"Surgery? Doctors?"

He sighs; he changes gear. *Where* **are** *we going?*

"So, what we got in there, then?" he asks me, jerking his head at the window.

I shrug.

"Little drama going on?" he fishes.

In the back of the ambulance, even through the glass, even through this stupid plasticky-rubbery helmet, I can hear Beardy—at the top of his voice—telling the soldier that he is a brilliant, brilliant, brilliant microbiologist. "Best in the world, mate…best in the ✳ world," that kind of thing.

"Hush-hush, is it?" the driver asks.

I do not reply. I want to go home. I want to "And then I woke up."

"Just trying to make conversation." The driver sighs. "Ah! Here we go!"

We pull up at a gate. There are no crowds of the useless here. It is just a gate in the middle of nowhere. I *will* my guts not to lurch, but they ignore me.

"All right, mate?" grins the driver, rolling down his window.

"All right?!" A soldier at the gate grins back. "What you got in there, then?"

"Drunk guy and a kid."

The gate soldier speaks into his walkie-talkie: "Exit confirmed."

"Confirming exit," a walkie-talkie voice says back.

"On you go," says the gate soldier as he steps back and swings open the gate.

"Cards later?" the driver yells.

"Lamb to the slaughter!" the gate soldier yells back.

"We'll see about that," the driver laughs to me as we bump out into the night.

It is such a starry, moonlit night—so bright I can see exactly what the sky is thinking. It is happy to light our way for now, but it is cooking up other plans; a fat slice of sky is already missing, smothered by nimbostratus, a cloud so thick with rain not a single star shines through it. That's pretty much how my brain feels: dark and deadly. Erm, and dense and dim. Obviously, the plan is to escape… It's just that the precise details of how I'm going to do that are not known to me.

"He took me to the cleaners last night," my driver is saying. "Totally skinned me."

I do not respond. On the track ahead of us, puddles glisten.

"You want in?" the driver asks me.

I glance at him, wishing he'd just shut up so I can think. The driver hates the puddles, swears at them a lot as he tries to weave slowly around them.

"C'mon," he says, in between a bout of swearing, "you want in on the game? I could get you in."

A random star in my brain twinkles feebly in the gloom: *My enemy's enemy is my friend.* (That's what my history teacher said when she was trying to explain some of the jaw-droppingly "as if!" pacts that got made in World War Two.) *My enemy's enemy is my friend.*

"High stakes, though," the driver is saying. "You need serious— and I do mean serious—stuff to put on the table. You got that?"

I nod. I am just looking out of the windshield, desperately trying—trying to think.

"I'm not talking cash, mind. It's gotta be jewelry—good stuff— maybe a nice piece of art. None of that modern nonsense—"

He swears, then shuts up for a moment as he maneuvers slowly around some more puddles. My enemy's enemy. I take a deep plasticky-rubbery breath and then remove my helmet. I am almost certainly going to need to shout, and it will only get in the way.

"Proper paintings, that's what people like," he says, and glances at me—does a shocked double take when he sees that I am just a kid. "I'm a Turner man, myself…" he says, but I can see his brain has moved on to a different subject: me.

No going back now.

I fling open the door and jump out.

"✸!" he shouts, braking. "What the ✸ hell do you think you're doing?!"

What I am doing is scooping up a double handful of puddle water, and I am back at the door in a flash.

"Get out!" I tell him, my gloved hands dripping.

Shaking, they're also shaking, and my voice has found its natural frightened squeak.

He stares at my hands in horror for 0.1 micrometers of a nanosecond—then he's out of the ambulance.

What's supposed to happen next is I get in and drive off.

What actually happens is the soldier gets out before I can do that, gun waving between me and the driver because he can't work out what the problem is, only that there is one.

"She tried to ❋ kill me!" shrieks the driver.

"No, I didn't!" I snap at him. "I was just *threatening* to try to kill you!"

"Put your hands in the air and back up!" barks the soldier at us; his breath, like all of ours, pants out white, hot with human fear in the cold night air.

"But she—" the driver protests.

"Both of you!"

Wondering if I've got the guts to start throwing water around (H20 versus bullets…hmm…) I look down at my cupped hands, but most of what was there has dribbled away. The gun herds us together as we back up—carefully, to avoid the puddle!—raising our hands. From mine, water drips down.

"See!" shrieks the driver.

"I was just trying to scare him, that's all," I shout at the soldier. "I was just trying to scare him!"

I am now scaring both of them. My hands are gloved, but my head is bare. Puddle water drips trickle down my face. I blink them out of my eyes—and spit when a drop reaches my mouth. I am not sure what is scaring me more right now: the gun, the overall situation—or the water itself.

Anyone who has seen what the rain can do would understand this; even for a FREAK like me, the fear makes my skin crawl and twitch.

"What the ❋…" breathes the soldier.

"There's a cure!" I squeal. Ha! I have been out of that base for five minutes, and already I have blabbed—but this hardly counts, does it? This is *emergency* blabbing.

The soldier shakes his head, reaches for his radio.

"There is! There is! They've got a massive tankful of phage!"

A frown flits across the soldier's face.

"The cure! It's a…rockety thing! From my nose! It's—ask *him*!" I dare to point at the sorry figure of Beardy, who is clambering drunkenly out of the ambulance.

"Are we there yet?" he says and staggers, clinging on to the soldier to stay upright—and in that moment, when the soldier is distracted by Beardy, I scoop up another handful of puddle-water. Can't risk it draining away, so… OH. I slurp it up.

"Hey!" shrieks the driver as I run at the soldier.

Pretty nasty situation this. I am in a face-off with an armed man, and all I have is—

"She's got a mouthful of water!" the driver helpfully shouts.

I do mean that: "helpfully." I give it a quick slosh around my mouth to make sure the soldier gets it, but this negotiation is going to be tricky now that I can't speak. (Do I expect to die at any second because I've got a mouthful of rainwater? YES, I still do.)

Me and the soldier eyeball each other.

"Well, that's not going to hurt anyone, is it?" slurs Beardy.

Me and the soldier do a "You what?" eye flick at him; then it's back to stare-you-down. In my head I am doing an emergency read-through of my mental notes for the *Ruby Morris Guide to the Rockety Thing*, but—annoyingly—they fail to mention whether this is true.

"I said, it's not going to hurt anyone, is it?"

I give the water in my mouth a threatening slosh. The soldier flinches; the driver is gasping.

"I swear," Beardy slurs. "I so totally promise you…"

"Is there really a cure?" pants the driver. "Is there?"

"Yeeeesss!" goes Beardy. Uh, he sounds like a great-big grown-up version of my stepbrother, Dan.

The soldier brings his gun up under my chin.

"Spit it at him," he tells me.

I turn my head to the professor.

"Ooo! So scared!" says Beardy. (Dan!)

"Not him!" yells the soldier. "Him." He jerks his head at the driver.

"✸ hell, mate!" pants the driver.

"Your choice," the soldier says to me. "Bullet or spit."

"Bored now," sings Beardy. (Dan!)

"You run, you'll get a bullet anyway," the soldier tells the driver.

"Go ahead," Beardy tells me. "Spit! Only could you please hurry up?" He waves a drunken finger at the clouding sky. It is possible, I suppose, that he isn't quite as drunk as he looks—but then he staggers a bit, and I think maybe he is.

"Do it," the soldier tells me.

I turn my head to face the driver—who stands before me…panting, weeping, and unsure who to look at with pleading eyes: me or the soldier.

I am going to do it. I am, because I don't see—I cannot see—what else there is to do…but my eyes slide to the right as a small child climbs, shivering, out of the ambulance. The Princess tugs at the soldier's sleeve. He looks down at her, and I see it; I see him do that tiny, melty, guilty, flinchy thing that most *decent* adults do when small, scared eyes have spotted their badness.

TWOOH!

"Oh my ✸! Oh my ✸! Oh my ✸!" wails the driver, collapsing into floods of tears the second I spit the water out onto the ground.

"They'll kill her," I tell the soldier. "If you turn us in, they'll kill her. That's what they've been doing: experimenting on kids. They KILL KIDS."

"That true as well, is it?" the soldier asks Beardy.

"I'm a lab man," Beardy mutters, suddenly sounding very sober.

"It's true and you know it!" I shriek.

"IS—IT—TRUE?"

"Yes," says Beardy.

For a moment, everyone just stands there, breathing white puffs of hot fear. The driver is sobbing.

"Great," says Beardy. "So now we've all established that, can we please discuss this someplace else?"

Everyone looks at him.

"Someplace inside?" he says, pointing at the sky.

Nimbostratus: now half the stars tucked away. The moon glares down at us.

The soldier nods.

The Princess gets back inside the back of the ambulance, but no one else wants to join her—which is fine by me; the way everyone's so jittery, it's probably best if we all keep an eye on each other. We pile into the front.

"Shift over," I tell the soldier, who has taken the driver's seat. And he does; he actually does. He sort of looks fairly composed, but there must be so much going on in his head, he's as useless as the bawling driver—or Beardy, who would probably manage to turn the ambulance over in about 0.1 micrometers of a nanosecond (assuming he can even drive).

I bump down the track. I don't care about puddles. When I get to the end of it, to a tarmac road, I hesitate.

"Go right," weeps the driver.

"Go left," says the soldier.

Beardy shrugs. He has no clue.

"Go right," blubs the driver.

I angle the steering wheel to turn right.

"I've got kids," the soldier says. "I've got kids."

His radio crackles.

"I've got a daughter. *Her* age," he says. "Turn left."

"Hey! Wassup!" a radio voice says.

"Road's bad," he speaks into it. "We're coming around the long way."

He clicks that radio off. "We need to think this thing through," he says.

I go left.

"Ah, come on! No!" wails the driver. "For Pete's sake! I just wanna go home!"

"Oh, shuddup," I snarl at him.

The four of us stare out of the windshield—stare hard at the road ahead, like we're going to see the future appear out of the dark.

At least, that's what I was doing—from the way their hands clutched the dashboard, I think the others may have been more concerned about the road itself.

Right on cue…it starts raining. Awesome.

I seriously step on it.

CHAPTER SEVENTEEN

I saw there was a garage ahead of us—a fancy car showroom. I spotted smashed glass, and because the place had already been well and truly busted into, I drove straight on in, with only a small amount of further smashing as the roof of the ambulance collided with the remaining bits of window. I screeched to a halt at the end of a long line of fancy cars whose prices looked like the answers to math questions I'd rather not be asked.

The prof, the soldier, and the driver bundled out immediately and plonked themselves down in the funny little potted plants and seating area they had—so you could make-believe you were at home on the sofa, chatting about which car to buy (or what to do about the apocalypse, in this case). The discussion pretty much reminded me of radio programs my mom and my stepdad would have on: people going on and on about stuff. Angrily. It got even angrier when Beardy claimed that the people in charge wanted to use the cure as some kind of international bargaining thing ("More like a ✳ card game!")—though quite what trinkets they might want in exchange was not known to him (most probably nuclear missiles, a few countries, oil reserves, that kind of thing).

To be honest, I wasn't really listening that closely. Every time it

felt like my brain was tuning into a thought, I'd just tweak it back
to the matter at hand: gotta get out of here, Ruby.

The Princess, whose sign did not show her name but said "Nil
by Mouth," watched from the side door of the ambulance as,
in near darkness, I worked my way through every car in there;
each one, same thing: battery dead—and no jumper cables to be
found. Useless.

I splopped plastickly-rubberily past the discussion panel, ignored:
ghost girl in a biosuit. There was a dinky coffee machine and a store
of creamers, so I grabbed the lot of them, went back to the ambulance, and—ah! Saw the machine they use to start stopped hearts
with. I dumped the creamers and inspected it. It's basically a giant
battery pack, isn't it?

I had a go with it on a car.

It didn't work.

Mighty ✳ cross about that.

I took it back to the ambulance (lights still on inside) to get a
better look at the instructions—like maybe it was possible to turn
the thing up?—when the Princess tapped me on the arm.

"Yeah, yeah, just give me a sec," I said.

It's all probably sounding a little weird to you, the whole situation and the not even speaking to the kid—it sounds a little weird
to me—but I tell you, I was so trying to keep my brain tuned in
on what I needed to do. Anything else at all could not be handled.

I didn't get the instructions, but I thought it was worth another
go anyway. The Princess tried to pull me back—

"Yeah—one sec!" I jumped out of the vehicle and—she slammed
the door shut behind me. "What the—"

Headlights from the road rippled along the line of cars. I hadn't
even heard the engine. I ducked—way too late.

Prof Beardy, the soldier, and the driver—they'd ducked too.

I peeked—saw the taillights of a big, dark army truck disappearing.

"We need to get out of here," the driver—who'd stopped blubbering but was still freaking out—said.

Yeah, I thought. *Need to get out of here.* I ditched the heart-starter, and as I speed-crawled/splopped plastickly-rubberily for the ambulance, I had a genius moment. Hanging on the wall by the "Let's pretend we're at home on the sofa choosing our car" area was a huge road map of Britain, so you could see all the places you could go once you'd bought your fancy car.

I dragged over a spare chair and tried to pull the thing off the wall. It wouldn't budge. There was some random mini-tree in a pot, a thing that had probably once looked totally plastic and now looked totally dead. So I grabbed it by the trunk and swung the whole thing at the glass. Big smash. Big mess. I tore the map out. Unfortunately, it was stuck down at the edges, so there were quite a lot of places we wouldn't be going to.

I turned around and…there they all were, staring at me: the prof, the soldier, the driver.

"I just want to go home," I told them, trying to scrumple the map into a more manageable size. "Please just let me go."

I felt my frightened heartbeat.

"I'll keep my mouth shut. I won't tell a soul. I promise you! I just want to go home. Please. *Please!* Just let me go."

"I could take you," said the driver, getting to his feet.

"Siddown," said the soldier. He sat.

"I'm just a kid," I told them.

I am so not. I was. Once. That's gone.

"I don't know how I got like this! I promise you I don't!"

"Clinically speaking, she is no longer relevant," said Beardy.

Another set of headlights—army truck—blasted us.

I stood and I pointed at the gleaming ambulance. The elephant in the fancy car showroom. "They'll see that," I said. "Next truck that comes past, they'll see it."

The soldier, who was the only one I really needed to pay attention to (gun), nodded.

"Get out of here, kid," he said. "Take the back roads."

The problem with maps, even complete ones, is you need to know where you are in the first place. I didn't know where we were. All I knew was that I needed to avoid the main roads. That thought came through the hiss in my head loud and clear.

We drove around for ages burning precious fuel and—it turns out, getting nowhere. We hit a main road. I have this horrible feeling that it looks vaguely familiar...but we're going to have to go for it. I kill my headlights and turn out onto the road.

We're in a forest, right, surrounded by trees and I am peering at the road in the darkness and... *Ru? Wasn't there a forest on the way to the army place?* a tuned-in voice in my head kicks up.

"Yeah!" I say out loud.

Thought so. You're going the wrong way.

OK. OH-KAY. I need to turn around, is all... Oh, but headlights are coming toward me, blasting through the trees.

GET OFF THE ROAD! shrieks my head voice.

Parking place on left: I swing into it—the kind of place you'd have parked to go for a charming country ramble—but not good enough, not far enough from the road—but there's a track, leading into the woods. We are...GOING DOWN IT.

I accelerate into it, and immediately we're hitting stuff, bouncing left and right and bumping along, through darkness and bracken and brambles and bushes—some brambles so high they smack against the windshield, smear ink-dark blackberry-blood spatters across the glass.

Bash-splat-splat-bash-splat, go the brambles as we bump, bash, bump, lurch, slide, smash down that track—and in the middle of it all the ambulance conks out. I try to restart it without stopping. One hand on the wheel, one hand messing with the ignition key, both feet messing with the pedals. Won't restart. All gas gone. Engine noise gone—all you can hear is the bump, bash, bump, lurch, slide, smash (and the bump, bash, bump, lurch, slide, smash of my heart) as we freewheel down the track.

Until we stop. I flick on the headlights for ONE SECOND, for long enough to check. We have gone far enough, I think. I hope. We're deep in the forest. It's night. It's raining—the Princess hammers on the glass between us. I get it. I kill the lights. We sit. In silence. Hoping.

I am holding so many thoughts away from me. So many thoughts. The effort of it hurts. I sit, holding back the thoughts and the feelings that latch on to them, screaming. My eyes do that adjusting thing, the way they do in darkness. After a while, I can see it all: the trees, the ferns, the brambles…

After a longer while, the rain stops. I see a fox creep across the path.

It got wet; it shakes itself. It comes sniffing up so close to the ambulance I can't see it anymore.

An owl hoots.

I let one thought—ONE THOUGHT—in, and I weep for a while, thinking how much Simon, my stepdad, would have loved this nighttime nature stakeout…and then I unravel. The hiss in my head tunes in to the shrieking panic: What am I going to do?!

I get out of the cab—for one second, even through that biosuit, I feel the wildish night wrap itself around me, and I shrug it off and open the back door to the ambulance.

I'd have said sorry to the Princess for waking her, but she is sitting awake in blue light, wrapped in one of those silver-foil blanket things they give to marathon runners.

So no one has slept.

"Hey," I say.

I slam the door behind me. She scrambles down from the bed for the patient, so I can sit.

"It's OK. You stay there," I tell her, reaching behind her to try other switches—there are tons of them—but now only this blue light in the middle of the ceiling works.

I have to respect what she has done. In my absence, she has been through that ambulance; a little pile of stuff she hasn't touched lies next to her: teensy cartons of water, even teensier clear plastic tubes of—I can't even tell what it is; the light is too dim and I can't be bothered to read it. And the showroom creamer, also untouched.

"You did a good thing," I tell her, thinking about how she tugged that soldier's sleeve. "You were brave."

She does not respond.

"This all we've got?" I ask.

I rummage where she has rummaged, find clear plastic tubes of other stuff. I look at her; she shakes her head, telling me no. I look closer. "Saline"—that's what I see on the label. Wouldn't want to drink that. Smart kid.

I split our pile, peel and glug a mini water carton first.

Breaking into the next one when I see she's not drinking, I look at the sign around her neck—and it comes to me, what it means: "Nil by Mouth." No food, no drink. That's what they make people do before operations, isn't it? Like when Simon had to have his knee messed with. (Bird-watching accident, overly hasty exit from a private wood. Chased by angry landowner. Tripped on own binoculars. Didn't like *that* part being mentioned because he shouldn't have had them off his neck anyway. "Keep binoculars on neck at all times" is one of the many bird-watching rules.) (I might have *mentioned* it anyway—that and the *trespassing*.)

"Halfsies," I tell her.

She shoves the whole pile at me.

This is why they chose kids to experiment on, isn't it? Not just because kids trust adults…but because they have no choice but to trust them. Those kids back there in that "hospital," they would have just done what they were told. That's what kids do, isn't it? They trust adults until…they can't trust them anymore. And still, they trust them.

Ah, my ripped-out heart.

I hardly feel like any kind of adult—but to the Princess, I am. I must be. And not only that, but she has also realized she needs to keep me alive.

I get it, kid. I get it. Ripped-out heart hates it—ripped-out heart says:

"Halfsies."

And shoves half the pile back.

It is more than half the pile. I am not saying this to make myself look good; it's what I did because it's what Simon, my stepdad, did for me—made it look like we were sharing, equal, when he went without.

Yeah, right. I am so thirsty I could force her to swallow those mini creamers whole so I don't have to see them. I swig down my next water carton and crash out on the floor.

✹! ✹! ✹! ✹!

Just knowing she's there, just sitting there, is going to keep me awake.

I sit up.

"Look, kid, I can't do a story right now."

The Princess just stares into space. She's probably relieved; I do remember my last story didn't go down too well.

"I can't...you know. I just can't. And I can't talk about any stuff either, OK? I just can't. I can't..."

What the ✷ is this? My voice is going all...wibbly-wobbly. I tune out a million thoughts. I'm great with kids, me. Argh—my Henry. Babiest brother-brat beloved. Dan. Brother-brat beloved. Tune out, tune out.

The Princess just sits there.

"How about a song?" I ask the kid.

I can't read what the kid thinks like Darius could, but I am guessing that face is a no. I don't blame her. I do remember—though I can hardly bear to—the last time I sang to her...and it was awful, and not just because I can't sing, but because...it was a lullaby— same as my mom sang to me...same as any kid's mom would sing.

"Yeah—you go to sleep or I start singing," I threaten. Empty threat: I want my mom so bad I couldn't sing if I tried.

She lies down and shuts her eyes. She is so not even slightly asleep.

I lie down. I am freezing ✷ cold.

How did this ever come to be? How did it ever come to be that I am lying on the floor of an ambulance in the middle of the woods, freezing ✷ cold, and...

I shut my eyes. I want to sleep. I just want to sleep. ("And then I woke up," etc.) I cannot sleep.

"What you have to do," I tell her, as much as I am telling myself, "is shut your eyes." I look to see whether hers are shut—they are open again, just staring into space. "You SHUT your eyes," I tell her.

She does shut them.

"And you see what's there. Not the scary things. You don't look

164

at those; you just look at the colors and the shapes…and all you do is tell yourself what the colors and the shapes look like."

I shut my eyes. I have to.

"So there they are," I tell her. "The colors and the shapes. Every time a bad thought comes into your head, look away from it—just look at the colors and the shapes. Tell them to yourself. Tell yourself the colors and the shapes."

Bad thoughts, bad pictures come into my head.

That's how come I discovered this in the first place. When you can't put your head anywhere else, "See only the colors and the shapes. Only the colors and the shapes."

Am I telling her or telling me?

"There's a blue-speckled orange mist," I say out loud, "a blobby slide of black over a green blob…gray diamondy things with purple blotches…a red soup with pink flecky bits."

CHAPTER EIGHTEEN

The kid pokes me awake. I'm not great in the mornings anyway, but…

I know it's late; the door to the ambulance is open and the heat of a sunny day is cooking up the greenery outside. The scent of warmed forest wafts in, of trees and leaves and moss that are thinking quietly about winter, and must have had their most peaceful, people-free summer for thousands of years, I guess—up until last night, when an ambulance came crashing through. I don't suppose the SOUND OF A HELICOPTER FLYING OVERHEAD bothers them too much—*BUT IT BOTHERS ME.*

HOW DID I SLEEP THROUGH THAT?!

I'm up on my feet, peering out of the ambulance door—can't see the helicopter for the trees, but that's fine. I can't see it, so it can't see us. I don't know whether it is anything to do with us, but I do know WE HAVE GOT TO GET OUT OF HERE.

I'd go nuts at the kid for not waking me sooner, but…I can't. A couple more creamers have been drunk. The rest of the tiny pile? She hasn't touched it.

"It's OK," I tell her. "It's OK. You drink that stuff. It's yours. You drink it."

I am desperate to glug it. All of it. I look at one of the little tubes full of clear liquid—sucrose solution. Takes a nanosecond to swig it down.

Really…could life be any more horrible?

"Just drink up, huh?" I say, as I go to try to restart the ambulance.

It's pointless. We *are* out of gas. It makes nasty noises.

Nice day for a walk.

I return to the back of the ambulance and grab the map.

"C'mon," I tell the kid. "We gotta walk."

She hesitates for a second. She's right. I'm in a biosuit, aren't I? She's in a hospital gown.

I rummage. I find scissors and…great big super-tough bags.

I can't fool myself; they're body bags.

Well—great. They're strong, and there's tape too, also pretty strong stuff, and so I can make her some body-bag shoes and a nice, snug suit.

"All done," I tell her when I've taped that plastic suit tight around her, complete with hood.

"C'mon," I say, stepping down from the ambulance.

I offer my hand.

She takes it.

What do either of us feel? Not much. A moment of warmth through tape and plastic.

She hops down. Lets go of my hand. I pull on my plasticky-rubbery helmet. I've taken enough chances.

We walk out of the forest, me and that kid. I go first. With gloved hands and the scissors from the ambulance, I snip brambles in our path.

It is a slow journey.

We reach the main road. It is quiet…but I know which road this is. It *is* the road to the army base; any second, they could come.

"We've gotta run now," I shout through the helmet at her. I am so thirsty, the words feel sticky in my mouth. "Can you do that?"

For the first time, the kid nods at me.

And we run; boy, do we run.

The breath of life pants in and out of my lips, of her lips. All you can hear is our muffled breathing, our muffled panting as we run; our muffled feet, slapping muffledly on the silent road and the map; our map, the only thing we carry, flapping. Muffledly—I can hardly hear it…but I do hear a vehicle. Yes, I feel the Princess's hand squeeze mine; she hears it too. We dive off the road and hide, panting, in bushes at the roadside as an army truck passes.

We wait until it is quiet again.

We run on.

It's hopeless, this. A couple of minutes later, we hear another vehicle. We dive off the road again. We wait, flattened, cowering… In front of my eyes, I see earth, insects scurrying to flee the human apocalypse that's just landed on them. I watch one tiny bug run, screaming tiny insect screams, and see—behind us, through a hedge—there's a field…other side of that, there's houses.

The ambulance scissors won't cut barbed wire, but—OK. I pry it open so the Princess can get through. Me, I have to scramble over it—and the ✸ wire rips the thigh of my suit and a glove.

The Princess grabs my hand and we run around a field of corn. I suppose because I am a **FREAK**, I could just run straight through it even with holes in my suit—but I don't.

I've got a kid to think about.

We hit the outskirts of a town, clamber over a fence, and—

It is a bit of a nightmare. I'm sure it would have all been very charming and all that—cute town green, charming church, ye olde shops—but it has been so visited (not by ye tourists, but by ye desperate people like us, heading to or from the army base) that nearly everywhere has been broken into already. All ye stuff—ye anything to drink, ye snacks, ye cars—has gone.

We leave the main street, wander along this suburban road.

We may as well be in a desert. There are no cars left. I don't even have to go look in those houses, doors smashed open, to know there will be nothing left in there. The way it is (and I am sorry to have to say this), even the dogs have abandoned this place; what bones remain are picked clean and scattered.

Marlborough—that's where we are—twinned with the Sahara. If a camel came wandering down the street, I wouldn't even think I were hallucinating.

I know I'm not hallucinating that helicopter. We duck into a stinking house until it passes.

It's hopeless. There's nothing but a school at the end of the road. I turn around. The kid doesn't follow.

She looks back at the school.

"What?! You're kidding me?"

She doesn't budge.

"Seriously?"

The thing to know here is despite all my finely tuned looting skills and experience, the one thing I really, definitely, totally avoid at all times…is schools. It is not because of the terrible memories of mathematical humiliation. It is not even exactly because I imagine the beeps of cell phones and kids all over the country going, "Hey, someone in Dartbridge just texted me to say this guy called

Andrew Difford says Ruby Morris is a lousy kisser." It is because. It is just because.

We stroll into that school via the kitchens. Everything is gone—but not in your usual Marlborough way, smash-and-grab chaos, but in a neat way. I suppose the French chef at the army base could have sent out a raiding party, then thrown a tantrum at the sight of so many giant cans of baked beans, etc., but taken them anyway.

The kid doesn't seem as devastated as I am; she just goes wandering off through the school, and I follow. Something isn't right here, because I'm pretty sure she's supposed to be following me… but that thought fades as the real reason I don't go into schools comes battering down on me. And it's bigger than just every classroom, every bank of lockers, every wall display of artwork we pass reminding me of my friends—MY FRIENDS—who are now all dead… All that is bad enough, to be reminded… But what squeezes my heart tight with hurt in this place is the thought that it was the same here, the same in every school, everywhere. Rubys and Leonies and Saskias and Caspars—and even nerd-boy Spratts—were free to roam these corridors.

Well, not free—but you know what I mean. Giggling about longing for the next party, for the summer—or for the next math class, depending.

I mean, obviously, I am unique (that's right, because I am a FREAK), but you take my point. (We were all unique.) It is the most unfair thing, what has happened to the world—and to us, most especially. Kids, I mean. *Young* people. We never even got a decent share of life.

The Princess stops outside a door. The staff room. I am too done in with sorrow to do much more than raise my eyebrows. She tries the door—locked. I shuffle off…but she's not going to budge. Stubborn little thing, stood there in her body-bag outfit.

My squeezed heart loosens, just one tiny bit. I cave, pathetically—become the kind of "mother" I so often wished mine had been, one who does just exactly what her kid wants, all the time.

I shouldn't be doing it, because we need to conserve energy here, but I do a fire-extinguisher job on the door. It swings open onto enemy territory: tables, textbooks, and comfy seats, where teachers can relax as they prepare for the next round of torture.

Looks like the executive desert to me. "There," I say, setting the fire extinguisher down, but the kid has already gone in.

Staff rooms, I notice immediately, tearing off my helmet, smell different than the rest of the school—which is no bad thing right now. Even though no one much has been here for months, it still smells different. In the corridor, there is still your classic school smell: dinners and kids, and then janitors mopping up after it all. Inside the staff room…there's an alien smell. Not mold, not anything like someone's been here any time recently, but… T-E-A-C-H-E-R-S.

I wedge the door shut behind us, just to block out the scent of the past for a moment—and I hear this beautiful, beautiful gurgling.

WATER COOLER!
WATER COOLER ALERT!

The kid must have been in an even worse state than I realized because she's managed to get her little head shoved under the tap, gulping what she can. I grab teachers' mugs, peel her off the tap, and fill one, hand it to her, and fill one for myself—then have to give that to her because she's already drained hers. She's gulping as I fill another and I remember something…

"Just slow down," I tell her.

She's not going to, so I have to take hold of her hand on the mug and pry it away from her face; she glares at me.

"Slow down or it might make you sick," I tell her.

Her stomach, agreeing with me, gurgles violently.

"Like this," I say.

It's killing me to demonstrate, because all I want to do is gulp too, but I sip—pause—sip. In the next pause, I release her hand; she eyeballs me as she takes a sip that's more of a glug, then pauses for a trillionth of a nanosecond, then takes another gluggy sip.

It's only when we're on our next mugfuls that I bother to think about whether that water will be OK. It's not going to have the killer-bug in it (What do I care? I am a **FREAK**), but it has been sitting there for so many months... Water can go funny after a while. I'm peering into it, looking for any worrying signs of greenishness or reddishness (i.e., badishness), when the Princess wanders off, gluggy-sipping, then wanders back, still gluggy-sipping but managing to clutch an enormous family-size tin of cookies—which she dumps on the floor. Luxury, chocolate cookies.

Our greedy hands dive in.

A helicopter flies overhead. It doesn't stop or anything freaky like that; still, it's scary...but not scary enough to make us lay off the cookies.

Cranked up on sugar, we revive and carry out a thorough search of the staff room.

We discover the Lost Property box.

The kid has no choice but to work out an outfit of sorts from it, and I cut her out of her plastic so she can dress. She looks like a secondhand-store kid. She is walking lost property.

Me? Kids my age are more careful. I can't find stuff big enough to fit me. I am forced to dress in teachers' clothes—specifically, the PE teacher's clothes. An absolutely dreadful tracksuit, and sneakers that aren't much better.

In an effort to console myself, I am also forced to contemplate using teachers' makeup, but I can't quite bring myself to do it. I put it to one side as emergency reserve and carry on rummaging.

We pull together a brilliant haul: tons more cookies, sweets, chips, fizzy drinks, boring crackers (but, hey, there's jam too!). Plus, there're three whole other unopened drums of water for the cooler. Awesome! The frustrating part is that there're cans of soup and dried noodle snacks, but obviously, no electricity to work the microwave or kettle to make them truly yummy. The kid seems not to mind and is ladling cold soup into her face (I really am worried she'll make herself sick) when I have a brilliant idea of my own.

Armed with cutlery, bowls, water, and goodies, we trot off to the science labs. It's all gas Bunsen burners in there, but in the store cupboard (another fire extinguisher job) there's one of those alcohol burners in among all the stuff that's used for "Look But Don't Touch" teaching, just in case the kids accidentally blow themselves or the school up. Superb.

I try to force the kid to put safety glasses on, but she's not having it unless I do too, so I do. I get us both lab coats too.

See how good with kids I am? See how much fun I can be?

The Princess doesn't even crack a smile, but I sort of somehow know she's not un-into it, if you know what I mean. Could be because there's food at the end of it.

We cook up a feast. She gets hot soup, clutching the glass beaker with a massive heat-proof glove, and I get a glass beaker of water on the boil for a noodle snack.

Afterward, she throws up.

It's probably just the dehydration and the pigging out on an empty stomach, but still it makes me go a little panicky, worrying that she's "got something"—not the killer-rain something, but a *something* something, like kids used to get. I ask her a ton of questions that get no answer. (Does your head ache? Is your throat sore? Do you feel hot? Cold?) I make her lie down in the staffroom under teachers' coats, giving her a lecture about how didn't I tell her not to glug so much water, followed by another mini-lecture that goes like this:

"You know, it really would be a lot easier if you spoke to me."

That's it. End of lecture.

I plunk myself down. I wait. I know she doesn't want to go to sleep, but I can see she's going to fall asleep—fighting it, every snoozy dragging step of the way. I feel like I could sleep too, but I need to stay awake, so I can get on with the other thing I feel I need to do, which is panic. I don't want the kid to see me do that.

She sleeps…like a princess…silently.

I've gotta get rid of her.

CHAPTER NINETEEN

I do not want to be lumbered with a kid.

I mean, I know, to a lot of people I still am a kid…but—uh—you know what? Me and this kid? It is NOT going to work.

I've already demonstrated—in a "Stay back, kids, this is dangerous" science-teacher demo way—that I cannot take care of her. I don't WANT to take care of her. I am way too young for this sort of responsibility.

The whiteboard in the staffroom is filled with hideous staff reminders about exams. I wipe the whole thing clean.

I write on it:

BACK IN 5—RING BELL IF PROBLEM. RX

and I put a massive old school bell on a desk right in front of the whiteboard.

Then I leave, to panic where I won't disturb her.

I go to the gym—when would I ever, voluntarily, go to a gym?!—and I chuck a ball at a net. At a net; it's meant to go into the net… but this isn't PE. This is thinking. I miss hoop after hoop—same way I'm missing thought after thought. In the end, I just kick the thing, hard, against the wall. Still I miss some, but this is how the kicks go:

Kick.

Where now?

Kick.

Home.

Kick.

That's the first place they'll look for you.

Kick.

All right. Shut up. I know. I'll look for Dad.

Kick.

That's stupid. You know that's stupid. And it's pointless. It's stupid and pointless.

Kick. **Kick. KICK. KICK.** The ball goes flying. I get it back.

Kick.

Got a better plan?

Kick.

Go back to Xar's.

Kick.

He scares me.

Kick.

Yeah, but everyone else is OK.

Kick.

Excuse me?!

Kick.

They're just no good in emergencies, that's all.

Kick.

I'm not taking the kid there. I gotta get rid of the kid.

Kick.

Really?

Kick.

Yes! Have you seen how the kids are at Xar's?! Running wild! It's a completely unsuitable environment for—

Kick.

OK, shut up. I know.

Kick.

Salisbury Cathedral. That's where I'll take her. Nice, kind, useless people there. They'll take proper care of her.

Kick.

You're really going to dump her?

Kick.

YES!

I give the ball a massive kick—and I miss the ball, again.

We've got supplies; we need transportation.

I leave the ball where it is, rolling, lonely in a gym…where it will probably never be kicked again. Slowly, over time, it will go flat. No one is ever going to pump that ball up. (On the positive side, no one is ever going to stand there screaming at a girl like me to "*PASS! PASS! PASS!*")

I case the joint; there are cars dumped here—not many, but in any case, they're all keyless or fuel-less or have dead batteries. I am just about despairing and considering leaving the school grounds to comb through the Marlborough leftovers when… Hurray for school janitors! Rounding the building, I see garages—and in one I see… this funny little three-wheeler flatbed truck. It is worth a try. But it is locked! Boo for school janitors! But there has to be some place where the keys are kept. The garage our getaway vehicle is in has other garages and sheds close by; I investigate them, pull up doors onto smelly goalposts and hockey stuff. One I have to smash open, only to find a Tutankhamun's tomb of things for the school carnival: tables, streamers, a pirate scene on hardboard with holes where the faces should be, throw-a-wet-sponge-at-the-math-teacher's-face. For fifty pence. Bargain.

I slouch back to the janitor's garage, just to give the three-wheeler thing a kick.

The keys are hanging on the wall, aren't they?

My hands are shaking so much, I can hardly get them in the ignition. It purrs into life—purrs? It judders, gnarrs, and whirrs, like a lawnmower. WHO CARES? IT WORKS!

I switch it off. I race back across the playing field. If our PE teacher had been alive to see it, she would have been astonished. And I would have been forced to join the track team—so, hey, one for the list of things I'm glad there'll be no more of. Being forced to join the track team, not the PE teacher. She couldn't help herself, I don't suppose. She just liked PE, and I didn't.

My genius brain shouts, *GET A BETTER MAP!*

"'Kay!" my genius self answers.

RUBY THE GENIUS RIDES AGAIN!

Or not… Of all the many, many books they have in the library, there is no ✱ road map. I suppose that's understandable; why would kids need a road map? EXCEPT THIS ONE DOES— LIKE, NOW! I'm rummaging through shelves like a lunatic, desperately flicking through the geography section, tossing books aside (or flinging them, in the case of *The Rain Cycle* and its depressing blue maps of global precipitation) when I hear the bell I left the Princess with clanging. It is so loud. It is so, so loud. It is louder than the helicopter that is passing overhead. I could run back out to the garages and find something to defend us with—a javelin! They looked good! I should've grabbed one! But that bell clangs so loud I feel like I have no time. I grab the biggest, heaviest book I can see—an encyclopedia—and run.

I pelt down the corridor, book raised, ready to strike.

She's standing there; there's no one from the army coming to get her. She just woke up and got scared… I see that, I feel that, before I even get to her. And what was I going to do? Fight them off with a hefty book?

I get to her. I do scan the staff room just to be sure.

"I'm sorry," I tell her. "It's OK now. I'm here."

I don't mention that I am going to ditch her ASAP.

Me and the kid load up the three-wheeler lawnmower-truck thing with supplies. I decide to wait until dark before we leave, so I do end up fiddling around a little with teachers' makeup, supplemented by more glittery and gorgeous items that must (surely?!) have been confiscated from young innocents like me.

Helicopters and distant truck sounds all day. Can't be about us, but don't want to find out for sure. So we wait; then we putter off.

OK, so it's not that simple. We haven't got that much gas, but that part's OK. The lawnmower truck isn't greedy; it just putters and futters along. It is also a very good thing that Salisbury is still there, clinging to the bottom of the ripped and mud-grubby showroom map. What is not so good is that the useless map only shows us the main roads, so we only know what to avoid and not the roads we *should* take.

It is a fairly unpleasant experience. My stomach churns with fear the whole way. Thank goodness it is dark because we end up puttering past army camps and camps of the useless. Every time we do that, I think that's the end of us. We'll be spotted and dragged back inside that army base…because we can outrun no one. We putter… past an airfield at one point—plane coming in, helicopters unloading people. Busy little bees, the army.

I should try for another car, but I don't. Too scared to stop.

And if anything, this whole, horrible journey just makes my head know for sure: I cannot take care of a kid.

♦

Outside a Salisbury fish and chips place, we conk out.

I've read you can make a car go on used cooking oil, but I've never tried it. I could try now or…

The night is starry and clear. It cannot be that far to the cathedral. I get out. I recheck the sky—all around. I check the kid's feet, like she's a pony; her body-bag hoofs are tattered, but I think there are enough layers left to get us where we need to go.

"C'mon," I tell her.

I offer my hand, but she climbs down alone.

"There're nice people here," I tell her.

We pad through silent streets toward the cathedral, past signs that were left out months ago. Sheets with welcome messages carefully written out on them, now rain-run into weeping gibberish. Balloons to say, *Hurray! You're here! You're gonna be OK!*… Yeah, they're all popped. Hanging limp and tattered.

The kid and I march toward the cathedral—to the people, the useless people, where I once—officially—belonged.

When we reach the green around it, we zigzag through a graveyard of cars to that massive stone building, where beautiful electric lights are no longer burning.

I do not want to believe this is a bad sign. I do not want to believe it until—until we see…

The ancient doors of Salisbury Cathedral are bust in.

Like, smashed.

All dark in there. All dark.

"Hello?!" I called.

We ventured inside.

"Hey?!"

Ahead of us, I saw the tiniest light flickering. We walked toward it, past pews on which all sorts of stuff was dumped—luggage, clothes, and all kinds of random stuff. The leftovers of what had been normal human life.

There was a lady, kneeling down in front of the altar, on which a single candle burned. Next to it, a goldfish in a bowl. Maybe God had been replaced with something easier to care for.

"Margaret?" I whispered.

She looked around. It wasn't Margaret—a lovely lady I had met once, a long time ago. It was some other old lady.

"Hello, pet," she said.

She carried on praying.

"Excuse me, but where is everyone?" I asked.

She didn't answer.

I laid my hand on her shoulder—in a polite, nervous sort of way.

"Excuse me. Where is everyone?"

She didn't answer. I sank down to my knees alongside her, and I craned my face in front of hers.

"Please…where has everyone gone?"

It took a moment for her to focus on me.

"The army came, pet," she said, like that explained everything. Which I guess, in a way, it kind of did. "People ran away."

I thought about the people I had met here. Sagal, in her wheelchair, trying to get out through the parking lot full of cars. Her dad ranting in Somali. Sagal probably finding time to get embarrassed about the whole thing. Whether anyone would have helped them.

I swallowed. I unthought that. I breathed. Plan A thwarted.

I didn't want to get saddled with an old lady any more than I wanted to be saddled with a kid…but to leave her there? I couldn't do it.

"Do you want to come with us?" I asked.

She clutched my arm. Stared into my eyes.

"You can bring the goldfish if you like," I offered.

"Oh no, Trevor's not mine," she said. "I'm just minding him for someone."

I felt my sad heart beat.

"We could just leave them a note about the goldfish. About Trevor. Or…I mean, we could take him with us and—"

"I'm staying put. No offense, but you're just a little un, aren't you?"

Lady, I am the *oldest* little un you will ever meet.

"Let's face it. Our Trevor's probably got more common sense. You should get home to your mom and dad. Best place for you."

I stood up.

The Princess had sat behind us in a pew.

"Come on," I told her, holding out my hand.

She didn't take it—not immediately—but she did take it, a little way farther on, as we walked out, down the aisle.

"It's a disgrace, i'n't it, Trevor?" I heard that lady mutter. "It's all just a ✷ disgrace."

I stood at the smashed-in doors. It *was* all just a ✷ disgrace.

I barely looked at the sky. I just walked out, the kid with me. Plan B: Xar's. He's a loon, I know, but there are other people there who aren't (Grace). And there are other kids there. The Princess… she'll be OK there, for a while. She'll be OK. I'll leave her there. I'll go back and get her when I find a better place—or I won't need to, because ***everything's going to be OK.***

Thinking about it, it didn't seem like a good sign that there was more than one car to choose from on the edge of the giant parking lot. I s'pose it meant that people had kept on coming there, but I s'pose it also meant that people hadn't left—which you'd think they would have done if the army had come…in the way the army seemed to have come, wrecking those doors.

Anyway, I got us a car.

Flipped open the glove compartment, saw a Carpenters CD. Shut the glove compartment.

CHAPTER TWENTY

I got us to Xar's.

It seemed so quiet as we crunched up the drive, but I suppose it was pretty early for party people. I thought I saw the downstairs curtains twitch. Then, at one of the big upstairs windows—the biggest—the curtains were drawn back, swept back, like it was a theater. King Xar—in white, um, snug-fitting underpants—stood at the window. I didn't know what else to do, so I waved. He didn't wave back. A punky-looking girl appeared next to him. She didn't wave either, but then Xar said something to her; she turned and shouted something into the house, then turned back and gave me this little wave. That was a welcome, right? I was being welcomed? There was no smile on her face.

Then the massive front door swung open and one of the Court I recognized, this cheerful-looking fashionista girl (in fashionista pj's) appeared, waving frantically. That was a welcome.

"C'mon," I told the kid.

"Hi," said the fashionista as we crunched in over a tarp spread across the hall floor. She seemed a little flustered.

"Sorry, didn't mean to wake you up," I burbled. I felt nervous—so would you. I didn't really see why they wouldn't want us there, but it's a funny old thing, knowing you've got nowhere else to go. It is not nice. It is especially not nice when you can feel there is a kid standing so close by you, you can hear her every breath.

I wasn't even sure whether the fashionista had heard me or not; she just stared at me in the gloom of the hallway. The aftermath of another big party night, I guessed.

"Ladybird…" said Xar, slouching down the stairs.

In another time and another place, I would have been quite distracted. Mercifully, he had put some trousers on, but they were the loose, linen-y, hang-on-your hips kind. Also white. Shirt draped across his arm. Bare chest. Um, tanned. Um, muscly. Um. The guy was hot, OK? A bit scary and weird, but HOT.

"Um," I said.

"So how's your little friend?"

"Dead," I said.

Just then a door crashed open and Grace—lovely, HUGE Grace—came waddling out of the kitchen in an intoxicating haze of TOAST SMELL, carrying a breakfast tray.

"Ruby!" she gasped.

"Grace!" I beamed—but Grace was not beaming; she looked horrified—she looked, pleadingly, at Xar.

My eyes looked lovingly at the breakfast tray.

"The thing is…" I said to Xar. That toast, on the plate, on the tray…it smelled so good.

Butter. Melting. You can get it out of cans, don't you know? Bread too! Hadn't I discovered that in the deli in Dartbridge? And gorged myself stupid…ooh! So goooood!

PULL YOURSELF TOGETHER, RU.

"Look, we want to stay here," I tell Xar, the words bubbling in a pool of drool.

"Sure you do, Ladybird," he says. "But you've got to see it from our point of view. Why would we want you?"

WHAT?! Um—because?! Just because?! Hello—APOCALYPSE? Kindness of your heart?!

"Still, let's not be rude to our guests, *Grace*," he says.

She holds out the tray. Plate on it. Butter dripping. Whole tray rattling.

Uh! I need *sustenance*!

"Enjoy," Xar says.

I guess the kid must still be feeling sick or something because she doesn't seem to want any, but me? I don't need telling twice; I grab a slice of toast and a mug of tea, stuff toast into my face.

Xar shivers, pulls on his shirt.

"And then it's bye-bye, I'm afraid," he whispers, smiling, and slouches back up the stairs.

The kid. I feel the kid breathing next to me. Grace, tray rattling, starts to sob. I flip. On the spot.

I yee-haa.

What's to lose?! I glug tea to try to get the enormous glob of toast in my mouth swallowed.

"We've got nowhere else to go!" I shriek after him, half choking on toast. I slug more tea.

"Not my problem…" says Xar in a quiet voice, slouching out of sight.

Now Grace is bawling.

Ruby Morris Decision: blab.

"They've got a cure," I bellow. "There's a cure!"

King Xar pops his kingly head over the stairwell.

"There's a cure," I say at him.

Xar speed-slouches back down the stairs—*Yeah, gotcha now*, I think. I do know I kind of said I wouldn't tell anyone. I don't much care right now. All I want is a safe place to stay and more toast. I just REALLY want—MORE TOAST. I cram another mouthful in.

I chew, nodding—bravely, meaningfully—at him. He just stares back. Speechless, I guess. Grace stops bawling, but her breathing is all jagged and weird. It's a horrible sound.

"You can go now," Xar tells her, and she shuffles back to the kitchen, gasping weirdly.

"Ladybird," says Xar, breaking the silence. "We need to talk."

He holds out his hand to me. "Forgive me," he says.

It goes without saying that I'm basically never going to forgive Xar, but I am prepared to accept everything he has to offer by way of an apology, which consists of a breakfast the French chef would be hard pressed to improve upon in Xar's private suite.

It is important to note that, in my mind, what this apology also consists of is us being able to stay, and for that reason I am prepared to tell him EVERYTHING.

And so I do that, lounging on a ginormous sofa with the Princess.

She is listening. I know she's listening. She shows no sign of it…but I know her enough to know that's what she's doing. And I don't get so caught up in telling it all that I completely forget she is there. When I get to the most horrible parts (which, for me, are the kids on the ward and the "sampling" of my family), I find myself glancing nervously at her and trying to find a way to say what I need to say without letting my own horror splurge out any more than it demands to.

Xar does show signs of listening. He sips some kind of green herbal tea from a china cup so thin the light from the lamp behind him shines through it, making pretty ripples on the fancy plaster ceiling where fat-cheeked cherubs cavort among fruit and flowers. He cocks his head this way and that as I speak, frowning and making "mm-hm" sympathetic noises of encouragement when I struggle to say how it was. And when I have finished, he asks many questions I can't really answer, and one that I can:

"Did you tell them about this place?"

"No."

And then me and the Princess lie sleepy eyed on the sofa while Xar improves his understanding of what a phage is from a bunch of books that look even tougher to get your head around than anything I dared pick up in Dartbridge Library.

I keep thinking he's going to ask me another question, but he doesn't.

Finally, "So could we just get some sleep now, please?" I ask.

Xar looks up like he's surprised we're still there.

"We're really tired."

"Sure," he says, and waves at his ginormous four-poster bed, even huger than the one in the dressing-up room. He goes back to reading.

"Isn't there somewhere else we could sleep?" I ask.

Xar looks up—a flicker of annoyance. "No," he says, like it should somehow be obvious. "All the rooms are taken."

"Oh, er…" I start up, thinking Grace wouldn't mind if we bunked with her.

"You'll find it perfectly comfortable," he states, and goes back to his book.

I don't really want to go to sleep there, in his bed, but I'm too tired to argue it. I pull the sleepy Princess off the sofa and haul her up into that bed. She's out like a light. So fast I'm not even sure if she was awake in the first place.

Me, I get in too—but as soon as I lie down, my eyes zap open. Wide-awake.

I shut them, I try to do the color-shape thing, but my mind is buzzing.

I give up. I just stare at the window, and I watch the light behind it get stronger and stronger as dawn, finally, comes.

CHAPTER TWENTY-ONE

S wear to ✸ I'd shut my eyes for two seconds when Grace shakes me awake. She looks as terrible as I feel.

"I'm so sorry, I'm so sorry, I'm so sorry," she blurts into my face. "Look, I kept your stuff for you," she says, shoving a plastic bag of my clothes at me. "I took care of it. I'm so sorry. Please forgive me? I'm so sorry."

"About what?" I say, really, really annoyed, rubbing my eyes and—ARGH—feeling like I am being tortured. Whatever part of sleep she just woke me from, it's the one that hurts most to be dragged out of.

"They made me do it."

Whu—?

"*He* made me do it."

Whu—?

"But you're OK, right? You're OK?" says Grace, stroking my stumpy hair.

"Yeah, I'm OK, Grace," I whisper. The Princess is still asleep beside me. I look to where Xar was sitting—he's gone.

"I'm so sorry," Grace blurts.

"OK," I whisper-hiss at her, getting out of bed and leading her away from the Princess—and away from me; I'm leading her to the door. I don't know what this is, but I do not want to hear about it now.

"I didn't want to do it," she gibbers. "I didn't want to."

"OK," I say again. I just want her to go. I was asleep! "Later!" I open the door.

"I didn't want to do it even before I saw it was you," she says.

Whu—? My sleepy mind wakes up enough to shut the door.

"Grace?" Weird prickly things happen up and down my spine. My guts—the guts that I have been trying so very hard to ignore—they lurch. "*What?*"

"They told me I had to," says Grace. "It's how it works. If you want to stay here, you have to prove yourself. It was just my turn, Ruby. I didn't know it would be you. I didn't!"

My head is really not wanting to try to make sense of this.

Grace rubs her belly, soothing the baby inside her. "I need a safe place, Ruby."

"Yeah," I tell her, thinking, *We all do.* "So *what* did you have to do?"

"Kill someone."

No… My head is not having it. Did she just say…?

"I mean, you know what Xar's like. He thinks everyone should die anyway. So you've got to prove you agree with that to live."

"*Excuse me?*"

"I know! It's totally ✱ up! But when he talks about it and stuff, it's like it kind of makes sense…kind of…"

I can't even manage to shake my head properly.

The apocalypse—it sure does bring out the best in people, doesn't it?

"…and anyway, tons of people died already," Grace is waffling on. "That's how you've got to think about it. Tons of people died."

"Are you saying… Grace, was the water in that tea bad?"

194

She nods.

"You were going to kill me…?" I can't look at her. I turn my face away and see the kid in the bed. "And her?! You were going to kill a kid?"

"You've got to see it from my point of view," Grace pleads…but I hear a snarl creeping into her voice. "What *else* could I do?"

I look at her again. I feel physically sick.

"It'll be the same for you," she comes back at me. "It's what you'll have to do."

I shake my head at her… *No.*

"You will!"

What the army have been doing, that was bad enough…but there was a point to it, wasn't there? A sick, disgusting thing (killing people) to try to stop a sick, disgusting thing (people getting killed). This?

"It's disgusting. It's sick. It's **mad**."

She stares at me. It's horrible. It's like I can see inside her brain, see that creepy little wiggly-legged 🦟 crawling all over it, laughing at the mess it has made—of the mind of a girl who (*I **must** remember this*) did not seem to be so different from me. Who cannot be so different from me.

"Grace…" I don't know what to say to her. I can hardly speak anyway. I feel like I'm definitely going to cry or throw up. Or both.

"But I chose the tea, Ruby," she gibbers on. "That was *my* choice."

I cry. I'd like to feel that it was my small, sad, human heart, but it is stress, exhaustion, and horror that make me weep.

"I just thought…you know, if you're going to have to kill someone…I mean, that's nicer, isn't it?" Grace is yammering on. "The other choice was a gun! I couldn't do that. I couldn't shoot someone!"

My face scrunches up in disbelief—in disbelief that is wafer thin. I am coming to realize that I could believe anything about anyone.

"I just did it for the baby. You've got to understand that! I just did it for the baby!"

I gotta stay calm here. I also gotta go. **GO**.

"Get up," I tell the Princess, who is now awake and listening. I pull her up out of the bed.

"We've got nowhere else to go!" Grace shouts, sobbing as I grab that sorry bag of stuff and drag that kid out of that room—and down the stairs and out of that place.

I stuff the Princess into the car. We've not got much gas left, but we are so going. We are SO going.

Trusted those people so much I didn't follow my usual rule of reversing into that drive, so I have to reverse out of it now.

Seconds, extra seconds.

I look back—for the gazillionth time—when I know we're not even going to make it to the highway. That in itself wouldn't bother me—am I not (I am so!) the queen of car grabbers? But I will not have time to grab us a car.

"I'm so sorry!" I tell the Princess, dodging stopped cars. "Those… people…are…very…bad…people."

Those people are after us.

A couple of cars' worth of them. Those I could outrun. I could certainly try. It will not be so easy to outrun the motorbike that Xar is on; he's right behind us, so close I can see him smiling. If I didn't have plenty of memories to make nightmares from already, this would be a stunning new addition. I do not want it—I refuse to have it—and I am a fearless driver. I am braver than Xar. I take a roundabout the short way (over) and watch Xar flounder and stop and have to double back. I'd laugh. I should be triumphant. But what I know is that we have no gas left. The needle is sinking into the red of doom.

It *is* empty. It's empty.

Gotta run. Jump out of that car. Some huge building towers above us; glass door all smashed in—in we go. More doors; the metal shutters covering them pulled back, ripped away—the doors themselves smashed in. Museum. Great big hall, steps straight ahead of us, and us straight up them and Xar's motorbike stopping outside, and take first exit off stairs, and it's a stupid dead-end tiny room, and back out and—

"Aw, Ladybird," says Xar, his voice echoing around the building. "What did you run away for?"

We stop, hear his footsteps. Then hear nothing but his listening.

"Come out, come out, wherever you are…" he says. And I hear him decide. He is coming up the stairs.

I take the Princess's hand, and we creep up another flight of steps.

It is a maze, this museum. It is an echoey marble and stone maze, with no way out and no place to hide. Stairs and more stairs and rooms and galleries that lead nowhere or back to more stairs. We creep-run past cases of dinosaur bones, then dead, stuffed things, glass eyes glinting in the dim light. I don't want to think about the dodo. Every exit door I try is locked; every window has bars outside it—and every possible hiding place is too small or too blocked up— too tiny a gap left even to shove a Princess into.

At the end of the geology section, I realize we are back where we started, back at the stairs. I squeeze the Princess's hand. I want to tell her that I am sorry. That I meant to help, but that instead I have brought her to this place. Not the museum, specifically, because I have a feeling that she's the kind of kid who'd find it quite interesting. But to *this place*, where even the SAS… You can imagine looking it up in the index of the SAS book: "Trapped…in Antarctic, in Arctic, in desert, in forest—ah!—in museum, by nutcase." You can imagine frantically flicking through to the correct page. You can imagine the advice: "Hide." Maybe you turn over the page and read one of their terrifying case studies on the subject. These seldom end well and are generally included to prove the SAS's point. If you don't do what they advise, you will probably die. (They should have written books on how to be a parent: "If your child fails to heed your advice about keeping shoelaces tied, try reading them this cautionary tale. 'When on a family picnic in the alligator-infested swamps of Florida, little Bobby Jones failed to tie his shoelaces and…'")

I'm going on about the wrong things again, aren't I?

"Awwww, Lay-dee-bird," says Xar, "where'd you fly to?"

It's what I do, isn't it, when…

He's behind us. Could we make it down the stairs to the door? We're not even going to get a chance—cars are pulling up outside. We go up instead. We have to.

…It's what I do when I can't bear…

It's useless. Useless, useless, useless paintings. On into the historic pottery section, crammed with ornaments and plates and glass and—under the huge cases, there are gaps that look just big enough to stuff a kid into. I pick one by the wall and shove her in.

…how horrible a thing is.

Other footsteps coming into the building.

The echoey sound of Xar's footsteps, coming up the stairs.

I back away, on through the pottery, as his voice booms out, "I think we should have ourselves a little bonfire, don't you?"

And I hear…splintering wood…

I know what he's doing; he is tugging and tearing a painting off the wall and I hear him fling it off the balcony, down into the hall.

"Ging Gang Goolie, children," he yells.

Oh, and this thing, it is very horrible.

The museum fills with the sound of the members of King Xar's Court building a fire. Know what that sounds like? Stuff being smashed and broken and dragged and thrown, echoing so loud it's like the building itself is being smashed to smithereens around you. But not loud enough to block out the sound of Xar.

"You have been a very stupid girl," he says.

He grunts loudly, tearing another painting from the wall.

"But I don't want you to feel bad about that."

He starts on another.

"Because people *are* stupid."

And another.

"Don't you think so, Ladybird?" he roars.

I guess the paintings get dumped over the edge, because there's a pause. In the mess of noise, it's him I'm tuned in to, him I'm listening for—oh ✳.

He smashes a glass case.

"IT'S PEOPLE THAT ARE THE PROBLEM," he roars.

He's in the gallery behind me, where the Princess is hiding.

"PEOPLE *DESERVE* TO DIE."

Smash, smash, smash, smash...all those pretty things my grandma would have loved. And in between the huge smashes and the sound of whole shelves of stuff being swiped to the floor, I hear more *precise* acts of destruction—a pause, while he perhaps admires a thing, followed by single smash.

"IT REALLY WOULD BE THE BEST THING FOR THE PLANET."

There's a frenzy of smashing now, coming straight toward me—and all I can do is run away from it, through a labyrinth of cases... that ends back at the stairs.

"DON'T YOU AGREE, LADYBIRD?"

Over the balcony, I see how it is: a pyre of smashed stuff—of cases and creatures and things; on top of it a gorilla, coffins painted with hieroglyphics and solemn dead Egyptian faces...and Grace, standing there, keeping watch. She sees me. I shake my head at her, pleading silence. I don't know what her answer is because I hear Xar smashing his way right behind me, and I leap down the stairs, steps at a time, and back up the other side, through the smashed and torn remains of paintings and into the kingdom of pottery—which is not how I left it. All the superglue in the world won't put this right.

"LADYBIRD!" Xar screams—he's at the stairs—and I can't move now. Not from the terror, but because I cannot walk into this smashed-up place and be silent. I am trapped.

"They got out!" Grace shouts. "They just ran out!"

She is a terrible, terrible liar. Her pathetic lie echoes weakly around the building. I hold my breath; I am a thing, waiting to be smashed. There is a pause—the rest of the mob quiets; I hear their footsteps returning to the hall, even as Xar starts on Grace.

"Are you sure about that?" Xar asks. He doesn't ask it in a nice way. "ARE. YOU. SURE?"

"Yes!" cries Grace.

Really—she's such a terrible liar she may as well be pointing at where I went…which, for all I know, she could be.

"YOU. DON'T. SOUND. SURE. GRACE."

"It's because I'm scared!" she shrieks.

Now that does sound convincing.

"I'm scared you're going to blame me! I didn't have to say anything, did I? Please, Xar! Please! I'll do anything!"

There's another terrifying pause. My heart is in my mouth—for myself, and for Grace. I can hear her sobbing. It's a dreadful sound in this smashed-up place.

"Go and look for them," Xar instructs in a bored, irritable voice.

There's a scuttling of Court feet.

"Not you, Grace," says Xar.

In the silence that follows, I hear only her sobbing—and a sloshing sound... Within moments, the stink of gas reaches my nose.

"YOU ARE THE SECRET AND THE KEEPER OF THE SECRET," he roars, so loud I jump. I hear this sinister shake, shake, shake... Matches. That'll be matches. "AND YOU SHOULD LEARN TO KEEP QUIET.

"Here you go, Grace," he says.

It is so quiet you could hear a pin drop—or a match strike. And another. And another and another.

"Ladybird! Your house is on fire!" Xar shrieks, laughing his head off.

The crack, the spit, the hiss of flame. The choking stink of foul smoke. Of fire burning ancient dead things and smashed-up wood. Of fire burning treasure.

"Ging Gang Goolie," says Xar.

He waits, you know, until that fire really gets going, until my chest starts to heave and hurt from the smoke, and I have to crouch down into the broken stuff.

"See you around, Ladybird," I hear him call.

I can't know for sure whether he's gone, but when my chest won't hold out any longer, I start coughing. And I can't stop. I don't know if it's possible for this stone and marble place to burn to the ground, but I do know we're going to choke to death if we stay—so we must go. I fish the kid out from under the smashed case, and we run to the stairs, down the stairs, and—I can see how we can get around this fire to the door. There is a gap between the edge of the pyre and the wall, but the doing of it is another matter. The heat! I can't even get near that gap—but we have to—this massive old wood-and-canvas plane falls, crashing from the ceiling. "We have to!" I shout at the Princess.

So we do.

It is only a few seconds, but I feel as though I am going to burst into flame.

Me and the kid stagger out, coughing, sucking in air and coughing again, eyes weeping, lungs weeping, mouths spitting.

I am expecting Xar to be there—or Grace, with a breakfast tray, being given a second chance. The street is deserted. I grab my sad little bag of stuff from our abandoned car.

We need another car—now—but I am too scared to walk down the long shop-lined hill ahead of us. Nowhere to hide but small shops that would burn so much more easily and quickly than a museum, so we walk in another direction—not back toward Xar's, but away from all this.

There is no point dwelling on what just happened. There is no point letting smoked-out lungs stop us. We do try to keep the coughing and the spitting quiet.

All. I. Want. Is. A. Car.

I try car door after car door after car door—and there are more and more cars to try; there's a hospital, and the road that leads to it is choked with them. I find one that will start, but it is so blocked in I can't even smash and bash my way out—and the noise it makes terrifies me. We have to give up and start again—and behind us, the smoke from the museum fire swells up black into a clear sky…and a small plane passing overhead banks, turning, dropping lower and lower, circling.

No time to gawk. "C'mon," I cough at the Princess.

I find us a car, on the other side of the hospital. Way I find it is: I put my hand on the hood as I stumble on a dead something I don't want to describe. The hood is warm; not sun-warmed like others had been, but proper *engine* warmed.

Got a fear about that; look around, see no one.

Maybe they're on their way to toast marshmallows on Xar's little bonfire. The keys are in it; they're either kind or they're planning to come back after the campfire sing-along.

If they did come back, they'd find their car gone.

I have nothing left but Plan C. Plan C for the C-grade girl. When we reach the place where we have to make a choice on the highway, I stop. I pause for a moment, freaking out about the fuel I am burning while I also freak out about…

All I want to do is go home. I head that way…and then I pause again. Freaking out.

Plan C is shaky.

I want to go home…but I also don't want to go home. Not just because I am being sensible—like, if the army really is looking for me, I suppose that's where they'd go. And not even just because…I cannot bear the thought of what they might have done to my mom, to Simon, to the babiest brother-brat beloved. Whether they—their bodies—would even still be there. I know that my dad won't have rocked up there while I have been away, that I should have stopped believing that could happen a very long time ago. I don't want to go home because there is too much hurt there already.

If I go back there now and there is more hurt, I fear I will lose "home" forever.

From my sad little plastic bag of stuff, I fish my sad little crumpled list of addresses out of the pocket of my jeans…but I already know there is only one place I want to go. It is first on my list, but was the last on Sask's neat, geographical version.

I reverse off the on-ramp. I turn around. I am scared to let another lovely place be destroyed, but if I can't go home, I can go to the next best place: my grandmother's.

This really is Plan C. This really is all I have left.

I already know my grandma is not going to be there (alive). My dad is not going to be there (alive). But I am alive, and I…I need the comfort of my grandma's. I just need a safe place to be still for a second. We'll go there. Then we'll work out what comes next.

I forgot. "We" won't be working anything out. I'm in charge, and I've got a kid to take care of.

Then *I'll* work out what next. Then *I'll* work it out.

We cough and spit museum smoke. We listen to music. We hide under a bridge when a helicopter goes overhead. I don't speak because I have nothing to say. The Princess doesn't speak because she doesn't speak. After what I have just managed to put her through, I seriously doubt whether she will ever speak again. I start to feel like we are driving into oblivion, that when we get to the end of this road, Lancaster probably won't even be there. That there will just be this enormous, planet-gobbling white fog, into which we will drive and disappear.

CHAPTER TWENTY-TWO

It upsets me a lot that I have trouble finding Grandma's. I know the house very well, but it is like I know it from a dream. That's how it is with places you go to when you're a kid, isn't it? You know them in a kid way, so some things—like the color and shape of the cookie tin or the bush with the squishy white berries ("snot berries," me and Dan called them)—you'd know instantly and never forget, but other things—like precisely where the house is—are a little hazy. It was never my responsibility to remember exactly how to get to Grandma's.

We drive up and down the wrong lane before I find the right lane and the house—and the back door is open, which I am very pleased about because I think it would not have felt nice to have smashed my way into my grandma's. I am even more pleased that there is no spicy-sweet stench of anything I don't want to see, only a colder version of how my grandma's house always smelled: of cookies, with a hint of mothballs and Chanel. I tour the house, sniffing it all in, saying a silent hi to the ornaments I love best and winding the grandfather clock—the first time in my life I have done this without supervision. The house feels so much better with its tick-tock back, but a tick-tock will not save us. The Princess, meantime, has gone through the cupboards and there's nothing for us here—not even an empty cookie tin, because the tin itself has gone.

"We need to get something to eat and drink," I tell her, winning today's prize for stating the SCREAMINGLY OBVIOUS.

I hate it so much that we are going to have to get back in that car, but I would rather have driven a thousand more miles than been confronted by the sight that awaits us outside: there is a guy standing there with a shotgun.

He raises it as he sees us.

I swear I can't take any more. I swear I can't. We stop in our tracks—of course we do—but my body? It hardly even tenses.

"All right?" says the man, glaring at us. "Who's with you?"

"Loads of people," I tell him.

"Yeah? Where are they?"

"They're just coming."

He lowers the gun. I am fooling no one. "What are you doing here?" he asks.

"This is my grandma's house," I tell him. "I've got a right to be here if I want."

"Oh yeah," he says. "She must have been a popular lady, your nan."

I don't know what game this is. All I know is that I don't want to play it.

"Lot of people been coming up here the past couple of weeks. We've had the army visit, for a start."

"So what," I tell him. I don't even have the energy.

"And another guy come up here. Kid with him, and a woman. Guy said he was her son."

I can't speak. I actually cannot speak.

"That your dad, then? Or your uncle?"

I think I do not even speak the word. I think my lips just make its shape: "Dad."

"You'd better come and speak to Bridget, then," he says, and turns to walk away. "We're just up the lane," he says.

I take one step and the Princess pulls me back, her other hand grabbing at the car. From somewhere in the fog of shock that I now am, a lone brain cell responds.

"We'll drive," I shout.

He stops and looks at me. "Please yourself," he says.

We drive. He walks ahead of us. I wish he would walk faster. I am shaking all over. The Princess puts out her hand and squeezes my arm. It is not a reassuring squeeze; it is an "Earth calling Ruby" squeeze, as hard and as mean as she can manage.

"OK, OK…but I have to. I can't not. We'll stay in the car. We'll just stay in the car till we see."

It's farther than just up the lane, but it is not far. On a bend in the lane ahead of us, there is a big house, set back from the road on its own little hill. The guy waves at the house and people come out. Men, women…I see kids try to sneak out and get shooed back in. They all look normal enough (e.g., no weird costumes), but I don't much like it; there are a lot of them and only two of us, and the way the road runs, the only way out of here is going to be driving right past the house—and I can't see what might be around the corner.

I can't tell you what this feels like; I want to know what they know. I need to speak to them. I have to speak to them. But I am so scared, even my mind feels like it is shaking. That's what it feels like: as though an earthquake crack is opening up inside my head, splitting the thinking of the me that wants my daddy and the me that was born on the night the rain fell.

"Hey!" shouts the guy as I force myself to turn the car around. The lane's too narrow to do that easily, so I have to make a nine-hundred-point turn in long grass at the gateway to a field. By the time I've done it, they could have all easily swarmed up to the car, but they don't. They just stand in the lane outside the house, watching.

"I have to do this," I tell the Princess, watching them all back in my rearview. I check our doors are locked, and I reverse—at speed. I want them to see how fast I can move. I burn rubber. I stop.

The woman I'm thinking must be Bridget is the only one who comes to the car. Though perhaps not old enough to be a proper granny—her hair's not even gray or anything—she looks as craggedy and weather bashed as the moors. I do not roll down my window.

"Hello," she says to me through the glass.

I glance at her. She is smiling—a little. Not some huge, welcoming grin, but a small, worried sort of smile. I don't want her to see my desperation. She is not going to hear it either, because I am finding it hard to speak. I check on the rest of them in my rearview; they've stayed where they are. I look back at her.

"Have you girls come far?"

Her voice, muffled, comes to me like a voice I am imagining. I can't speak.

"Do you want to come in and have a cup of tea? Are you hungry?" She glances back at her people, shrugs at them.

"Barry said he thought you might be looking for your dad?" She crouches down at my window.

"Are you looking for your dad?"

I can't even nod. I am so dehydrated, so tired, and so cried out already that I can't believe there could be a single tear left in me, but I feel the first trickle escape.

This, apparently, counts as an answer.

"We haven't seen them for about a week," she says.

I feel my breath starting to suck and drag like I am back in the fire.

"I'm telling you that just in case, OK? Just in case they've moved on. It isn't the most sensible place to set up home."

I feel my mouth open like words want to come out, but they won't.

"And if they're not there, you come back here. We don't bite."

JUST TELL ME, LADY, my mind yowls.

"Do you hear me? You come back here."

I nod. Ferociously. LADY…

"Do you know where Overton is?"

I shake my head.

"Do you know where Morecambe is?"

Of course I know. I know. I know. I know. Sort of. I've been there. I know.

"I'll come with you," she says.

That earthquake fault? It's widening.

"You can follow my car," she says.

I watch her in my rearview as she walks back to her people; she is shaking her head. Not some great big no of a shake, but some sad little thing. She goes into the house, comes out a few moments later—with stuff that she hands to another woman and keys that she jangles in the air. For my benefit. She knows I am watching. She knows. The other woman comes to the car.

"Bridget thought you might like these," she shouts at my window.

There're cookies—a whole packet, unopened—and water—a big bottle.

I wouldn't take them, but the Princess grabs my arm again and squeezes tight, so I lower my window—just enough.

"✹," says the woman.

I don't know what that's about. I don't know if it's about the gap I am prepared to open the window by, being barely large

209

enough to get the water bottle through. I don't know whether she's looking at us and being horrified. I don't know. I don't care. I drag the cookies and the water into the car. I check the seals, that they haven't been opened. I check them all over. I think they're OK—the Princess seems sure; she snatches them out of my hands, glugs water, stuffs cookies, offers them to me...but I could go for a million miles on empty now; I am just watching the road behind us.

That Bridget woman comes up behind us in a Land Rover.

I start up and I move off.

I don't pull over the first place I can—where I turned, where the lane is so narrow. I worry I'd be boxed in too easily. (The split—do you see?—the earthquake split.) I drive onto a bigger road and pull over where I know we could bolt and run no problem. Bridget goes ahead.

I follow her because I have no choice...but all along I am thinking if one single weird thing happens, I heard what she said, and I will split and go get a map and go work out where I am and where Overton is for myself.

No weird thing happens. We go what even I think is a funny route around Lancaster. We do not go through the middle of it. That doesn't make me panic too much; I remember what it was like, back in the normal days. Sitting in traffic in the center of the city with my dad swearing. We cut up away from the city, then down onto a road I heard that swearing on—the river, warehouses on our left—but it's all clear now; only the side running into town is choked with traffic that will never move. We turn left again.

We go on.

The Princess squeezes my arm.

"Get off me," I tell her.

Looking back, this was very bad of me. But all I am doing is looking forward. All I am doing is wishing, hard.

And I remember…

I believed so much in those fairies my mom told me about that I climbed up and climbed in and waded through that ancient well because I saw—half-buried in the mud—an apple. The red-and-green cheek of an apple, under the water…the water that, hundreds and hundreds of years ago, doomed, desperate people (lepers, mainly) had believed could cure them. At seven years old, I didn't know anything about that; the head of my seven-year-old self was such a muddle of fairies and wishes and longing, I thought I saw a magical fairy apple. A gift that they had given back. Do you see? It had worked! You give things to the fairies, and they give back and—the mud in the well was horrible. I remember that. It was horrible and so deep…but I plunged my hands down into the dark water and the mud, and I grabbed up the apple, and I bit into it—but the apple was mush and did not taste nice, and I heard my mom shriek, "Ruby! What HAVE you got?!"

I swallowed it anyway…because that's what fairies do, don't they? They like to make things difficult for humans. They like to trick people. But you cannot let them beat you. No. You have to show that you are brave and clever and then they will have to grant your wish.

I wished for my dad.

I choked.

And then I threw up so hard it came through my nose. I remember that. It came through my nose.

How hard am I wishing right now? I am wishing so hard I don't feel anything except that wishing. Not my thirst, not my hunger, not my fear. Certainly not the Princess's arm-squeeze. I feel nothing but the wish.

The car in front of me stops. I am wishing so hard, I forgot about who was driving it, about how we came to be here. This woman in the car in front of me gets out. She points. I get out. I follow her pointing finger.

There is a house. It's a big, modern place with a bunch of fancy cars parked outside. (I am my father's daughter.) I go to the house. I go into the house. I am shouting. I think I am shouting. There is no one there. I come out of the house. The woman is there. She grabs my arm. I don't hear what she says. I don't hear it. She's pointing again. On the shoreline I see them: three figures. Boy, woman, man. Man.

"*Daddy!*" I scream.

I hear my voice as if it is far away and long ago.

The man turns.

It's my dad. It's my daddy. It's my daddy.

"DAD! DAD!" I scream, pelting at him. Sound comes crashing back in. "DAD!"

When I get to him, I fling myself at him.

And then I punch him. Not around the face but—smack, smack, smack, smack—into his chest.

From the earthquake crack inside my head, a subterranean something, a monster so terrifying it makes the troll-me look like a teddy bear, lets go of the many dreadful things it was clutching tightly. All of them. All at once. They are too big and terrible to stay in my head, and they come out in the form of a raging, weeping, screaming, punching, slapping fit of:

"Why-didn't-you-

why-didn't-you-
why-didn't-you-
why-didn't-you
come back for me?!"

Not even as clear as that, because I can't get the words out properly, because I am bawling so much. Because I am raging, weeping, screaming, punching, slapping.

I sit on the table, shuddering with geological-sized sobs. Brother-brat beloved Dan sits on the kitchen counter. The woman that was with my dad (it is not Dan's mom) has left us to it. My dad is sitting in a chair, but back to front—so he's got something to lean on, I suppose. He has his arms resting on it, his chin resting on them. Still he manages to talk, quietly. He stops every time a sob goes juddering through me; then he carries on. The Princess sits on a chair the normal way around, stuffing herself with more cookies from the pile of food Dan's put in front of her.

After the first rain fell, my dad went looking for Dan and Kara. He found only Dan. Kara had died on the very first night; my brother had survived because he had been at his mate's, indoors, on the Xbox. Then they came to get me. They got to Dartbridge, wrote the message on the wall. They went to look for Grandma. Grandma wasn't there. They came back for me. They were *coming back for me* when they got stopped at an army checkpoint. They didn't run like I did; they went to a base. Not Salisbury, one in the Midlands. It seemed like the sensible thing to do. They asked if I was there. The army "checked" their Apocalypse Lite computer system. They got told I was dead.

A massive sob shakes through my body.

"Ruby…" my dad says.

He gets up off his chair, takes me down from the table like I'm a baby. Scrapes up another chair and plonks me on it. He sits back down, close to me. He strokes my hair. Dabs a dish towel at my tears.

"You wanna see my room?" I hear Dan ask the Princess, sliding off the kitchen counter.

Incredibly, she goes with him.

My dad waits a moment. Waits for me to calm down. I cannot take my eyes off him; if I look away, he might disappear.

"They told us you'd been reported dead. They told us everyone was dead."

"They lie. They tell terrible lies. They're terrible people."

"Hush," he says, and he leans and puts his arms around me. "You're safe now."

My daddy. I'm with my daddy. The dream I dreamed, the wish I wished. It's come true.

"You're safe now. You're with us. Ru! You smell like a bonfire!" He laughs.

His arms fall away from me; his hand reaches out—and takes the hand of the woman I had been in too much of an emotional meltdown to be introduced to. My dad draws the woman to him; his arm scoops round her waist.

"Ruby," my dad says. "This is Tilly."

He beams up at her. She's younger than him. By, like, about a million miles. She smiles an awkward smile at me. I decide two things: (1) that smile doesn't fool me; she looks like a total ✳; and (2) I have been here before.

My dad has a long history of inappropriate girlfriends—or "floozies" as I heard my mom tell my auntie Kate. Whatever-her-name-is is just the latest chapter in that history. My dad isn't looking at me anymore; he's gazing up all dewy-eyed at what's-her-name. I've seen that look before. My dad is in love.

Any doubts about whether this horrific turn of events could actually be true are totally erased over the food my dad serves up, calling it lunch when it's got to be nearly the end of the afternoon already. My dad is in Sunday supplement mode, when he'd attempt glossy, try-once, never-again recipes with nice pictures and fail, but it's worse than it ever was because now he's totally improvising, trying to turn canned items and dried stuff into gourmet dishes. The results are as horrible as ever. The dried sausage is OK, if a little chewy, if you scrape the beans and garlic-paste tomato sauce off it. My dad doesn't seem to have noticed I am no longer a vegetarian. Dan does.

"So how come you're eating meat?" he pipes up.

I roll my eyes at him. "Because," I say.

Because the world is in meltdown and I got hungry, and the stuff that used to seem to matter doesn't seem to matter anymore: that's what I want to say, but I feel like I can't…because my dad isn't just in weekend-chef mode; he's in lurve. Know what that means? It's the same every time there's a new girlfriend; me and Dan get introduced, then my dad chatters on so much no one actually gets to speak to anyone else. We don't usually mind because they don't usually last all that long (though if the rain doesn't get her, Tilly might be around for a bit, under the circumstances). In any case, today I'm so tired and frayed, I'm as silent as the Princess. Dan's pretty quiet too, and Tilly seems happy to just let my dad run on. So he does.

The upshot is that, basically, my dad is loving the apocalypse. He doesn't have to go to work anymore—he hated his job—and all the things he's gone on about doing if only he didn't have to do the job he hated, he can now do. This house *is* only temporary; he's on the hunt for a bigger (For why? I glance at Tilly: Is she pregnant?! Are there going to be more of us?!) and better place, where he can do all that solar-power stuff, where he can grow biofuel, and vegetables, hydroponically (I don't even know what that means).

He doesn't stop for a second, telling us how marvelous it's going to be.

I don't get it. Like…everything's for free now, isn't it? Like…who cares about how much gas or whatever you burn? There's so few people left, all that stuff he's going on about, what does it matter now? I don't say anything about that. I don't even say, "Yeah, but what about when the water runs out?" I just smile a little and try to pull myself together. Or at least not to lose it again.

As my dad clears away our plates, I tell him the food was lovely. I've said that so many times before—"That was lovely, Dad!"—it's our joke, from before Dan was old enough to get it. I don't even know how old I was the first time I said it—but he'd laughed, and we'd laughed about it so many times since. He's OK about stuff like that, my dad; he knows he's a terrible cook, but he never stops trying. He always thinks the next dish will turn out better. Today, he doesn't even seem to notice that I've said it.

I'm thinking how I'm really going to have to excuse myself from whatever Dad's got planned next—my head hurts and I want to lie down—but what Dad has planned next most certainly doesn't involve us anyway.

"I could do with a nap," he says, yawning and giving Tilly yet another hug.

Yeurch. *They're going to go and do sex, aren't they?* Thinking that, I sound about eight years old, even to myself. I look away from the horrible sight of my dad going all smooch gooey—and catch Dan's eye for a nanosecond. I deduce, instantly, that he doesn't like it any more than I do. My brother-brat and I, we need to talk.

They smooch off.

I have—literally—walked through fire to get to him. And he smooches off.

CHAPTER TWENTY-THREE

There's just us kids left in the kitchen. It is all somewhat weird.

"We'd better go out for a while," says Dan gloomily, as he pulls a sex-is-disgusting face.

I pull a face back. Yeurch. The thought of my dad doing it *is* revolting.

"I could show you my stuff," the Danster says, doing excited "secret stuff" eyes.

It's going to make him happy, I can see that. I do also think how Dan is just like my dad. You can tell he's desperate to show us things, and I already know I'm going to have to listen to him go on about them. But he's a kid, still, isn't he? And isn't that what every kid wants? Someone to take an interest in their stuff?

We traipse outside after him.

There is a massive, crumpled heap of plastic right outside the house. Dan has got his very own bouncy castle. I'm not quite sure where this fits in with my dad's vision of our lovely eco future…and it certainly doesn't fit in with Dan's now.

"*A bouncy castle?!*" I laugh at him.

"Dad got it," Dan mutters and shoots me a weary look.

My dad isn't always exactly the best at, um, knowing what is *age-appropriate* for us. Sometimes it's a total disaster (I got a pink bike with tassels on the handles for my twelfth birthday); sometimes it works out really well for us because it means you get stuff other kids can only dream of. Dan got to go deep-sea fishing (in a storm) when he was seven (there was a Kara storm when she found out); and me, I've had tons of stuff—a laptop that was nearly as big as me (I spilled cola into it about ten minutes after I got it) and the gift that has turned out to be most excellent of all: my dad let me have a go at driving the car when I was thirteen.

"They're mine too," Dan says, pointing at the paddock, showing off. "Thunder and Lightning."

You don't have to be some kind of genius—as I am—to work out that Thunder must be the little black pony and Lightning must be the little white one. They don't look stormy at all; they look fat and lazy—and mean. The Princess is entranced, heads straight for them.

"You don't touch them!" I yell after her.

Dan, on a showing-off mission, takes a step after her. I take a step after him and grab his arm. Brother-brat turns to face me. So... before I even ask one single question, I detect a thing—and then realize a thing. The thing I detect is...my brother-brat has become a teen. It's not just that he's grown—like loads!—or that I feel muscle in his puny arm. It's that...

"Dan!" I say, and I grab him in a hug. He's gone awkward. He's embarrassed. He doesn't one hundred percent want to be hugged. The thing I realize is...

"I missed your birthday!" I squawk, as I let him go.

It's such a stupid thing to say, really. What? Was the whole apocalypse thing going to pause so I could go find my brother and wish him a happy birthday and then get on with the whole survival thing?

"Happy birthday!" I squawk. "Happy thirteenth!"

Dan shells out a kind-of smile. A "thank you, but don't go on about it" smile. "It's good to see you, Ru," he says.

Whoa! Mr. Grown-up and Sophisticated! *It's good to see you?!*

"Yeah!" I say—and I do what I dreamed I would one day get to do again: I ruffle his hair.

Oh my ✳! He'd always pretend he didn't like that, but he did really—and now…

"Gerroff," he says. Not too nastily, but…he means it.

He's a teenager! So that must mean, does it, that I can talk to him like a teenager?

"So how long has all that been going on?!" I ask him, rolling my eyes in the direction of the house.

"I don't know," he says, kicking the grass. "I don't really care."

He's a teenager! My brother-brat's a teenager! I want to hug him all over again and tell him that I get it and—oh, I have this terrible thought:

"I'm sorry about your mom," I tell him. I see him crumple into himself. "I'm so sorry."

"Yeah," Dan says, and kicks the ground harder.

"You know my mom died too…"

It hurts so much, I can't look at him. I look at the Princess.

"YOU DO NOT TOUCH THOSE HORSES!" I screech at her.

Dan's "tour" doesn't get better. It gets worse, so much worse. My Xbox-loving brother has picked a fine time to discover outdoor pursuits. The ponies are bad enough; he's got a quad bike—no helmet!—and he's built himself his own assault course. He's doing us a demo on that, the Princess attempting to follow, when I see what he's about to dive in to…sloshing around inside the tire hanging from the tree, I see rainwater. A dark, deathly puddle of it, cradled, waiting. Sight of it—I've been getting madder and madder—I grab hold of my brother. Hard.

"NO! NO! NO!" I shriek. "That's enough, Dan! Are you crazy?! Look!"

I shove his head so he sees what lurks.

"I'm telling Dad!"

"✳ off!" says Dan.

He's never, ever said that to me before. We call each other all sorts of names, say all kinds of terrible things—but that? Never.

I see kid terror on his face—and teen defiance.

And what I feel is…stuff that lay deep in the earthquake fault, raging and clawing to get out. What I feel is *angry with my dad*.

"I so am," I inform him. I march off.

"Don't care!" Dan shouts.

My dad… It's hard to imagine him getting worked up about anything, but the brother-brat has kid fear that he might.

"If you tell him, I won't even show you my other stuff!" Dan shouts after me.

He's desperate now, I can tell. I hesitate—not because I want to see the Danster's "other stuff," but because I hear his desperation. I turn around.

"What other stuff?" I say. My hands… Are they on my hips? They're on my hips. "What stuff, Dan?"

My hands are clenched into fists by the time Dan has finished showing me and the Princess his "other stuff."

In a cottage down the road, my brother has his own petting zoo. There are creatures in cages, but most are free-range. Rabbits and guinea pigs hop and scuttle around what was someone's front room. A gerbil stands alert on the top of the sofa…

"Moses!" my brother shrieks, hopping through creatures to get to him.

The Princess, eyes saucer wide, joins in the futile recapture attempt.

A friendly rabbit hops up to me.

"Dan! Have you been touching these animals?!"

"Yes!" says Dan, fishing around under the sofa.

I hear the unspoken "Dur!"

"It's fine! They're all from pet shops and people's houses and stuff!"

They better be OK; my brother and the Princess are lying on pet poo and pee to try to reach Moses. Seems like my brother is about as keen on cleaning up after pets as I was.

"It stinks in here, Dan!"

"Yeah..." he says.

I hear guilt—and irritation.

I pick the rabbit up—too cute!—and take a tour of the room, petting the bunny. Dan's dragged the dining-room table in and set up a vast hamster city on top of it. (Guilt attack about Fluffysnuggles, the abandoned hamster.)

"I don't think you're meant to keep hamsters together, Dan."

"Mmm...no. They fight sometimes."

They're also doing other things; weensy batches of hamster babies huddle together. Thought crosses my mind:

"Does Dad know about this?"

Dan sits up and shakes his head solemnly at me, studying my face. Am I going to split or not?

"He ate a rabbit, Ru. It was someone's pet."

I stroke the bunny in my arms.

"Wow, Dad killed a thing?"

"Uh-huh," Dan says, watching me closely. "He looked like he was going to faint or be sick or something," the brother-brat informs me. "He broke its neck. Like..."

The Danster does a twisty thing, complete with sound effect.

"Euwww," I gasp, not just because the thought of that happening to a bunny—let alone *my dad* doing that to a bunny—is a truly

223

horrible image, but also because I sense this is what Dan wants. It would have upset him. It must have upset him, to see that—and I feel that he needs to know he was right to be upset.

"It was pretty gross," Dan says.

"I'll bet."

"But Dad said we shouldn't get sentimental about it."

"Suppose not…"

"He said it might be the last fresh meat we ate—you know, until he starts the hydro-whatsit farm and stuff."

"Ah-huh."

My brother-brat…he's looking at me so hard. He's looking at me to check…what I think about the hydro-whatsit farm…and about my dad.

I cannot have another earthquake brain split happen here and end up falling down the middle. I have to stay on a side. I'm gonna stay on my dad's side—although obviously I'm gonna have to talk to him about what that side should be like.

"Guess he's right," I tell Dan, shrugging.

He looks at me, stares at me. I realize we are having the conversation I wanted to have, but not in the way I imagined we'd have it.

"I think we'd be better off if we stuck with those other people," he says. "You know, Bridget and the others?"

"They're OK, are they?"

"Yeah…" says Dan. "I mean…they sort of seem…kind of *organized*."

I don't know what to say. And then I do know what to say.

"I'll talk to Dad," I tell him, nodding.

I have been here for five minutes. I haven't even seen the half of how bad things are, but I already get what my brother is saying.

Dan grins. He's relieved. He's so relieved.

He's such a beloved brat.

"The rabbit tasted pretty good though," he says, strictly for the purpose of shocking me. He dives back down to rummage for Moses.

"Anyway, you don't need to tell Dad about all this," he says from under the sofa, "because he's scared of snakes and stuff."

Snakes?! Excuse me?

There's a flurry of activity—the Princess grabs Dan; he looks up, and she points under the sideboard.

"Moses is so smart," Dan tells her. "We'll never get him now."

But—oh boy—they are going to try; they reposition, totally caught up in the game of gerbil hunting.

"Snakes... Dan...*snakes?!*"

"Um, yeah...they're in the conservatory," he says, grabbing a random guinea pig for the Princess. "She can be yours if you like," he says *magnanimously* (good word: means looking like you're really being kind and generous when it's really no sweat). He hands the guinea pig over. "What do you want to call her?"

"She's not big on names," I chip in, heading for the conservatory.

It's a fairly terrifying sight: there are tanks with creatures I wouldn't want to touch in a million years...and not even the SAS would go near.

"Dan, there's a ✺ scorpion in here!" I call in disbelief.

He doesn't even answer, too busy giggling in kid mode.

My brother-brat has amassed a "World's Deadliest" collection of creatures.

How—HOW?!—has he been able to do this?!

Yeah, I am SO going to have to talk to my dad.

Unable to bear the horror of the conservatory, I wander into the kitchen. Oh, my brother has truly excelled himself. But the first thing I see is my grandma's cookie tin—and I pick it up and I cuddle it.

It's such a sty in that kitchen, anyone would need a cuddle. It takes a few minutes to see the true scale of his stupidity and naughtiness—but you can smell it right away. Above (high, high above) the smell of human and animal food is a jumble of weird, chemically burned smells, more powerful than the stink coming from the front room.

The kitchen isn't just an animal-feed restaurant; it isn't just a Dan snack bar. It's a lab. The contents of one of those advanced chemistry sets—the kind of thing a kid like Darius Spratt probably had when he was five but is really meant for older teens—are scattered all over the table. And I mean scattered: there's powder and liquid stuff spilled out of tubes and containers. A mess in which half-eaten packets of cookies and chips lounge. This makes me and the Princess's science-lab excursion seem as carefully controlled as anything they would dare to do in school. This glass rod, intended for the stirring of lethal boiling mixtures of toxic chemicals, is shoved in a bowl of noodles. My brother has been cooking up instant noodle snacks on top of a Bunsen burner that is connected to a MASSIVE gas canister—in glass beakers that have had 🔶 knows what in them. It is beside the point that I may have just done a similar-ish thing myself. The beaker I used looked very clean indeed, whereas Dan's—

I pick up another beaker that still has 🔶 knows what still in it; stinky, scorched chemicals coat its sides. I sniff and choke.

"Ru?" Dan says. He's leaning against the door; the Princess stands behind him, petting her new guinea pig.

I shake my head at him, still choking. He shrugs…uncomfortably. He knows this is bad.

"I'm trying to find a cure," he says.

Oh boy, this is worse than bad. On the table, there's a bottle of clear liquid. On the bottle there's a label; a label Dan has drawn a skull-and-crossbones on. He has copied it very accurately from the labels on the various other lethal substances.

"What's in there?" I ask quietly, pointing at the bottle.

"Water," says Dan. He goes into emergency squeak-speak. "I use gloves! I'm really careful! Look!" he squeals, shoving his hands into a pair of proper hospital-type gloves…

"STOP!" I bellow, before my idiot brother can grab the water. "Don't you touch another thing in here. Don't you EVER touch ANY of this stuff again."

A distant bell clangs.

He looks like he's going to cry.

The Princess shuffles, bothered by the bell that keeps clanging.

"What is that?" I ask.

"Dinner," says Dan.

Unbelievable. My dad is letting my brother run wild.

I AM GOING TO HAVE TO HAVE A SERIOUS CHAT WITH MY DAD.

"Come on, then," I tell them, shooing them out of the room.

I stand, holding the front door open—and holding my temper.

"You'd better leave Pretty here," I hear Dan tell the Princess. "She'll be OK."

It'd be hilarious—if I wasn't so mad. That guinea pig is the ugliest one I ever saw.

I stalk back to the house, the kids trailing behind me…then Dan comes trotting to catch up with me. "Ru," he says, "you won't tell Dad, will you?"

Honestly, I feel so exhausted and sad just looking at his worried face.

"No," I tell him. "But you're not to touch any of that stuff again, OK?"

He's relieved, I can see. Brother-brat beloved nods.

VIRGINIA BERGIN

"We'll get rid of it. And we're gonna have to get rid of the scorpion and the snakes."

His mouth opens in protest.

"You can't keep stuff like that. You just can't."

His mouth clamps shut in a tight line. A further thought looms up in my mind.

"What do they eat anyway?"

The tight line of my brother's mouth wavers.

"What have you been feeding them, Dan?"

"Casualties," he mutters. "From the hamster wars. I wouldn't kill things, you know that."

Yeah, only yourself, I think. *Like I want to kill my dad right now.* "Get inside," I tell him.

He grabs the Princess's hand, and they run for the house.

"You're not the boss of me!" he shouts over his shoulder.

Brother-brat be-teenaged beloved.

Dinner is pretty much a rerun of lunch, only, my dad and Tilly-Dilly are now drinking wine, so they're even more oblivious to the plight of the children around them. Dan is keeping a watchful eye on me, just in case I change my mind and tell on him after all—or make out like I'm going to—which, in our old life, would have been tempting.

You'd think my dad would use this occasion to consider the responsibilities of his new family, but apparently my explanation for the existence of the Princess is enough for him ("She's just a kid I found. She's doesn't speak"), and even more shockingly, it appears he is in no hurry to listen, with tears in his eyes, to the heart-rending account of my survival—elements of which, like the fact that I am a **FREAK**, would have to be missed out. I mean, I guess I will tell him that ("YOU SHOULD LEARN TO KEEP QUIET"), but as

228

it's the sort of thing that's way off the imaginable scale of terrible things to tell, and as I'm ~~dog dead~~ very tired, I think it can wait until tomorrow. Or the day after. I've had enough trauma, and there is no telling how he will react. If I can even get him to listen.

Tonight, he is listening, enthralled, as Tilly tells us all about a zoo trip she once went on with a bunch of kids and how it all went horribly wrong when one of the kids freaked out on the "treetop" walk climbing thingy and refused to come down the zip-line.

I am listening to a woman I don't know, telling a story I don't care about, from a time that no longer exists. About a subject—fear of heights—that I do not find in the least bit funny.

Though I am keeping my mouth shut, I am raging internally. Not because it is a really boring story—it is, though my dad seems fascinated—but because I have this weird feeling that the real point of this story is not even how Tilly saved the day, and isn't she so marvelous, but what a pain kids are. And what idiots they are. And even though I have just seen for myself evidence of the truth of this, it makes me mad. And when my dad laughs, it makes me furious. Seems to me there might be a lot to be said for being silent like the Princess. Seems to me sometimes it might be better not to speak.

"Right, bed, then?" my dad says to Dan when dinner is done.

I expect Dan to kick up; he'd kick up even if it were one in the morning…but it's only half past eight and it's not even a school night, is it?

"Sure. Night," says Dan, and kisses him AND Tilly.

He really is a little creep, and I make sure he knows I think that with an "I'm wise to you" stare when he has the nerve to come and kiss me good night too. He grins like a monster at me. Brat.

"You can sleep in my room if you like," Dan tells the Princess. "I don't mind sleeping on the floor."

The Princess trundles off after him. You'd think someone

would go with them to make sure the whole bedtime thing happens in a sensible manner—but no. My dad is fiddling with the DVD player. He can rig up a generator, but he can't do basic "Press play" technology.

"You wanna stay up and watch a movie with us?" he asks.

This I would have snatched at. This would be such a gorgeous thing…in the past. Right now I would rather eat second helpings of what he just served up for dinner than sit and watch a film with…I can hear her, Tilly, clattering away behind me, clearing up dishes.

"No thanks, Dad. I'm really tired…"

BECAUSE I JUST CAME THROUGH MONTHS OF TERROR TO GET TO YOU, I think—and I try to think it hard enough so he comes to his senses and says something a little more meaningful and sympathetic than…

"OK, night then, Ru," which is what he actually says.

He does then manage to tear himself away from fiddling with the DVD player for long enough to give me a kiss. "It's good to have you home, my lovely girl," he says, then goes back to pressing the wrong buttons.

I could sort it out in a second.

I take pity on him; he is my father after all. I set the DVD up to play. He beams. "Night, Dad," I say. My heart feels melty and strange.

"Good night, Ruby," the Tilly woman dares to say. "We could have a chat tomorrow, if you like?"

I do not like.

I squeeze a lemon-juice smile at her for the sake of my dad.

I'm not in with Dan. I've got a room all to myself. I bang on his door as I pass, though, and shout for him to shut up and go to bed, because I can hear him messing about, laughing.

It goes quiet, and I hear a massive *thump!*

I know exactly what he'll be doing, building himself a Dan nest on the floor—which is just a good excuse to fling bedding around and jump on it.

Before the rain, I'd be in there doing it too…or when I got older, I'd pretend to disapprove and then—*thump!*—randomly fling myself down on it too.

It was really funny.

Part of the fun was you knew you were going to get told off; only I bet that doesn't happen much in this house. It is going to tonight. I wait until there's another massive *thump!* then fling the door open—for one tiny second, I hear what I couldn't hear outside: the Princess, making this sweet, soft, breathless giggling. She stops immediately; she's standing on the bed, about to take a dive into the pile of duvets. The brother-brat has a pillow at the ready, to dump on her when she lands.

I'm instantly distracted (and shocked) by the state the brother-brat's room is in. Like really, anyone would think he'd been holed up here for years, not weeks. It is a terrifying boy-mess of items and clothes—and from the smell of it, I wouldn't be surprised if he has pets lurking in here too. He's also been having a go at his own graffiti art; the walls are colorfully sprayed with his own name, over and over. Brother-brat's working on a tag for himself.

"It's good, isn't it, Ru?" he says. "I wanna do the sitting-room wall, but Dad says I've got to practice first."

"It's brilliant," I tell him. "Now, you two! Go to bed!" I shout at them.

It's not proper shouting; it's that pretend shouting parents do—you know, playful with a hint of I-might-flip-out-soon-for-real.

Dan does a comedy dive onto his nest—but the Princess isn't ready for this. She just sinks down onto the bed. She thinks I am totally serious. More stuff inside my heart feels strange. I can't handle this.

"Night," I say and shut the door.

THUMP! Dan flings the pillow at the door.

I lie on my bed for ages. Even when those kids finally shut up, giggling and bed-bombing, I cannot sleep.

I just want one night of not thinking. *I am safe*, I tell myself. I do feel safe. Safe for now.

This house my dad picked is not a good house. The piece of land it's on sticks right out into the estuary; there is WAY too much water around, but at least the house is modern, so it's all double-glazed and sealed up…but, boy, with that oil-fueled stove going, it is HOT. I feel like I can't breathe. I get up and—it's raining out. Not pouring down, but feeble stratus-type rain.

What do you care? Just open the window, freak.

I take hold of the handle…I twist it open…but I can't do it. I can't put my hand out into the rain. That was how my mom died, wasn't it? Just putting her hand out into the rain. Just trying to help someone.

I use some random shoe that must have belonged to the people who lived here before to poke the window open. Let the shoe drop out of the window. Deliciously cool air floods in. I breathe. I stare at the rain. It's falling so quietly.

Go on, freak, just do it, the rain whispers. *Put your hand out. Dare you.*

"No," I tell it, out loud.

I go back to bed.

I can't sleep.

It isn't even proper autumn yet, is it? The summer has been hanging on. There's only going to be more rainy nights like this—and days. I should be feeling glad, that I am here with my dad and Dan, but when I think about that, when I think about the winter coming, when I think that there could be days on end—weeks!—stuck inside... WHAT IF IT SNOWS? There will be no snowball fights; there will be no sledging; there will just be...more terrible meals with that woman.

If we can even get food. I've seen what my dad has stored, and I have to say that it's pretty poor. He has clearly not read the *SAS Survival Guide*. Even his DVD selection is not great. For all his talk about how he's going to do all this wonderful stuff... I think about what I heard my mom tell my auntie Kate, that my dad was basically just a dreamer. And I'd been so mad about it, so hurt for him because he'd said so many times it was just his stupid job that was holding him back.

I'm going to be stuck in this house for weeks on end with the brother-brat preferring the Princess's company to mine, and my dad preferring that woman's company to mine, watching the same DVDs over and over without even a guinea pig to keep me company because my dad will only try to kill and cook it.

This is quite bad. See what I mean about apocalypses, and how they can get worse?

And I could go back down there right now, and I could say, "Father dearest, I am both the secret and the keeper of the secret."

And my dad would say, "Huh?"

And I'd say, "THERE'S A CURE."

And I wouldn't be able to explain it properly, and a whole lot more terrible stuff would start up, and all I want is to be still and quiet and sleep and just not have to deal with another thing.

So I don't want to tell them about any of that.

I could just run away.

But I can't run away, can I? Where would I go? In any case, I feel the terrible weight of responsibility—and not just on my shoulders. It crushes my whole body into that bed. If I go, Dan will be at the mercy of these people—these people being my father and that woman. The Princess too. They'll be left to run wild without a single clue about how to behave properly and how you're supposed to grow up—only they won't live long enough to find out.

It is possible, I suppose, that my dad is just having a bad reaction to the whole apocalypse thing—that, just like I did, he's having a temporary phase of not coping. That seems the kindest way to think about it, and not that my dad is a bit of an idiot and a lot of a dreamer and in lurve. I mustn't think those things, especially the idiot part. After all, I am his daughter, and surely that would only make me a bit of an idiot too.

By dawn, I have decided how it must be. Until my dad snaps out of it and gets with the program (and gets an *SAS Survival Guide*), someone is going to have to take charge around here, and that someone is me.

The freak, whispers the rain.

"Oh, why don't you just shut up!" I shout at it.

My door opens. That woman, that Tilly, comes in. It is too late to pretend to be asleep because she has actually had the nerve to just step right into my room, where I am sitting bolt upright in bed and—and maybe I just shouted so loud that you can still hear it ringing in the air.

"Are you OK?" she asks.

I find it hard to speak.

"I heard you shout…" she says…and—OH NO—she shuts the door behind her and pads across the floor and comes and sits on my bed. OH NO.

"I'm OK," I manage to say.

I know for a fact I can't possibly look it. I rub my piggy-feeling eyes. "Your dad is—"

"Don't talk about my dad," I blurt.

"He's asleep," she carries on gently. "Do you want me to wake him?"

"No!" I say, horrified. *I just want her to go.* "I'm fine!" I tell her. Her face crinkles.

"I really am fine! I'm absolutely fine."

I curse my own chin for wobbling, my own breath for doing the sucky thing.

"I'll get him," she says, getting up.

"NO!" I grab her arm. "Please don't."

"You're upset…"

GET IT TOGETHER, RU—that's what I tell myself. I hear the rain laugh: *Yeah, freak.*

"Look, Dilly—"

"Tilly."

"There's really no need to get my dad up. It was just a bad dream and… I'm…just so happy to be here, that's all."

There is a pause. Oh yes there is. During which she looks at me and I don't look at her.

"That's not really true, is it?" she says, and before I can go on about how it is true, she carries on. "It's OK. I get it. You'd rather I weren't here, right?"

I look at her. Lady…of course I'd rather you weren't here. But— trust me—you are pretty much the least of my problems.

She sighs. She looks out at the rain (does it speak to her too?!). She looks back at me. "But here we all are," she says.

There is another almighty pause. I look at Tilly; I don't like her any more than I did before, but I do get that maybe stuff has happened to her like it happened to me.

"That's what I was crying about," I tell her.

"Yup. You and me both," she says…and that's when I notice Tilly—so why was she up so early?—has been crying too.

"Are you sure you don't want me to get your dad?" she asks.

I shake my head. She looks doubtful; she's going to get him, isn't she?

"I can deal with this," I tell her.

"Me too," she says—after a moment.

Any other adult I have ever known would give me a kiss or a hug right now. Tilly doesn't; she just flashes a twisty smile at me and leaves.

The door closes. I flump back down on the bed. I close my eyes. I just want to sleep. Oh, I just want to sleep.

Freak, the rain whispers at me.

I want to ask it to let me forget. I already know it is never going to let me forget.

CHAPTER TWENTY-FOUR

It's late when I wake up. I know that even before I see a clock. I know it because I know about days now in a way that I never used to. I feel time—not in a seconds-and-hours way, but in what I suppose is an animally way; how many hours of light are left, what kind of sky there is. Even before I look.

Today there is late September heat and sun streaming in through the window...same way it used to stream in through the window when you were at school, going, "Hey! Sorry I missed the summer and all—but ain't I just lovely now?"

The ✹ sun; it always comes too late.

And it is late—in the day. Couldn't put a number on it, but I know it's afternoon.

I get up. I go and pee in the chemical toilet in the bathroom. It stinks. I sniff my pits; so do I. Uh! What does it matter? I'll sort it out later.

I feel thoroughly depressed already...but also, weirdly, thoroughly determined. I will eat some breakfast; then I will wash; then I will start to sort this whole mess out. I can't even be bothered to clean my teeth, or—I glance in the mirror—even clean my smudgy, tired face.

I plod downstairs. I am in my (BIG, BAGGY, FLOWERY)

hospital-issue underwear and skanky PE teacher's T-shirt. I have not washed since I got here. I care not. Why would I? This is my family. We're in an apocalypse.

"Oh, and here she is," I hear my dad start as I slouch straight for the kettle.

Aw, shuddup, I want to tell him. *I'm gonna save you, all right?*

But not right now. All I want right now is a big fat cup of tea, and then I'll start.

"Nice underwear," Dan snickers.

"Shut it, weasel face," I tell him.

I check that there's water in the kettle; I shove it on the stove. I grab a cup, drop a tea bag into it. There's a carton of creamer there. I pick it up, shake it. It's empty. Uh. Gonna have to speak to people.

"So is there any more milk?" I ask, turning around.

They're all there, eating lunch. There's my Dad. There's Tilly. There's Dan, grinning his head off. There's the Princess. There's Darius Spratt...

D-A-R-I-U-S S-P-R-A-T-T

I can't breathe.

"Hi, Ruby," he says. That's a perfectly normal thing to say, but the voice he says it in is NOT normal; it shakes about all over the place.

Oh ✳. Oh my ✳. Oh my ✳.

I feel like I could faint on the spot.

And then I do breathe, mainly for the purpose of sucking air in so I can screech. I am in underwear. Like, basically, I am naked. I screech. I screech and—I run.

Tilly runs after me, comes busting into the bathroom.

"Is he your—?"

"NO!" I shout at her, pacing, scrubbing my face with a baby

wipe. That teacher's mascara? Not waterproof. (Why would it be? They don't cry! They only make kids like me cry!) Yet again, we have a classic zombie look.

I don't even know what I'm doing; the Spratt has seen me in a million worse states, I'm sure, but I'm on some kind of weird autopilot—I think that's what it is. That if I can just manage to look normal, I'll feel normal. Having some clothes on would be a start. I don't really care about what clothes, just as long as I am wearing some... But not that! I shake my head at some offering from Tilly's wardrobe. Or that! Another wardrobe offering.

I dive for my room and pull my teacher's tracksuit bottoms back on.

Tilly flings down a pair of underwear—WUUERH! "They *are* clean," she says.

She looks the other way as I put on used but clean underwear. Tilly holds out a T-shirt; it is white, plain white—not like mine, which is apocalypse gray. I put that on too.

I return to the kitchen...but I am not composed. Nor is Darius; he looks all red and flustered and nervous and emotional. I need to be alone with him, immediately. I need to speak to him. That earthquake fault-line in my head? It's shuddering again; it's closing, and the two great lumps of me—the past me and the rain me—are smashing up against each other. It feels fairly overwhelming.

Because I am having difficulty standing, I sit down at the table—where a cup of tea and a hideous lunch are waiting for me. My idiot brother is grinning his head off at me. Even the Princess looks ever-so-slightly amused. My idiot father appears to be... URGH! What is that look? Is that...*fatherly concern*?! HE HAS GOT SOME NERVE. Sheesh!

"So, well done, Darius, eh?" my dad says in a weird, stern kind of voice. "He's managed to track you down, Ruby."

"Yeah," I breathe. I am guessing Dar has had the sense not to mention that the last time he saw me, I was standing, crying in the pouring rain, or surely Father Dearest would have a few questions to ask about that.

"Would you prefer some cereal, Ruby?" Tilly asks after I've inhaled the stink of garlic coming off the lunch and shoved my plate away from me. I find I'm grateful she's there, because she's the only one who's actually behaving like people are supposed to behave.

"Um, yeah, sure, thanks," I manage to say, even though I'm pretty sure I couldn't eat a thing. I pick up my tea, attempt to slurp it. "Ah ✹!" I swear.

I look up. Why are they all looking at me? Why can't they just talk among themselves?

"So you were saying, Mr. Morris?" says Darius Spratt.

This is marvelous, because (1) it indicates that all that has gone on is my dad going on, and (2) it's going to take the heat off me—but REALLY! Could he PUL-EEEESE just sound a little less like some sort of creepy prospective boyfriend-type person?!

Tilly puts a bowl of cereal down in front of me, and I ladle a comforting spoonful into my mouth, dagger-eyeballing the sniggering brother-brat and even giving a quick mini-eyeball stab to the Princess, who's definitely SMIRKING.

I hear my dad telling his version of how come he ditched out of the army base. His version sounds like a reasonable, well-thought-out explanation—the kind of thing you'd get an A+ for in school. "Well, it just seemed to me to be somewhat oppressive," he says. "Undemocratic," he says. Then he uses words like "Orwellian" and "fascistic." At one point, he even comes out with "Kafkaesque."

I'm not really listening. Dan already told me Dad went AWOL from the army camp because he hooked up with Tilly in the hangar line waiting to be processed—I mean, really!—and when he realized he was going to have to get up even earlier than he did pre-apocalypse, and work harder and not go out for long lunches and not be able to "do things" (Dan-speak) with Tilly because there was a shortage of family accommodation, so they were all crammed into the same room, he did a runner.

I slurp in spoonfuls of breakfast cereal, waiting for the moment I can extract myself and Darius from this hideous situation.

"So you said you were at an army base," my dad says finally, after he's finished going on about totalitarianism.

"Um, yeah," the Spratt says. "I guess I'm quite good at math and stuff."

I could kiss him for being so vague. For sounding so dumb. I pounce.

"So, come on, Darius," I say brightly, in a voice that comes straight out of some wholesome family TV show and sounds weird and strange to me and must sound utterly bonkers to my family. "Let me show you around."

I scrape back my chair, pick up my unfinished breakfast, and scurry into the kitchen area. Dan scurries after me, no doubt outraged by the thought that it's only *his* stuff there is to show.

"Oh, Ruby, dearest, let me help you with that," he says, trying to grab the bowl off me. "Ruby's got a boyfriend, Ruby's got a boyfriend," he whispers at me as we do tug-of-war over the bowl in the kitchen area. I win: I let go right at the perfect second; milk sloshes over him.

"Shuddup," I growl at him.

"Ooooo!" he whispers. "I'm so scared!"

Tilly strides between us and mega-eyeballs him. Dan hands her the bowl.

Maybe I've got things wrong about this place; maybe there is some sort of control—and a sense of decorum. Coming from Tilly, a stranger.

"Come on, Darius!" I call in a slightly less-wholesome way.

"Yes, do come along!" trills Dan—and Tilly points a finger into his face to shut him up.

I shove my feet into boots that must be Tilly's, and me and the Spratt walk out into the sunshine.

It is unseasonably warm. At this point, there is not a worry in the sky. At this point, there is nothing but cirrocumulus floccus fluff. A meringue cloud sky, all sweet and puffy.

I am puffy (of face—not enough sleep), but I am not sweet.

"Did you say anything to them?!" I viper-hiss at the Spratt as we walk away. I glance back; oh my ✳. They are ALL watching from the huge, scenic double-glazed patio doors. *What ARE they like?!* I make out like I am showing the Spratt around. I point at Thunder and Lightning, the ponies.

They have their pony butts turned to us. They do not want to get involved.

"Of course I didn't!" says Dar.

I sigh with relief and point at the massive crumpled heap of the bouncy castle.

"Ruby," Darius says. "I thought you were dead."

I cannot look at him. "How did you even get here?!"

"I drove. Oh, Ruby, I thought you were dead…"

I cannot have one more word of this conversation here, with everyone watching. I feel very, very confused. I don't know what this all means. I must stay on mission. I do an emergency think.

"Wait here," I tell the Spratt.

I stride back to the house; I don't have to go inside because as soon as my snooping dad sees me coming, he's out of those doors…

"What is it?!" he says. "Are you OK?!" Whoa! Does he really

think…that the Spratt has somehow molested me when—hello?!—
we've just been standing right there, with everyone watching?

"Yeah, we're just going to go into town and stuff," I tell him.

My dad's face clouds quicker than the sky is about to.

"I need things, Dad."

"What kind of things?" he blurts.

"Steven…" Tilly says. I could—maybe—get to like her.

"Clothes and things."

"We've got clothes. Tilly's got clothes," my dad gibbers.

"Steven…"

"And things. Tilly's got *things*. Haven't you?"

Uh. Could he get any more embarrassing?! Is my dad really, seriously, meaning *tampons and sanitary napkins*? Oh…my…✳.

"She probably needs *condoms* for her *boyfriend*," Dan chips
in, super-helpfully.

My dad actually cuffs him around the head. Not hard—my dad's
not like that—but not playfully either. But Dan is grinning his head
off. The Princess gasps out a little wheezy laugh; Tilly bites her lip,
trying hard not to do the same. Only me and my dad are not finding any of this in the least bit funny. I'll never be able to say for sure,
but I suspect we're on about the same level, horror-wise, though for
different reasons. I have to take control of this situation now. This is
not a negotiation. I have made the classic mistake of telling a parent
what I intend to do.

"We are going into town," I say. Oh: my dad's face. I make a
concession, it being the apocalypse. I give him precise information.
"For an hour," I tell him.

Urk: see my father's face calculating what could happen in an
hour. Have never had to deal with this before.

"Dad, I've driven, like, all over the whole country. I *know* how to
take care of myself. I've been on my own for months and…"

243

I have to stop myself. Not just because he looks horrified, like he's only just realizing all this and his imagination is adding a ton of stuff that didn't happen to the TEN TONS of stuff that did, but because I feel I could quite easily have another total, screaming meltdown (probably ending in me yelling, "FATHER! I AM BOTH THE SECRET AND THE KEEPER OF THE SECRET!"). Plus, this line of persuasion is not working.

"Oh, Daddy, please…" I try.

Cumulus-congestus look on his face. A downpour of no is about to happen. I must evaporate it. Heat must be applied. I have a Ruby the Genius moment.

"He's the *school nerd*," I tell my dad. "I am so not even about to…"

Whoa! I have kind of just mentioned sex, without actually saying "sex." This is the wrong direction to go in.

"Dad, he's a *nerd*," I say—and roll my eyes. (HE'S JUST A NERD WHOM I ONCE KISSED PASSIONATELY IN A CLOSET AND WHOM I… My feelings are so confused, I couldn't speak the next part even if I tried.)

"Steven…they'll be fine," Tilly says.

Behind her back, behind everyone's backs, the brother-brat is doing a horrific smooch pantomime. Next opportunity I get (coming up real soon), I am going to be so horrible to him.

My dad looks at Darius, standing, shuffling awkwardly, on the lawn. The sight seems to reassure him.

"OK," my dad caves. "But *I think he likes you*," he whispers— doing this comedy eye-bulge/watch-out thing.

Dan snorts with laughter.

"He's a *nerd*," I say to my dad, and I comedy eye-bulge back. Right: discussion over—swift exit. "Thanks, Pop."

I've never called my dad "Pop." My dad smiles at me—and I remember how much I love him for being like this. It's a new one,

this situation, but he has always been prepared to be on my side…
even when he didn't really get where that was. At this moment, he
certainly doesn't, but I am his Ruby, his girl. And I always will be.

I get the brother-brat back straightaway. I give him the tiniest mean
look as we're leaving and watch him panic.

"Ruby…" says Darius, the second we get into the car.

I can't look at him. "Wait," I tell him. "Please. Let's just get away
from here first."

Dan and the Princess come running after the car, but by the time
he gets to his zoo in a cottage, me and Darius are already confiscat-
ing his most lethal pets—in silence. The brother-brat is also silent.
He can't say a thing about it.

"It's for the best," I tell Dan.

He does this pouty thing.

"They're too dangerous."

Super-pout.

"They'd die in the winter."

The pout twitches; he knows it's true. Yeah—pout all you like.
Game over.

"And anyway, if Dad found out, he'd probably make us eat them.
Snake stew, Dan."

So we load them up. Dan even helps, mainly so he can whisper
his little good-byes to them. He's given them all names.

"Now you go back to the house, and you stay in the house," I
tell him.

I've seen the sky; the sky looks like the beginnings of questionable. Some stratocumulus starting to hang out on the horizon.

"You're not the boss of me," Dan mutters.

He kisses the bunny he's clutching; the Princess has hold of "her"
guinea pig, the one hilariously named Pretty.

"Go back to the house, Dan."

He scowls at me. Because I can't kiss him anymore, I kiss the bunny in his arms.

"Please?" I whisper.

And my brother-brat, he amazes me.

"I am happy you're home, Ru," he whispers back.

"I love you so much," I whisper. My brother blinks; his nose twitches like the bunny's. I am so glad I told him that.

Me and the Spratt drive away. There is this horrendous few minutes more of silence as we bump out onto the main road. I feel like the whole world really is disappearing.

I can't drive. I stop the car. We kiss like we are falling off the edge of the world.

CHAPTER TWENTY-FIVE

We are leaning against each other, forehead against forehead, in a car that has not moved.

I do not want us to talk. I just want us to stay here, fallen off the edge of the world.

"I thought I'd never see you again," I tell him.

"I thought you were dead."

"Why did you come here? How did you find me?"

"I made you a promise."

I remember. A long time ago, when I had thought I was about to die, I asked Darius to do this. To find my dad and tell him I was dead.

"But how...how did you find me?"

Even before I've got the question out, I know the answer. I *see* the answer. I know it before Darius tells me that he tried my dad's house, in London, then he went straight back to Dartbridge, to the school. He looked at my records; he found my house. I see the kitchen door. I see, written on it in Saskia's neat handwriting, the list of every place I was going to look for my dad.

The Lancaster people said the army had already come calling...

...but that was before I ran away.

I am the secret, and the keeper of the secret.

"Ruby…" Darius whispers. I trace my finger across his lips, and he kisses it…but I keep it there, keeping him quiet.

"I'll tell you. I will tell you. Just wait."

I leave him in the car, saying I just want to quickly say thank you to the Lancaster people. There are only a few of them at home, guarding the kids like proper responsible adults should do. I stand in front of them and I tell them… Well, I just kind of ramble on. It goes something like this:

"So…the thing is…if anyone else shows up asking for me… please just tell them you don't know where I am. Or my dad. Yeah— um—please just don't tell anyone about us."

There're mumbles, mutters, concern. There're mumbles, mutters, concern in my own head too. This plan is a terrible plan, the main flaw being that it's not going to work. It's just like the Internet is back. It's just like posting a thing and hoping people won't have opinions about it, when you so know that if you post something, EVERYONE is going to have an opinion about it, whether or not they actually, like, saw what you originally said. Instead of just going Thumbs-Up, Like, Favorite, and moving on, they're going to say stuff about it. Some of them may even ask questions.

"Why?" would be the main question here. No one asks it. I think that Bridget lady might have done, so really it's probably just as well that she's not there.

I see how it is: although it is the apocalypse, I'm still just a teenager to them. I am, basically, a kid with pubic hair and more problems.

We are taking Dan's creatures to the Butterfly House. It is high on a hill outside town. We went there so many times with Grandma. I remember it as a warm, tropical paradise, filled with gorgeous butterflies.

It is like an autumn out of a nightmare fairy tale. It is bone dry and weepingly sad. We scrunch in over a carpet of dead leaves and butterfly bodies, their wings still so shockingly pretty it hurts to tread on them.

From dead plants draped with the webs of desperate spiders, butterfly cocoons still hang, so easy to spot—bright green, bright blue, bright yellow. The weird worst thing is that the door was not locked; it is the weird worst thing because it makes me have some random thought that if the butterflies could have somehow realized this, maybe they could have all piled down onto the door handle and gotten out. That maybe the weight of all of them would have been enough to set them free.

It is a stupid thought.

Darius looks so worried. I know I'm going to have to tell him now. I know I'm going to have to tell him.

I find that I cannot stand. I sit down on the leaves and the wings, and put my head in my hands and say it:

"I am a freak."

I hear Darius scrunch down beside me. He puts his arm around my shoulder. I can almost hear his brain trying to calculate an appropriate response. As usual, it's a disaster.

"I don't think you're *that* much of a freak," he says.

"Muh-hoo, muh-hoo, muh-hoo," I go. It is a feeble crying that is as dry and thin and ugly as this greenhouse freakish autumn. It is not a mighty troll crying. It is the crying of a freak.

"Oh, Ru, sorry... You know what I mean. You're not really a freak."

"You don't know," I muh-hoo, "you don't know."

"Or, I mean, you know, maybe I am too," the Spratt blunders on. "Probably in many ways a lot of people are."

I look up at him. "Darius. I AM a freak."

He smiles this sweet little worried smile. "I still love you," he says. The sweet little worried smile falls from his face, replaced by a look of devastating seriousness. "I love you," he says.

I stare at him. This is what you're supposed to wait your whole life to hear, isn't it? Someone who really does genuinely, truly, completely, and utterly love you telling you that they love you. Of course, any which way you'd ever dare to imagine such a moment, it wouldn't IN ANY WAY, SHAPE, OR FORM BE LIKE THIS, WOULD IT? YOU WOULDN'T BE HEARING IT SITTING IN A DEAD PARADISE FILLED WITH DESPERATE SPIDERS, WOULD YOU?

AND IT CERTAINLY, IT CERTAINLY, IT CERTAINLY WOULDN'T BE BEING SAID TO YOU BECAUSE THE PERSON SAYING IT HAS JUST COMPLETELY MIS -UNDERSTOOD SOMETHING YOU ARE SAYING.

WOULD IT?

I breathe. I wonder what it would be like to just whisper back, "I love you too," and then take it from there. (Never mentioning the whole FREAK thing again.) I wonder what it would be like to say that to Darius Spratt, period. And you know what? Part of me feels more scared of that than anything else.

"I am both the secret and the keeper of the secret," I tell him.

The little worried smile creeps back onto his face...

By the time I've finished explaining, there's no smile and nothing little left. We are way beyond worry. We are into BIG FROWN territory. The Spratt is deeply, deeply troubled.

"Ruby..." says Darius.

Then, just like Xar, he asks many questions I can't really answer, and one I can:

"So do you think the army is after you?"

"No."

"Hn."

We have not fallen off the edge of the world. It has gotten colder. It has gotten darker. Time is not going to wait for us, not now.

"We'd better go," I tell him.

"Ru—wait," he says.

He grabs my arm. I glare at him. He's going to say something I don't want to hear. I know it in my cold bones. Worse than that, I know it in my head. I know it exactly.

"We need to tell people about this," says Darius.

"No, we don't."

I shake loose and stomp out to the car, yank open the trunk, and grab up a tank of deadly things. The Spratt is hot on my heels; he is not going to let this go.

"I wish you'd just let me explain," he says, taking the tank off me.

"You don't *need* to explain," I tell him, grabbing another tank; the lid falls off—which would be pretty alarming, but whatever Dan has got in there is hiding under a bunch of bark and leaves. "I get it. But there are other people who know about this stuff, Darius—they're probably sorting it all out right now."

The thing in the tank stirs. Best not hang around; I stomp back into the greenhouse.

"Yeah—what if they're not, Ruby?"

"Well, they will be. It's all going to be OK. *Everything's going to be OK.*"

I dump the tank far from the door; Darius—following me—does the same.

"You don't know that," he says. "You saw it for yourself how they're trying to shut people up. What if there's been some kind of coup or something?"

"❋! You sound just like Ronnie!"

251

"The conspiracy kid?"

"Yeah, Ronnie. My friend Ronnie."

Who kept a whole school supplied with terrifying information that people only ever took seriously for kicks. Who knew the rain was coming. Who is now dead. But he died knowing he was, finally, right about something.

All I want to do is live.

"I wish I'd never told you." I kick the tank over.

"But you did," he says, kicking his tank over.

"Yeah, well, I wish I'd never."

And I stomp back to the car for more. It was horrific, what happened after I blurted it to Xar, but somehow this is even more awful. This is different; this is Darius. *Hn.* How did this ever happen? I care about what Darius Spratt thinks.

"But, Ru," he says, as I load up his outstretched arms with the last batch of deadly creatures.

"What if...?"

"What if what?!" I say, stomping off...but I am not so lost in where I am now, feelings-wise, that I do not totally register that the tank I am carrying has the scorpion in it.

"What if...?" the Spratt says, kicking over his tank—just lizards. They look harmless enough. They scuttle out, rustling across dry leaves.

I watch them go, disappearing into the gathering dark. I see the scorpion scuttle after them. I back off; a tarantula starts to climb a dead plant.

"What if what?" I snarl.

"I mean...this isn't just about you, is it, Ru?"

"*Don't you think I know that?!*" I screech. "Don't you think I know?! I'm scared, Darius. I'm scared and tired, and I've had enough."

We stand there for a second, still as still can be, staring at each other, our eyes glinting in the last of the dying light like we were stuffed things in the museum. Creatures rustle around us, crackling through the dead stuff. That place, that greenhouse, it is suddenly very scary.

"We can't let these things go, can we?" I say out loud.

It is what we are both thinking, I know. On this point, I know we are in agreement. It is as clear as the moment, months ago, when we realized we couldn't take Whitby the puddle drinker with us—only not nearly so heartbreaking. These creatures are NOT cuddly.

"Look, Ru," Darius says.

I remember that he's not supposed to call me that, but I am too weakened by the horror of everything to point that out right now. The Spratt bends to examine a cocoon. I peer at it. Inside it, I see life. I see a new butterfly, wriggling.

The Spratt yanks up part of a metal drainage grid; I don't get what he's doing until it's done. He flings, high, at the glass and a pane shatters.

The butterflies have a way out now. I mean… I'm not a total idiot, OK? I do realize if any of them do get out of here, they'll probably snuff it anyway, but I did see a weird thing once about butterfly migration (thank you, Simon) and if they figure out where they are, they can go thousands of miles to the nearest nice place. Maybe. A chance is a chance, isn't it?

That's a pretty brilliant thing for a nerd to do (especially the one I am arguing with) to give them a chance, and I turn round to tell him that and—

WOOOOOOOAAAAAAARRRGGGH!

TRRRRRRRRRRRRRR!

Just a few feet away from us—like, REALLY, don't ask me to get specific about DISTANCES right now!—a RATTLESNAKE lies coiled, head up, tail up—rattling—ready to strike. Either the snake has cottoned onto our plans, or I guess there weren't enough hamster casualties to go around and the snake wants a snack. I grab hold of the Spratt. We stand there, face-to-face, and for a minute fraction of a microsecond, he doesn't get it and probably thinks I'm going to kiss him again or something before his eyes swivel and he gets it and I feel him—

"Noh!" I breathe, squeezing his arms hard to hold him still. "Don't move," I tell him, as quiet as quiet can be—and it even comes out like "Don't 'oove" because I am too terrified even to let my mouth move enough to make the words.

TRRRRRRR!

Dar wants to run; I feel it. Oh, man! I just want to run too! But if you do that with a rattler, it'll just strike. The SAS were very clear about that.

"Noh." I can't even shake my head. All I can do is attempt a mind-control stare, trying to force that no deep into the Spratt's mind.

In his eyes, I see the question, "Are you sure?" Which is just as well because when he tries to say it, I can't really understand it, and also it comes out at the sort of low, buzzing pitch that I suspect would annoy any snake.

I death-ray stare to the max. "Shu-uh," I breathe at him.

It is not working. He's a runner; I can feel it. He bolts, snake will strike, and—NEW PICTURE: me and the Spratt lying dead among leaves and butterfly wings with deadly stuff crawling all over us.

"Is ore scare ov us an ooee are ov it."

TRRRRRRRRR!

The Spratt stares into my eyes; his bulge with fear—same as mine. The snake is clearly failing to understand the situation—but SO IS THE SPRATT. I feel him strain in my grasp.

TRRRRRRRRR!

"I read it in uh ook," I breathe into the Spratt's face.

That he registers: ook. *Ook* means "book" means something Ruby read, not something she is making up or guessing at. I see that, but I need to gain complete confidence. *Thu Ess-Ay-Ess Sur-wy-wal Guide.*

I do not want to repeat those eses; I suspect the snake does not like them. In my mind's eye, I can see the whole page, all the advice about when to suck the venom out and when not, when to apply a tourniquet and when not... It's just I can't quite see which snakes they were talking about. All I remember is...

"Don't oove." My eyes plead with the Spratt's eyes.

If we budge an inch, we are done for. So we wait. Face-to-face, trying to stop each other from shaking—all me and the Spratt can do is wait, staring at each other.

I blink, slowly, when I hear the helicopters.

They have come.

CHAPTER TWENTY-SIX

The Spratt blinks slowly back.

TRRR?! the snake chips in.

Like, really, I am about ready to shout at it, but the *SAS Survival Guide* warns very specifically against any sort of agitated behavior when confronted by a frightened snake.

All I can do is stand, staring into the Spratt's eyes, listening. Way I hear it, the direction it seems to be…

The noise stops.

I want not to think it, but I know it. They've landed somewhere near my grandma's house.

The snake calms, goes quiet; still, we don't dare move because the snake won't do what the SAS promised it would do and CLEAR OFF.

I'm not holding the Spratt still anymore; we're holding each other up.

I feel a single, frightened tear slide down my cheek, but the SAS and the Spratt's gaze keep the rest back.

Don't. You can be strong. Ruby, be strong.

Though of course I cannot know that for sure. The Spratt could really be thinking: DON'T START BLUBBERING, YOU *FREAK*, OR YOU'RE GONNA GET US BOTH KILLED! In that moment,

I realize it is mainly me who thinks like that. It is harsh, sometimes, the way that I think about things, but perhaps it has its uses.

We hear something—not helicopters but a small, rustling something. I swivel my eyeballs slowly and see the something: a lizard, scuttling across dead leaves, probably wondering where the boy with the dead hamster snacks has gone. The snake doesn't swivel its eyeballs; it swivels its head. It spots dinner. Those leaves? Those butterfly wings? It hardly even ruffles them as it slides off after the lizard.

The Spratt and I reconnect eyeballs. Arms are squeezed—slowly. The blink of a yes is made.

We pelt out of that place, slamming the door shut so hard I can't be sure the gunshot that follows wasn't some weird kind of an echo.

It isn't some weird kind of an echo; in this new world—without many people, without people noise—sound travels.

When I hear the next gunshot, I flinch. Me and the Spratt stop where we are, hands on the doors of my dad's car.

Those people, those lovely, kind people—they've been found, haven't they?

They are being made to blurt; I thought they'd just blurt anyway, but it has taken a gun and a bullet—two bullets!—to make them do it.

We hear the helicopters start up.

We get in the car, and we DRIVE.

As I drive into town like a reckless speed-freak boy-racer psycho, killer, ✳ lunatic (yeah, we had them, even in sleepy old Dartbridge), swerving with insane gear changes around stuff, and even above the roar of an engine that is being made to go like it was not made to go, and the screech of brakes burning that we only get the slightest whiff of because we are going TOO FAST, TOO FAST, TOO FAST, I see the helicopters—two of them (For lil' ol' me? Like, really, the army needs to get a life!), their searchlights on in the dusk that's so much more dark than it should be because—yeah, great!—IT IS GOING TO RAIN.

It is worse than that. It is coming on dark as night because it is going to POUR DOWN.

And I realize there is NO WAY we are going to make it to my dad's before them, not all the way around through Morecambe, unless…

I am thinking so fast right now. Get a boat, cut across estuary, get family to safety. Simple, simple, simple—AS IF!—screech, screech, screech.

Unless. There is no "unless." By the time we make it to the slipway at the dock, the helicopters are landing, two fields away from the house. In the beam of their searchlights, a glimpse of the ponies (freaking out)…then they are down. I can't see anyone in the house, but the lights are being turned off, fast.

I kill the engine. I keep the power on though. We need it to see what is going on. We need it because we need the windshield wipers. It is raining.

Oh yes, the rain—✸ you, rain!—has shown up.

It pelts down, every tiny drop of it going "Ha!" as it hits the windshield.

From this place, we could have taken any old boat (there are tons of them, and it can't be that difficult to drive one, can it?); we could have gotten across the estuary to my dad's in minutes, so much quicker than the road…because the house is right there, right there in front of us, just across the water. That is high tide but turning; the earth and the moon are playing tug-of-war with the sea so hard that white rip-tide waves of foam froth in the gloom. But I would do it; I would cross that to get home. Right now, I would get out of this car and…

It is raining.

I am the most cowardly **FREAK** in the universe. Though I have taken so many risks so many times, though I have lost count of the number of times I have stepped out of a car or a house without thinking, this is a very different matter. I find that I do not have the guts to get out of the car. My hand thinks about it, but all it is capable of doing is feeling its way around the door handle. My hand doesn't have the guts to do it either.

Me and the Spratt, we sit there, watching. All you can hear is our breathing and the rain… "Ha-ha-ha-ha." Every drop, I hear it. Machine-gun laughter.

"They can't get out," says the Spratt. It is the first time he has spoken since we left the Butterfly House. Either he has been thinking, or he has been terrified into silence by my driving, or both.

He is right. He's got to be right. No one gets out of the helicopters. Inside, they are probably bickering about whose fault it is that they got here so late.

Brilliant.

For a second.

Then they get out.

I see them like a comic strip; strobe-freeze-frame glimpses of them, in between wipes of the pelting rain on the windshield. The rain is coming down so hard, it is a roar now.

FRAME ONE: Helicopters in the rain.
FRAME TWO: Helicopter door opens.
FRAME THREE: Figures in biosuits get out.

FRAMES FOUR TO FIVE: Figures in biosuits circle
the house.
FRAME SIX: No one can be seen.
FRAME SEVEN: They are back where they started. They
are outside the huge, scenic patio doors.
FRAME EIGHT: Where'd they go?!
FRAME NINE: This would be that picture where there
is nothing but a great big explosion. A flash of white
with zigzag edges, **KA-BOOM!** written on top of it.
FRAME TEN: ✺.

Before the shattered glass from the huge, scenic patio-door windows
has even hit the floor, I am out of that car.

I do not even shout at the rain; I haven't got time. I need a
boat—a boat—a…

I hear this weird, muffled scream; I look round. The car, the
Spratt, they are not where I left them.

In the worst kind of slow motion you will ever, ever see, the car I
just stepped out of is not where it was; it's—I just catch a glimpse of
it rolling off the dock and tumbling into…

"*DARIUS!*" I scream.

I am on the edge of the dock. It looks like the abyss. The nasty
version. The dark, swirling waters are already closing around the
sinking car—

Hiya, Ruby! yells the rain. *Ha! Ha! Ha!*

I am not even thinking—I am in that water before any part of
me has any say in it at all. I leap straight off that quay. Before my
feet even hit the water, my whole body screams that I am an idiot.
I never read what the SAS had to say about water survival (Why

261

would I? I only read the snake stuff because it was interesting. But water? I wasn't planning on going anywhere near it ever again!); I am, however, fairly sure that they would *advise against* jumping into a surging tidal river at night.

Too late.

It is not quite so shockingly cold as you might expect. And that would be the only good thing to say about it. Before I've even popped up spluttering, I can feel the tide grab me. I have to start fighting it right away. I dive down into the dark, swirling water. I cannot see a thing, of course. I cannot feel a thing; my hands flail about in darkness. I surface, gasping, and I know two things: it is hopeless and…I am being sucked out to sea. I am not going to save my family, and the Spratt is dead. I am about to join him. In the dark, cold waters, we are lost.

Or not. As I try for the shore, I can just make it out: this figure that emerges from the water, clawing his way back up the dock like Spider-Man. (Obviously there must be a ladder up the wall.) I scream and shout his name. When he gets to the top, he screams and shouts my name. I can hear him so clearly, even with the roaring laughter of the rain, but I think he cannot hear me. I see him turning this way and that. I see also… Well, he's alive, isn't he?

My own chances of staying that way are fading. This estuary, the way it flows, it curves this way, then that—so fast it's like being on a fairground ride.

Wheeee! Isn't this fun, Ruby?! shrieks the rain.

It is not fun. And just like being on a fairground ride; it is too hard to fight against the way your body is being pushed. So I stop.

I am drifting free, being swept into the open mouth of the sea. On the shore, the helicopters are taking off. I see their lights sweep across the water. Not near me—they are far from me. The lights sweep across the water and hit the quay and hit the Spratt. This tiny little figure, waving.

Still looking pretty much alive, isn't he?

I see one of the helicopters swing around and hover.

I see a biosuit winch down and grab something up. Not a something: Darius.

They've got Darius...and Darius is alive.

Could it be that I am not the only FREAK on Earth?

The shock of that...it's almost enough to drown me.

The rain seethes. It pounds furiously on the water. I pull a sneaky move. I swim with the tide, but I am quietly cheating it; with every stroke, I claw just a little harder toward the opposite bank, and when the current swings around hard to finally spit me into the open mouth of the sea, I grab out at the water that has fallen off this ride. I grab out, kicking and clawing for the water that is more still, the water that is quietly rolling around laughing at what fun all this is.

They are looking for me now, I guess, the helicopter is crisscrossing the water—but this estuary is wide and dark. My hands find mud and, on my belly like a wriggling, flailing sea-thing, I haul myself up out of the water, away from the water, but too scared to try and stand because the mud is as sucky and as hungry as the sea. When my hands touch stones, I crawl and slip and stumble, then hit more stones—enough to run, hiding in reeds as the helicopter passes close...then gives up.

That wasn't what you'd call a thorough search, was it? If I'd tidied my room like they just searched for me, I'd be made to go back and do it again.

I watch the lights disappear into the night. There is only me and the dark and the rain left. But it is not done yet, this horrible thing that is happening. It is not done yet. I blunder my way through the night, taking the quickest route to the house, a route that is full of mud, of pits and pockets and gulleys and places where you start to sink so deep you have to fling yourself down on it to crawl in search of the next more solid part.

On the bank, wet through to the bone, a small child sits, shivering, hugging her knees.

She looks up at me. My heart, my brain, it jolts at the sight of her—how it can be that the rain does not hurt her either—but no more than this, not now.

I run on. I run to the house.

The truth isn't nearly so much like a comic strip when you see it. The scenic doors are indeed all smashed in. The house is dark, and no matter how much I scream, no one answers.

Outside, I scan the cars. I did not count them, did I? But there was a line of them, and now there is a gap in the line. One has gone.

My heart, my breath, my pain, my brain. I don't feel any of them anymore.

I go back to the Princess. I crouch down in front of her.

"Where's my dad?"

She won't look at me.

"Did they take my dad?"

She lifts up her head.

"Was he even here? Was my dad here? Have they taken him?"

She shakes her head.

"No?!"

Rain pours down her face. Still, somehow, I know that face is weeping.

Oh ✻ no. Please ✻ no.

"Did they take my brother?"

The rain, it hammers down on us. It *hammers* down.

"You need to ✻ speak to me," I yell at her. "You've got to ✻ speak!"

But she doesn't. I don't suppose she can. What she does do is get up, like a little, shaky old lady, and she shows me.

My Dan, the Danster, brother-brat beloved, lies in a little Dan-nest of reeds, where he had curled up to sleep for the very last time.

When I take hold of his body, I feel how it is already so cold. Dark smudges all over his sweet boy skin run in the rain. It is not mud.

I grieve so hard, not even the rain is fast enough to wash away my tears. I grieve louder than the storm itself.

The summer is over. For my brother, it will never come again.

I get a blanket from the house. When I wrap him in it, I feel how my hands are almost as cold as his. Almost. Though he has got so big, and I am so weak and so tired, I wrap him in it and carry him inside. I will not leave my brother to sleep in the rain.

I take him upstairs and I put him to bed.

"Just give me a minute, will you?" I say to the Princess.

She is standing in the doorway, head down, shaking with cold. Or fear. I don't know. Shaking.

Just for a second, something kicks in. I get Dan's clothes: track-suit bottoms, T-shirt, sweatshirt, socks. They will be too big for her. They are all we have. "You go to the bathroom," I tell her. "You dry yourself off, and you put these on. Then go downstairs and put the kettle on the stove. Can you do that?"

She nods her head. I shove the clothes into her arms. She looks up at me. Her mouth moves like she wants to say something. But she can't. She cannot.

"I just need a minute," I tell her. "With Dan."

She goes. I close the door and…oh, brother-brat beloved, I sang to you, didn't I?

Dan would have hated it. He used to do this howling-dog impression whenever I sang. But as I sing, I know even Dan would get it, that this is all I've got for him. It is not the right thing. I know Kara, his mom, used to sing to him when he was little, but I never knew what. I never heard that song. All I've got is what my mom sang to me. And I think…maybe it doesn't matter what song it is. Maybe the most important thing is that it is someone who loves you, wishing you sweet dreams.

CHAPTER TWENTY-SEVEN

I am robot Ruby. A machine, dead inside. I make tea; then I make noodles for me and the kid. I sit down. We don't eat. I try to sort out the thoughts. The thoughts have no order. I make more tea.

I remember another time when a cup of tea seemed like the best idea, a time when all my friends were about to die from drinking it. I delete that thought. I sip the tea.

I try to think calmly. I cannot think calmly. I am in the middle of a massive twisty, swirling mess. For once, it's not just in my head… but that's not a good thing. It is real and it is all around me. And for some reason, I am in the middle of it; not because I want to be, but because I *am*. I just am.

I am bone tired. I feel exhausted—like I am tiredness itself—but I *am* at the center of this storm.

I shut my eyes. And the robot shuts down.

When I wake up, it's light but still early. The Princess is just sitting there, staring at me, from inside a massive cocoon of blankets. I stumble to my feet.

The rain has stopped. I don't know when it stopped. I make us more tea. I give my dad half an hour by the kitchen clock. I feel like we can't stay here any longer; we have been safe for too many hours. Sooner or later, those ✳ could come back. I feel like…they are never going to stop. I have stopped caring about me, but I care about my dad, even though I don't know where he is (again). And I care about this kid. This kid, this *pesky* kid.

I bite the lid off a pen and chew it to a plasticky pulp, thinking what to say. And all the time, all the time, hoping my dad'll just come back—and then what, Ruby Morris? You'd still have to work out what to tell him.

I am no cure. I have saved no one and nothing. Darius? The Princess? I don't know how come they are OK. I do not know how come the rain doesn't hurt them. And I…do not feel OK. I feel I am a walking jinx, a human curse. That I bring terrible trouble to strangers and to people I love. To Dan, I brought death. I should not have come here. I should not have even left the army base. It would have been better for everyone if I had stayed locked up. I cannot bear to lose another person I love. I'm not telling my dad a thing.

I scrawl on the wall:

RUN AND HIDE. DON'T TELL ANYONE ANY-
THING. STAY SAFE.

It's that simple. It is what I wish I had told myself.

I do not write "Dad," and I realize I must not sign my name or even write a kiss. I must erase myself. But if I ever wanted to find him again? If it was ever possible to do that? I rack my brains…I rack my heart. There is nothing to be done about that. There will be no more messages.

"We have to go now," I tell the Princess.

She gets up; she is swamped in Dan's clothes. There is not much I can do about it except roll up sleeves and trouser legs. I Scotch tape a big fat knot into the waistband of Dan's tracksuit bottoms so they'll at least stay up—and all the while, touching those clothes, I smell the brother-brat. Too young still for proper Spratt-style stinky pits, but his own special cheesy feet smell and wafts of general Dan-smell, of farts and pets and using the apocalypse as an excuse not to wash. I think my heart is broken.

"I'll just say good-bye to him," I tell her.

She looks at me, so upset—and like she wants to say something again…but the words won't come.

I trudge upstairs. She follows me, right to his door.

"Do you want to say good-bye to Dan too?" I ask her.

She nods, the small, uncertain nod of a scared person.

"I can do it for you, if you don't want to come in."

She hesitates.

"It's OK, you know," I tell her. "You don't have to do this."

I open the door and go in. I leave the door open, and as I stand there breathing in the boy that lives no more and waiting for words that are big enough to speak this grief, she comes in after me.

For both our sakes, I keep it simple.

"Bye, Dan," I tell him.

The Princess reaches down into the jumble on his floor and picks up a random soft toy, the kind of thing Dan must have outgrown years ago—or not. It is old and battered and loved looking, a teddy I have never seen before. It is possible, I suppose, that it was his most precious one. That it had perhaps never been allowed to leave the house before…until the rain fell.

I force myself to speak.

"Do you want to keep it?"

She shakes her head. She steps forward and gives it to my brother.

If I don't leave this room, I feel like I will die of grief—or anger. I grab one of the Danster's spray cans. His favorite color. My least favorite.

Right across the living room wall in massive, dripping, orange letters I spray:

RIP DANIEL WOYSLAW-MORRIS

And this pleases me and the Princess as much as anything could possibly do at this moment when there is nothing pleasing whatsoever in the whole wide world.

I shove the Princess's feet in a pair of the Danster's shoes, and she scuffs slowly out to the cars after me. This is the only sensible thing about this place, that at least my dad acquired cars. I am his daughter. I am my father's daughter. But I have decided. That earthquake split in my head? I have chosen which side I must be on. I am not a little girl anymore. I am on the side where it rains, and **I am going after Darius**.

After we've stopped to let Dan's pets out. It's the Princess who reminds me—she just grabs my arm. I see the petting-zoo cottage. ✱. The cute pets are still in there, aren't they? (I mean, for crying out loud, can't there just be ONE moment in this story—*my* story—when a thing doesn't get messed up by another thing?)

"We cannot take them with us—you know that, don't you?" I tell her. "We just can't."

She nods solemnly.

"✱'s sake!" I swear—then apologize immediately. Not for the swearing, but for the sounding angry. "I'm not cross with you," I tell her. "I'm cross because it's like this. I'm cross about everything… I'm cross about Dan. Because I'm sad about Dan."

Man, I can hardly say those words.

"C'mon," I tell her, trying to get ahold of myself. "We'll let them out."

I get out of the car. I can hardly see the door through a blur of angry tears—but I will not let them pour, and this is not my heart crying, not really. It is some version of the troll me, spiny and raging.

We open all the cages. We pull apart the hamster city and set that down on the floor. We rip open every packet and sack of feed and dump it. And when we are done, we are left with two things: the Princess cuddles Pretty the ugly guinea pig, and I cuddle Grandma's cookie tin.

The Princess kisses Pretty and puts her down on the floor.

We leave the cottage door open. We get back in the car.

There's stuff in that cookie tin. I open it and smell Grandma. Slices of cake called "parkin." Just a few of them left, but—wow—the Danster must have had some willpower to hold off. Though I notice the slices look nibbled. Brother-brat. Beloved.

"Want some?" I ask her.

She just stares at me. She is as lost and frightened and upset as I am. More. She is just a kid.

"My grandma made it," I tell her, taking a slice. "She makes the best cakes."

I bite into it and—for the gazillionth time—I wish, I wish, I wish things could be how they were. "And then I woke up."

The Princess takes a slice too. She bites into it. There's a pause; then it disappears into her chops superfast.

"You want another?" I ask her, holding out the tin.

My heart is hurting. I want to feed the kid. I want to feed me… but in a moment, the last thing my grandma ever baked on Earth is going to disappear. No wonder Dan nibbled.

The Princess, munching, taps on her window, pointing: a bunny hops out of the cottage door. I crane over her to see. Ha! Then Moses bolts out!

VIRGINIA BERGIN

I've not seen cats or dogs lurking around here, but I want to go now. I just want to go while it all looks kind of hopeful, and while there is at least one slice of parkin left in Grandma's cookie tin. I snap the lid shut.

"It was my fault," she whispers.

Her voice is a little, raspy squeak. It is the first time I have heard it. Months, it has taken, for her to speak. The sound of it makes me furious. Not with her. With this. With *all* of this.

"No," I whisper back.

"I got scared and I ran outside," she says—so quietly I can hardly even hear it. It doesn't matter. I know it already. I can just see those kids alone in that house, scared stiff. Desperate.

"And Dan followed, huh?"

She nods. I punch the steering wheel. I have to apologize again. IMMEDIATELY. No—I have to do more than that.

"**Listen** to me," I tell her. "He would not have known the rain was still bad. He would not have *realized*. This was NOT your fault. It is NOT your fault. I will never, ever think that. No one would ever think that. *Dan* wouldn't think that. He's my brother and I know him and you have to trust me: he would **NEVER** think that."

Ugh. I can hardly breathe. My dad. My ✸ dad. WHY WASN'T HE THERE?!

Why wasn't he there?! Why wasn't *I* there?

It's like the snap of the cookie tin, the flash of the explosion, the single killer splip! of a drop of water…

I went out…and I didn't come back when I said I would.

I cannot bear to hear the answer to this question:

"Did my dad go looking for me?" I ask her.

She cannot bear to answer it.

"Did he?" I ask super-gently. For both our sakes.

The kid nods.

I don't know what happened. Whether my dad is alive or dead. (He's alive! He *must* be!). He went out looking for me…and what? The car broke down? He got trapped by the rain? He decided to snuggle up someplace with Tilly and lost track of time?

It…doesn't really matter what the answer is, does it?

He is not here…

And me?

I think I am pretty much entirely destroyed.

The most hideous thing outside my own head is that I am going to have to dump the Princess for sure this time. I cannot—I will not—take her with me. I gotta talk to the kid, haven't I? I've got to tell her that this is it; I'm dumping her. Like, really, she should be OK about it. She'll probably be happy about it. I mean, we haven't exactly been the best of friends, have we? And I don't suppose what happened last night has improved things.

It's just I can't think how to say it. I can't *bring myself* to say it. Kind of literally, since in my mind I'm already driving back down that highway, with this part over and done with. So I don't say it. Until, in the end, I'm going to run out of road to say it in.

Just around the corner from the Lancaster people, I stop the car. I clear my throat. I look out of the window. I clear my throat again. I turn and I look at her, and she's looking at me like she knows what's coming. Maximum Princess glare is in effect.

"Look, kid," I start. She doesn't like it already. "Princess," I start over. Her nose twitches like the first time I called her that, but her scowl tells me I may have mistaken what that nose twitch meant. With the Danster, it always meant he secretly liked something. With this kid, it is possible it means the opposite. Not got time for this, can't get into this. "I've got to leave you here."

✸! Could she make this any more difficult?! I can't look at her. I look out through the windshield.

"I feel pretty awful about a whole load of stuff right now, but I'm going to go and get Darius, you see."

Why does this sound like a bad fairy tale?

"And it's too dangerous for you to come too."

I cannot imagine specifics. I truly feel like this is the abyss. It's possible he's dead already. And if he's not, I cannot imagine what might happen—like, what? I'm going to rock up at the army place, tell them, "I've come to get my friend," and they're going to say, "Oh, OK, then. Would you like to come in for a cup of tea first?" and I'll say, "Oh, no thanks," and they'll say, "All right, then. We'll just get him," and shout "Darius! Your friend's here!" and that'll be that?

So I just stick to what I want to believe will be true.

"So I'm going to go and get him, and then we'll come straight back."

It sounds like the worst kind of bull✸ anyone ever told a kid. (It sounds like the worst kind of bull✸ I've ever told myself.)

"But I've got to leave you here while I do that…just in case it is dangerous. Which it probably won't be. But just in case it is."

There. Said it. I look at the kid.

Don't do that, kid. Don't go teary on me.

But she does, and I see her tears…and in them I see the rain, and the trouble it has brought me. So I say it: "And don't tell anyone… how you are. Don't let anyone see that you're different. Don't tell or show anyone the rain doesn't hurt you."

Still, her tears won't stop.

I can't handle it. I start up and drive to the house.

I'm not sure whether it's the whole mud-woman look—I'm still covered in it—that freaks the Lancaster people out, or whether it's just the sight of trouble. They are all outside, packing up to leave. Their welcome isn't exactly warm; it has been chilled by fear. But they are kind people, and I guess it takes a lot for kind people to stop being kind, so although people mutter and hang back, no one runs away. Only the children are discreetly bundled inside; their little faces pop up at the windows.

"Hello, Ruby," says Bridget.

No one is smiling. They do not want us here.

"About last night…" I start out. I hear the gunshots in my head. I see pain on faces. Oh no…please don't say…

"They killed Chrissie," spits an angry woman.

I don't even know which one Chrissie was.

"They murdered her," says the angry woman—one of the ones who bundled kids indoors. She is so angry with me right now, I can't even look at her. I bow my head.

"They didn't mean to," Bridget says quietly. "They just got scared."

"*Got scared?!*" snarls the angry woman. "*They're the army.*"

"We shot first," says Bridget. "We did shoot first."

Whoa. This ripple of tension spreads through the group and breaks, swirling around this rock of a man—the man who greeted me, glaring over a shotgun. Barry's glaring now too, but in the way anyone would do when, if they didn't glare, they'd cry.

"It was a warning shot," another guy says; he puts his hand on the glaring man's shoulder and squeezes it, which causes a tear to roll from the glaring man's eye.

Bridget nods, but other people don't. The tension, it's really choppy now.

"Who *are* you?" the angry woman starts on at me. "Who are you to bring this here to us?"

"All right, calm down, Catherine. You can see she had nothing to do with it."

That's what Bridget says, but when I look up, I can see Bridget's not convinced I had nothing to do with it. I look around. I have to speak.

I have to speak.

"I'm really sorry," I say. That sounds pathetic. It is pathetic, but it is true. "I am really, truly sorry. It's…I didn't think…"

"Oh, I can't listen to this!" says Angry Catherine. "Just go away, will you?"

"I'm going!" I snap—and catch myself. I know that this angry woman—these kind, angry, frightened people—must be feeling really terrible right now. Everyone around me is feeling really terrible. I am feeling really terrible. It is so unfair that I am feeling really terrible. But I must not yee-haa.

"This is all your fault, isn't it?" spits Angry Catherine.

I look down at my mud-caked shoes again. Nope, I cannot stop myself—I yee-haa.

"IT'S NOT MY FAULT!" I shout.

So there's this water barrel at the side of the house. A water barrel to catch the runoff from the roof, the kind of thing that would have been brilliant thinking in the days before the rain went poisonous but is now a cauldron of death; probably they worry about it every day, telling the kids NEVER to go near it. I march up to it. I plunge my hand into the water.

I could never have imagined what a group screech of horror would sound like until I heard one.

I've done it now. I cannot undo it. I take advantage of the washing opportunity and have a quick splosh all over my still-muddy face. Ever seen someone have an angry wash? I wash *furiously*.

"So that's why they came, right?" I tell my audience, wiping my face dry with a sleeve that is so caked in mud I can feel I'm just smearing mud all over my face again.

I stand before them; no one will touch me now—no one wants to come close.

"How…?" a woman asks. That's as far as she can get with the question.

"I don't know how come I'm like this," I tell them all—loudly but not quite shouting again, not yet. "But I am. That's why the army wants me. That's why they came here."

But they've got the Spratt, they've got the Spratt, they've got the Spratt.

"Oh my ✳," people are muttering. "Oh my ✳."

"You're immune?" Bridget says.

"I guess. They don't call it that. There's a thing on my skin, this thing called a phage and—"

"They could get a vaccine from you," some woman speaks up.

In a corner now, aren't I? How much more should I blab?

"Yes, yes," Miss Vaccine is explaining to someone. "An antibody. She must be carrying an antibody."

"So she could cure us?" someone asks her.

"Not cure: prevent. If she's immune…"

People glance at me. At the freak. This really is—in every way—a huge and unwanted step backward. Telling people **IS** a nightmare.

"…a vaccine could be made from her blood," Miss Vaccine declares.

Miss Vaccine is really starting to get on my nerves.

"It's not IN my blood; it's ON my skin," I scathe.

People mutter nastily at my rudeness.

"What is?" someone asks.

"A PHAGE," I yell.

"A what?"

"I DON'T REALLY KNOW," I yell, because I truly can't be bothered trying to explain it. "IT'S A ROCKETY THING. IT

LIVES IN MY NOSE—AND I DON'T KNOW HOW I GOT IT EITHER, SO DON'T START ON ME."

"Oh, wait a minute," says Miss Vaccine. "That rings a bell. Phage therapy! It's a Russian thing—"

"Oh, please," I super-scathe. "What do you know?"

She's one of the useless, isn't she? She has to be, or else why would she be here with these people instead of scarfing luxury nosh in comfort at an army base?

They really don't like my rudeness. Too bad.

"I mean, what? So you're some kind of *scientist*, are you?"

Yup, I'm scathing out. People gasp at my rudeness. They actually gasp.

"I am a keen amateur historian," she says.

Under normal circumstances, before the rain, someone saying something like that would force me to crack up laughing. Like, really, I wouldn't be able to help myself. Under the current circumstances, the fact that she is a "keen amateur historian" is somehow supposed to be some kind of explanation. I roll my eyes to demonstrate that it is no kind of explanation.

"If you knew your twentieth-century history you'd *know* what phage therapy was..." she starts up.

Oh, lady, I know my history.

Didn't Simon, my stepdad, test me on it when we were trapped in a car in a parking lot with hundreds of people dying? It's just that...

"It wasn't on our syllabus."

She smiles a lemony smile. "In any case, it's basic biology," she goes on. She's not even speaking to me; she's speaking to all of them. "Everyone knows about vaccines."

People nod. Honestly. What are they like?!

There is no point even trying to tell them they don't know

what they're talking about. This is all going hideously wrong, isn't it?

"You could help people," says Bridget, but in a vague sort of way, like she's thinking out loud. I wish she wouldn't. There are mutterings of agreement. The Princess edges closer to me; I do a microscopic head shake at her: stay back.

"I already did. There's a cure."

That's shut them up. Even the keen amateur historian.

"Yeah—that's right. They made a cure and—hey—guess what? They don't want anyone to have it. So if you want to *discuss* this further, you're just going to have to go to Salisbury and ask the army about it… but I wouldn't recommend it. They are not nice people. They kill kids."

The silence deepens.

"They've been experimenting on people. They were gonna experiment on her."

Hn. Telling Darius was easy in comparison to this, because he'd already worked out the whole Sunnyside thing, hadn't he? Telling Xar was easy because he's a psycho and so he enjoyed every minute of it. Telling the soldier and the driver was easy because Beardy was on hand to explain. Telling these people…is dreadful.

"I cannot help you. Do you understand? I can't help. So I'm going now, all right? I don't want to stay here anyway. But I want you to take care of *her*. She's just a kid on her own, and she has had nothing to do with any of this."

I gotta get out of here.

"I'm going to go and get Darius now," I tell the Princess.

I head straight for the car—going as fast as I can without it looking like I am running.

The Princess follows me.

"You can't come," I tell her, opening the car door. "You have to stay here."

279

I suppose this is how things were in olden times—before email, before phones, before there was even mail. You'd say good-bye to someone not knowing if and when and how you'd see them again. I reckon people must have kept it brief, or you'd be blubbering all the time.

She nods her head—but quickly, like she gets this already—and then…and then, she lurches forward and hugs me, tight, her face pressed into my tummy.

"You'll be OK," I tell her. I am looking all around—no one must see this, her touching me. I peel her arms off me. I crouch down to speed-whisper to her. "See? Don't tell *anyone*. No one must know about you; don't let *anyone* see the rain doesn't hurt you. Just act like the other kids. Promise?"

Her eyes have tears in them. Mine do too.

"*Promise me*, Princess?"

She nods.

It's bawl or drive. I get in the car. Slam the door shut. Start up. She knocks on the window. I do not have time for this. I can't do this. I hit the button and lower the window.

"Priti," she says. "My name is Priti. P-R-I-T-I."

"Priti," I say.

Oh, and she smiles.

Bawl or drive. I drive.

CHAPTER TWENTY-EIGHT

Here's how I would like the rest of this story to go:

I go and get Darius. (Like I said I would.) Somehow we manage to find the Princess—Priti—and the Lancaster people. And the Lancaster people are delighted to see me, welcomed me with open arms, etc. (Bit of a flaw here already, huh? They're leaving, and I've forgotten to ask where they are going.) And somehow my dad has also found them (and Tilly: she's allowed to be properly in the story now too).

And…we all muddle along—i.e., no one else dies and life is OK.

I would probably have to turn into some kind of slave-gopher for everyone, dashing out into the rain to get stuff, but I'd be prepared to put up with that just as long as they were really nice to me and didn't boss me around *too* much.

Oh, and I get to live in my own place, done up just how I please with absolutely everything I want. Not that far away from my dad and everyone, but just out of immediate nagging range.

And if, for some reason, I don't manage to get Darius (like I stand no chance)…well…maybe, in time, there'll be a new boy—and we can console each other because he, like me, will also have experienced utter appallingness and heartbreaking loss.

The End.

It might not be the happiest of stories, this story of my life, but at least it is not totally, gut-wrenchingly miserable and bleak. It is OK. And OK is the new spectacularly good.

The only trouble is…I cannot see him. I cannot see what this new boy will look like.

But, yeah. That's how it should go.

What happens in reality is:

As I drive off down the road, I feel like my heart is about to burst with hurt and fear and rage. It is too awful; every single bit of this is too awful. Like, really, I think my heart is going to—

BA-THAM!

FTHHHHH!

My tire bursts instead of my heart. I don't even know that's what's happened. All I know is I suddenly can't steer. The car *careens* into the hedge.

Careens, that is an excellent word. I read it in a book and now—right here, right now—I feel for myself what it means.

I have no control over this vehicle. It *careens*.

I brake. I stop. I glance in my rearview and see Angry Catherine being relieved of the shotgun. (Yeah… See the picture: People are tearing it out of her hands.) Still I don't get it. All I think is: crazy lady wants to kill me. I don't understand what has happened. I put the car into gear; I have to slam on the accelerator to make it move. It feels like the car is all crooked, limping, flopping about all over the place, and when I try to go on, it doesn't want to do it. I bump up and down, up and down before something bites the road, and I churn about—going nowhere—until suddenly the car decides to go somewhere and I sail—smash!—straight into the hedge on the other side of the lane.

My heart is pumping; I look into my rearview—all I see is the other hedge. I look around… All I see is a bunch of people marching up the road.

I switch off the engine.

I get out of the car.

"Stop!" Bridget yells.

Hello?! I am SO stopped.

She's the one who has the gun now. Priti tries to run to me—but a woman grabs her hand and pulls her back. Behind them is everyone else. Behind them, the glaring man, Barry, is cuddling Angry Catherine.

I put my hands up…I walk slowly to the back of the car. Angry Catherine, whom I might have to rename Psycho Sharpshooter Angry Catherine, has taken out my back left tire. As in, totally taken out: the dead rubber body of it lies in the road. I was driving on a wheel rim. Which explains the *careening*.

They puff up the road after me. Their breath snorts out white against the cold sky of this morning. They are like an angry, frightened herd of snorting things. And me? I guess I'm a rabbit. Suppose I could run. I have this feeling Bridget wouldn't shoot.

Is that enough to act on, ever? A feeling?

They stand before me. Snorting white puffs of human fear and anger. I feel like I have oh-so been here before.

I fold my arms. (As no rabbit has ever done.)

"Ruby, we just need to think this through," Bridget says.

"You call *this* thinking it through?" I rabbit-spit.

She is pointing a gun at me. I am being supremely teen ironic—as

in, "At gunpoint?! That's how you think you can sort this out?!"—
but no one seems to register that.

It doesn't really matter. All I do know is I have a gun pointed at
me…and, in fact, I am fairly deeply grateful it is in the hands of
someone who is saying, "We need to think this through," because if
it were up to Psycho Catherine, I swear I'd be dead already. Or that
historian, she'd be slashing open veins and drinking my blood.

"We just need to know more," Bridget says.

Uh. What is it with "adults" and needing to know everything?

"We need to know about the kids," says the woman who has
hold of Priti's hand.

"When the army came here the first time, they didn't just take
swabs. They took two of our kids," Bridget says. "They told us the
parents had been found."

Ah ✸.

I walk back down the lane. They part to let me go first. Even Glaring
Barry holds back Psycho Catherine to let me go past.

As I head toward the house, kids scuttle back indoors; kids' faces
reappear at windows.

"No," Bridget says. "The shed."

"You're kidding!"

Apparently not. They're afraid of me, aren't they? They're afraid
of the **FREAK**.

I go into the shed, and Miss Vaccine, the keen amateur historian,
shuts the door on me. (I see a glint in her eye that suggests she is
already thinking about where she can get ahold of a scalpel and a
syringe.) I hear a bolt slide.

"Cup of tea would be nice!" I shout.

When they bring the cup of tea and a blanket and some food, I get a glimpse of the outside world—which consists of a semicircle of adults sitting on chairs on the drive. Ha! They are sitting having a cup of tea and a chat with a shed.

Countries are probably being bargained for right now, millions of cars' worth of oil being shipped. Nuclear missiles are probably being pointed in different directions…but this is the British apocalypse, where we all have a nice cup of tea and talk to a shed.

It does occur to me to withhold information from them, but the way I see it, I've already messed things up by telling them stuff in the first place, and adult minds are mischievous and panicky things that can make two plus two equal a trillion, so I may as well give them the complete Emergency Public Service Broadcast. It will be factual overload, I'm sure, but better that than have their skittish minds messing with limited information. Plus, I want to get out of this shed. If they think I'm holding out on them, I could end up locked up with the spiders for days on end.

So I tell them EVERYTHING. I do a SUPER-BLAB.

Then I listen to their discussion. It is nothing like the radio programs my mom and stepdad listened to. It is, frankly, worse than that time our history teacher got us to listen to a debate in Parliament—and, possibly, even more nasty and shouty. And pointless.

They go on, a lot. When just one person gets to speak, they love it. The person speaking, that is. The rest of them mutter so loud, I can hear it from inside the shed, and when the person speaking has stopped, when it comes to the "discussion" part, you just so realize none of them were listening at all. They were just keeping quietish for a bit so it looked like they were listening, when all they were doing was cooking up what they wanted to say.

They don't listen to each other at all.

A variety of *cockamamy* plans are proposed—but in the end there are just two standout proposals:

1. They try to trade me in for their kids.
2. They keep me and make a vaccine out of me.

The "discussion"—a.k.a. blazing argument—becomes somewhat emotional and then fairly science-y as well as emotional (Miss Vaccine is having a field day) as Glaring Barry (husband of dead Chrissie) and Psycho Catherine (dead Chrissie's BF) are painfully forced to agree that the army are a bunch of ✱ who would probably just take me, say, "Thanks very much," and shut the gates again without letting the kids go.

Glaring Barry doesn't care; he thinks it's worth a try. He is not without support because everyone feels awful about the lost kids.

Someone points out that Glaring Barry could get killed trying—and then what? Glaring Barry says he doesn't care.

At this point, Miss Vaccine pipes up with the PLAN OF PLANS. She swears blind that it could be as easy as injecting some of my blood into someone else.

Uh. I have managed to keep quiet for ages, but honestly! "I told you! It's not in my blood!" I yell from the shed.

Like, really, I don't know why Miss Vaccine doesn't just go and offer to swap herself for the kids because the army would absolutely LOVE her. She's FULL of ideas. What she is coming out with now is that, as everyone really wants this whole thing to stop (quite a lot of people have wasted quite a lot of breath saying they wish this whole thing wasn't happening in the first place) (Dur!), and as the army are a bunch of scheming rats that no one can trust, they would be insane to lose this opportunity to find out whether a quick dose of my blood would fix everyone.

I have this terrifying vision of myself as a human pincushion, strapped down and getting stabbed by two dozen greedy needles while Miss "Keen Amateur Historian" Vaccine consults some weird medieval map of where a human's veins and arteries are supposed to be.

Glaring Barry starts on about the kids again, and Miss Vaccine tells him that as the army might not hand over the kids that were taken and/or they might be dead already (she is in charm overdrive; Darius Spratt couldn't do better) and given that he says he doesn't care if he dies, he should volunteer for testing.

A hush falls. Even Psycho Catherine has put a sock in it now.

"How would we do that?" asks Bridget.

"We'll just take some blood out of the girl…"

I HAVE A NAME—and, honestly, Miss Vaccine, how many more times do you have to be told IT'S NOT IN MY BLOOD!

"…and inject it into Barry."

YOU'RE A KEEN AMATEUR HISTORIAN.

No—oh no!—Bridget, sensible Bridget is *listening* to her.

"So, we take some blood out of…"

BRIDGET! THE WORD YOU'RE LOOKING FOR IS "NO."

"It won't hurt her at all," says Miss Vaccine.

RUBY. RUBY, RUBY, RUBY. MY NAME IS RUBY.

"Yes, but how would we test Barry?" asks Bridget.

"We'll do what the army's been doing. We'll dip his finger in water, and if he reacts, we'll chop it off."

BARRY! THE WORD YOU'RE LOOKING FOR IS "NO."

"And then I'm going for the kids," he says. "Whatever happens."

NOT IF YOU END UP DEAD, BARRY.

"Yes, of course," says Miss Vaccine.

AS IF. If he reacts and survives the whole amputation thing, Miss V is only going to want to have another go—and another, and another, until Baz is out of fingers and toes and she's eyeing bigger limbs. If he survives…

Mercifully, at this point someone notices the sky's looking

questionable (I could teach them all a thing or two about correct cloud classifications; I know twenty-four different kinds, did I mention that?) and they get a panic on and drag themselves and the chairs inside. Like really: they've been so busy discussing how they're going to save themselves and the world, they almost got themselves killed.

"Are you OK, Ruby?" Bridget manages to remember to ask.

"Yes. I. Am. Fine," I manage to say with superb control.

I guess they all make it indoors, because when I hear the rain start to fall on the tin roof of the shed, it is not accompanied by screams.

I carry on with what I was doing. Yes, that's right. While they have been cooking up the PLAN OF PLANS, I have not only hatched out but almost fully executed my own plan. The back of the shed is in a terrible state. The wood is very rotten. I have picked and picked and picked at it. When things got really shouty, I even snapped off big chunks. Now it is raining, and they are trapped inside. There is no need to be quiet about it. I kick a Ruby-sized hole in the back of it.

I should just flee, but I can't resist it; I go up to the sitting-room window…there they all are inside, going over the PLAN OF PLANS yet again, I shouldn't wonder. I actually have to knock on the window to draw attention to myself.

Psycho Catherine jumps up—to get the gun, I'll bet—but Bridget grabs her arm. Too right. Even if Psycho Catherine manages to clip me (rather than shoot me dead) it might only result in me— their only hope—bleeding to death in the rain on the front lawn.

"I AM GOING TO GET DARIUS AND THEN I WILL COME AND FIND YOU," I inform them, mainly for the Princess's benefit.

Priti. I must remember to start calling her Priti.

There is nothing they can say (although obviously they do anyway; I ignore every word of it) and there is nothing they can do. I turn away.

I turn back because the kid bangs on the window.

I look at her and she does a super-shrug, the kind of "dur!" shrug you shrug to idiots.

Ah. That's when I remember to ask:

"WHERE ARE YOU GOING?" I yell at them.

If this wasn't the apocalypse, this would be fairly embarrassing.

Bridget comes to the window.

We look at each other, this craggedy old-young woman and I.

"Spain," she says.

I hear the people behind her groan and kick up and complain. Not because they don't want a Spanish holiday, but because they don't want me turning up and spoiling it, I suppose—just in case the British Army is right behind me with their beach balls.

"We are going to—"

For the sake of those involved, I will not repeat the name of the place, and I had trouble repeating it at the time. Bridget spelled it out. As we know, I am *superbe* at French, but we didn't do Spanish at school. I struggled.

I seriously struggled.

She gave up on the spelling and she just said it…over and over, and I repeated it, over and over…until I had it.

We smiled at each other through the glass.

I keep saying it.

I get into one of their cars and leave.

I keep saying it.

Plan R has commenced.

PLAN R

It is a horrible drive. The rain has a right old laugh with me, coming down so hard I can hardly see the road, then easing off, then starting up all over again. When I have to get out of the car to look for another one (twice—this is not a good day), it's pretty consistently mean; it pours down on me, even throwing in some hail for fun, so by the time I get to the army base:

1. I am in a foul mood.
2. I am more concerned about getting a nice cup of tea than the consequences of what I am about to do.

Of course, (2) is not really true (though there is a microscopic amount of truth in it). The weather did hold me back, but I also dillydallied. Quite severely. It involved clothes shops (several) and a stop at a gym where I used up all the water and every can of drink inside their drinks machine and about a million towels *and* wrecked the exercise studio floor dyeing my hair an excellent shocking pink.

I looked, briefly, like a pale-faced human matchstick, so I plastered on a ton of makeup to even things out. No fake tan; I'm not messing with that again. I then sat and painted my nails, admiring myself in the mirror. Best I'd looked in months.

Seriously, I looked so good even the Danster would have said,
"S'pose you look all right."

Don't get me wrong; though I let my head toy with the idea,
there was never really any question about where I was going. So
that's why I did all that dillydallying, you see? On the off-chance
that when I rocked up to the army base they weren't just going to
let Dar go, and on the off-chance that I was probably going to end
up locked up in some hideous hospital room being poked at all over
again, and probably for the rest of my life, I just felt like I wanted to
grab a little bit of life while I still could.

I suppose there was another off-chance that I might end up dead.
(There: that will teach you not to run away.)

So, yeah, any way you looked at it… Well, as far as I'm concerned, the whole thing was completely justifiable. Necessary, even.
It was necessary. I'm fifteen years old, and I've had everything taken
away from me. This was what I took back.

This was all there was to take back.

So I rock up in a foul mood, the way anyone would be when they've
run out of stalling time and just have to get on with something they
pretty much know for sure is not going to be very nice and could be
very not nice indeed.

It's dark already, and it's ✹ raining. AGAIN. To cap it all, the
road to the gates is rammed full of cars and people (in the cars), and
it's possible that things have really heated up in my absence because
in among the normal cars and caravans and stuff that you'd expect,
there are a few more serious-looking vehicles: a couple of those bulletproof, tinted-window monster cars that celebrities and criminals
drive, a massive truck, and even a tank I guess someone must have
nicked from somewhere…that's stuck behind a VW van, surfboards
still on top of it.

And I look at it all and I don't think, *Oh yippee, maybe there's a revolution brewing and everything's going to be OK!*, I don't even think, *Wow, this could be a little scary*. I look at it and think, *For ✳'s sake!*—because you know what? I can't get the car through it. I am going to have to get out and walk.

I have spent what might be my last few precious hours of freedom EVER making myself look utterly spectacular and now I am going to get soaked. After hammering uselessly on the horn for a bit and realizing, for sure, that no one has the slightest intention of moving out of my way (in fairness, there is nowhere for them to go), I clamber about inside the car, stuffing my loot (I have provisioned myself for an indefinite future behind bars) into whatever bags I have, but one plastic bag must be sacrificed for the purposes of fashioning a crude rain-hat. (This word *fashioning*, it clearly has nothing to do with the word *fashion*.) And then I get out.

The reaction is immediate. There is hooting and tooting and shouting and screaming and—oh my word! Was that a camera flash?! I turn, dazzled by headlights, that flick off and on again.

Hn.

I can't resist. I do a superb, carefree, *Sound of Music* twirl in the rain—only I've got shopping bags where that nun-woman carried a guitar.

WHAT AM I LIKE?

I KNOW WHAT I FEEL LIKE, I FEEL…NOT LIKE ANY KIND OF THING I HAVE FELT BEFORE. I am not a cavewoman; I am not a troll; I am not a panda. I am not a shadowbeing; I am not a witch-fairy; I am not a plasticky-rubbery ghost. I am not a robot… Mom, I am still breathing. I am Ruby Morris.

I am floating free in space. I am free.

The mob goes berserko! Headlights, horns—people pound on

car windows; a whole busload of mean-looking guys start jumping about—but in a nice way, boinging up and down on seats. And everywhere, everywhere, amazed faces are pressed to windows.

I see a car door ahead of me crack open—whoa! NO! WAIT! I race to slam it shut.

"Noooo!" I bellow at the lady inside.

OH MY ✸! WHAT IF THEY ALL DECIDE TO DO THAT?! LIKE, REALLY, I HAVE GOT ENOUGH ON MY CONSCIENCE WITHOUT SOME MASS DEATH INCIDENT.

All around me is tooting, hooting, howling, flashing insanity—I gotta put a stop to this, right now. I dump my loot and clamber up onto a hood and scream:

"*NOOOOOOOOOOOOOOOOOOO!*"

at them all.

"*STOP IT! SHUT UP! NOOOOOOOOOOOOOOO!*"

—flapping my arms and tearing off my rain hat. And flapping and flapping and flapping my arms again until it quiets down—at which point, before I can open my mouth to shout at them all to *STAY IN YOUR CARS!* the pesky British Army chips in.

"DO NOT MOVE," a loudspeaker voice instructs.

Of course I do move, because I don't know they mean me, do I? I turn to look where the voice is coming from and nearly slip off the hood.

"PUT YOUR HANDS IN THE AIR."

Oh now, see…I think they must mean me. Up at the gates, in the floodlights, I can see soldiers crammed in the gatehouse, jammed in vehicles, standing at the gates in biosuits…with guns. I have made myself a perfect target, haven't I? That's what I think even before the spotlight hits me. I put my hands in the air, squinting into the brilliance of the light with the rain coming down like fireworks fall, a torrent of sparkling flecks of light.

I do recognize that I am now in extreme danger, but I am also pretty ✱ off.

"*I WAS JUST GOING TO TELL THEM TO STAY IN THEIR CARS!*" I shout grumpily at the light.

Apparently the British Army is not interested in what I was doing.

"KEEP YOUR HANDS IN THE AIR AND APPROACH THE GATE," I am told.

They're having a laugh, aren't they? How am I supposed to get off this hood without using my hands? What do they think this is, a PE lesson? I lower my hands to get off the hood and—

"*KEEP YOUR HANDS IN THE AIR OR WE WILL SHOOT!*" screeches the loudspeaker voice.

These. People. Are. Really. Annoying. Me.

Nevertheless, I recognize the key signs of someone wigging out (screechy voice, unreasonable demands), so I do it, what they say. I put my hands back up in the air and turn to position myself and… out of the corner of my eye, I see it: in the jam on the road coming from the other direction, there is a bright pink stretch-limo.

I can't see who's inside.

I do this really ungainly plunk of a jump down off the hood.

"APPROACH THE GATE."

Oh…oh no…my stuff. They're going to make me leave my stuff. I glance down at it; all my goodies, the rain poking its nose in *my stuff*.

"*I'VE GOT THINGS*," I shout at them.

"APPROACH THE GATE."

"*I'VE…GOT…STUFF.*" I do a little pointy thing with my finger— but it's useless, isn't it? They can't see what's down on the ground…I suppose, looking at it from their point of view, I could have a rocket launcher or something—but honestly, do I look like the type?

"APPROACH THE GATE!"

Ladies and gentlemen, we have a wig-out situation.

You ✳, I think, as I walk away, hands in the air, from my rained-on stuff. And this thought explodes in my head like the rocket launcher I seriously do wish I had right now, I'm so annoyed. Darius was right: I have no weapon against these people, except the only weapon I guess I've always had. My mouth.

"There's a cure," I say out loud.

But not loud enough. My mouth is afraid. So my heart jumps in and shows it picture after picture after picture after picture of things that do not give it courage—I feel no courage—but of the things that make me angry enough to dare to shout.

My mom, my baby brother, my stepdad, Simon—the people I have seen die, the bodies that are turning to skeletons—and Dan. Dan, lying dead in a nest of reeds.

"THERE'S A CURE! THEY'VE GOT A CURE! THERE'S A CURE! THERE'S A CURE!" I shout, at the top of my voice, all the way to that ✳ gate.

And when they open the gate, I still don't stop.

"THERE'S A CURE! THERE'S A CURE! THERE'S A CURE!" I shout as I am bundled in.

"THERE'S A CURE! THERE'S A CURE! THERE'S A CURE!"

I get stuffed into the back of an ambulance by biosuits and driven away at high speed from the honking, tooting chaos that has broken out behind me.

I can't see where we're going, but we drive way farther than the hospital. We stop somewhere; then we carry on, bumping along. I am guessing we must be on the track where I had that set-to with Beardy, the soldier, and the driver. We bump until we hit smooth tarmac. And then we turn right.

You know what? All the way I keep it up: "There's a cure, they've got a cure, there's a cure," I tell the biosuits over and over, until finally we stop and the doors of the ambulance open up. A canopy outside, the rain streaming down around it.

I step it up: "There's a cure, they've got a cure, there's a cure," I say over and over and over as I am led inside, through security doors, through more security doors, and into a…I don't know what you'd call this place…

A pet shop for scientists?

The lights are low, but in the gloom, you can still clearly see that there are rows and rows and stacks of cages of all sizes filled with all kinds of creatures. I detect the gentle stink of guinea pig amid the waft of other beasties (amid the waft of disinfectant).

And I seem to be about to join them.

There is a short corridor of cells. We can call this area the human pet shop for scientists.

The first cell door is open, a reading light inside it is on, and it is filled with a mess I can only describe as "scientist's bedroom"; every inch of floor and bed space is covered in books and papers.

"Hello there!" Prof Beardy calls cheerily.

All the other cell doors are shut—locked, I presume. I am shoved in my very own cell and told to shut up or else.

The last of the biosuits that brought me in turns out to be a woman; she hangs back to inform me that they'll bring me some food and some *proper* clothes shortly—which I could feel fairly insulted about as I spent a long time creating this particular outfit. (Not to mention the fact that there are several bags of other lovely clothes getting rained on out in the revolutionary traffic jam.)

She hesitates. "I don't know whether you're brave or stupid," she says quietly, "but you might want to think about keeping your mouth shut."

And before I can open my mouth to tell her what I think about that, the door is closed and locked.

I burst into tears.

So, that's Plan R for you. It went *terribly* well, don't you think?

CHAPTER TWENTY-NINE

I called the Spratt's room in the Apocalypse Lite army camp a cell, but it was just a really small room. This really *is* a cell, "hospital issue," with a bed, a table, a lamp, and a window—that's got bars on it.

I tell you, I'm gonna go nuts in a day here, never mind the rest of my life.

The fact that it is possible I have already gone nuts is beside the point.

I lie down on the bed. I am wet, still, but I am not cold. This place is airless and boiling. They switched the overhead light off when they left, but I've got one of those super-duper hospital-issue point-it-where-you-like reading lamps—which is fairly seriously marvelous because I could not handle being in this place in the dark.

I pull the lamp right down in front of my face and pretend I am somewhere else. On a beach, is what I try to think—but not a Devon beach. A beach someplace far, far away where there is no rain.

It is not even a Spanish beach. It is not anywhere in particular. It is just a beach. No one I know is there. I am alone. I am not even Ruby anymore. I am just a girl on a beach. There isn't even a palm tree for company. There is only the girl, the sand, and the sea.

Every time my brain starts up, I just shh it right back down. I shh and shh and shh—and sometimes it's my mother's voice I hear, and sometimes it's the sea.

And for a while it works, and then it doesn't.

Shh, shh, shh, I tell myself…but the beach won't come; the sea won't come.

All there is, is the girl. The girl lying on crisp white sheets, on a bed, on a floor, on some ground, on an island, on a planet.

The planet lies among stars and is turning.

!

I bat my lamp away from my face, leaping off the bed in fright as—KZZZZ!—the overhead lights snap on and some biosuit bursts in and dumps a bundle of clothes (that I know instantly there is absolutely NO WAY I will be wearing), then ducks outside and comes back again with my din-dins: a measly bowl of very un-chef-y looking soup (*canned?!*) (that I know instantly there is no way I will be eating) and a plastic bottle of water (for comedy value, I expect).

And that's it. The biosuit leaves again without speaking so much as a word.

The overhead lights snap off, and I pull the lamp back in front of my face and try to get back to the beach…but it seems to have been moved to a war zone.

At first I think I am imagining it, but then it comes again… GUNSHOTS. Distant, but—again! It must have stopped raining…because the revolution has surely started!

The SAS would have a fit, because instead of taking cover (which I'm sure is the sort of thing they would advise), I shove my lamp out of the way to get to the window—and I am greeted by the horrific sight of my own reflection.

My hair may be an excellent pink, even in the reflection I can so see that…but I have zombie mascara runoff in the bags under my unsleeping eyes. My head looks like a death skull. And when I grin at it, to reassure it, it's worse: my missing tooth and the glint of braces complete the effect. I press my forehead against the skull's, then cup my hands around my face; I see through her, through the bars, to the shadow of me on the wall of the building opposite. This is my view: a tiny gap and a blank wall.

And on that wall, there she stands: my shadow in a square of light. There is another square of light next to my square of light, and from that square of light that comes from the cell next door, another human shadow stares out.

If I didn't know better, I'd think…I wave at the other shadow. It waves back.

Oh my heart! It pounds. That nerdish shadow…

It fumbles with its lamp, and on the wall opposite I see a shadow-puppet dog appear, made by a nerdish hand.

Hn. I find a smile. It *is* him. I smile bigger. HE IS ALIVE.

I get my lamp angled and—ha! My silent, happy shadow dog appears on the wall.

His dog tips up its head. It howls love for me.

My shadow dog howls back.

KZZZZ!

In an instant, the dogs are gone, zapped into oblivion as the overhead lights in my room snap on. I don't even have time to make a dive for the bed before my cell door is yanked open.

"Hello, Ruby," says Ms. TVSOYMMSTTVCOMB. "How nice to see you've finally found a friend."

I switch the light off. My legs feel a little shaky. I have to sit down on the bed. Gunshots in the distance. Ms. TVSOYMMSTTVCOMB (she is immaculate, as usual) frowns at me.

"You've caused us a lot of trouble," she says.

That's the sort of thing they say in films, isn't it? The sort of thing they say before something really awful happens…torture, most likely, followed by death.

"But we'll discuss that in the morning, eh, Ruby?" she says—and yawns. She actually has the nerve to yawn. "After I've had a *chat* with your little friend next door."

"You're just trying to scare me," I tell her…but really I am telling myself.

"I haven't even started," she says, and goes to shut the door. "Oh! Wait! I almost forgot!" She chucks a pad and pen down on the bed—*my* pad and pen; there's the page full of death-ish doodles. "Just in case you remember something useful."

"I don't *know* how I got like this," I tell her—and I swallow, tasting the memory of a rotten apple that came from a well filled with water that only people more doomed than me believed could help them.

She hesitates, gazing steadily at me. I swallow again, wishing the rotten taste would just go.

"Oh, Ruby…you've remembered something, haven't you?"

I stare right on back at her, trying to produce THE GRIN OF INDIFFERENCE but failing. Failing. Failing.

"Hn," she says.

I feel a freezing chill crack through my bones as she smiles—icily—and shuts the door.

The second it locks, I grab my lamp. Who else in the world says "Hn" except the Spratt?! She's been on to him—questioning him—already! I need to communicate with him. I need to—*Stop*, my brain tells my hand, and the message reaches my heart, and my heart agrees. I make myself wait for the overhead lights to go off.

They do not go off.

After a while, I notice it: what I can only assume is a camera, hidden inside a small, dark, glass bubble, up above the door.

The SAS really would be ashamed of me. Very, very poor reconnaissance.

I lie down and shut my eyes.

After a while longer, the overhead lights do go out.

I am not asleep, not at all, but even though the darkness terrifies me, I do not switch my lamp back on. I roll over. I stare at the window. So dark in that nowhere space between the buildings, you'd hardly know there was a wall right there. But I know there is, and I know Darius is also staring at the wall. I wish we could just at least be together. I wish it so hard I can see invisible shadow dogs howl.

There is no let up. Every half hour, a biosuit snaps the overhead lights on and comes in to "check" on me. I know it's every half hour because when I got snappy and said, "Weren't you here ten minutes ago?!" my keeper checked his clipboard and his watch and said, "Twenty-eight minutes." Then, when he came back what felt like five minutes after that, he said, "Thirty-three minutes," before I'd even opened my mouth about it. "I'll try to make it thirty-four next time," he said. (Great, I am SO being guarded by comedians.)

Sometime, when it's still dark—proper dark, not even vaguely dawn—I hear some kind of alarm or siren join the random gunshots. I feel sick. This place, everything about it, makes me feel sick. Everything about everything makes me feel sick.

The darkness chokes me. Still, I will not switch on that lamp. I will not let them see my fear or my feelings…for the boy next door.

The overhead lights come on yet again; a biosuit pops his head around the door.

"Who's fighting?" I ask him before he can go again. "Out there—who's fighting?"

"Pretty much everyone," he says.

I crack. "Please! Don't go! PLEASE."

He ducks out of the door and switches off the lights. Ducks back in.

"There's a little bit of a disagreement about who should be in charge," he whispers, "and unfortunately the people who are in charge aren't that keen on discussing it. Do you understand?"

As a basic scenario, I get that.

"It's the army, isn't it? They're the ones in charge."

"No," he says. "But they are the ones with the most guns, so it's quite important that they make the right choice. Just be patient, sweetie," he whispers.

Sweetie. He called me sweetie.

"And try not to be afraid. You're safe here."

"*Ibrahim?!*"

He is silent.

"I'm scared," I tell him. "I don't feel safe."

"This place," he says, thumping the wall, "is bombproof."

Now I really, really don't feel safe—we could get bombed?!

"And we have *security*," he says. "Watching at *all times*. Trust me, sweetie: *everything's going to be OK.*"

He leaves and I lie back down. I try to sleep. I do the colors/shapes thing… It refuses to work…to begin with…but trust me: no matter how troubled you are, just keep going with those colors and shapes and… Trust me: just keep going. Just keep going.

CHAPTER THIRTY

Ah. Here we go. This is what a revolution is like when you're not involved in the exciting parts.

This is what a revolution is like when you are in the eye of the storm:

Nothing happened. (To begin with.)

I finally fell asleep and I actually slept because…after Ibrahim left, no came back. No one woke me up again until I woke myself up. In a somewhat cranky state. I'd be cranky anyway (who wouldn't be?), but honestly…more gunshots, more sirens went off as I prowled circuits of my cell, just like you see poor animals do in zoos.

Still, no one came.

You know what? Why keep quiet any longer?

It was *annoying*.

I yell and kick at the cell door.

There is a gap at the bottom of the door, a gap just big enough to shout out of.

"Hey?! HEY?! HELLO?! HEY!" I shout…just like I heard prisoners in Dartbridge Police Station shout—a lifetime ago, seems like.

And now I truly get how terrifying that must have been. What if no one comes?

I hear Darius kicking and shouting back.

I kick hell out of my door again.

I hurt my toe. I *really* hurt my toe.

I'm sitting on my bed, nursing that hurt toe, when Beardy opens the door.

I rush to get out, and he does this terrified, "No! Don't get me!" cowering thing that Dan would have done (which would have made me get Dan even more. Brother-brat beloved). But this is a grown-up, the most important microbiologist left in the country. I'm not about to get him, so I get a grip—the second the door is safely behind me.

"Ruby?! Ruby?!" Darius hollers.

"What's going on?" I ask Beardy.

"Time to go," he says, walking off.

I trot after him. (Going past the prof's cell, I see it's in an even worse state than it was before. Less in there, but oh so much more messy. It's kind of impressive.)

"Go where?"

"RUBY!" yells the Spratt.

"Yeah—just a sec!" I yell back. "Go *where*?"

"I'm not quite sure," he says.

Excuse me…

"I fired off a few emails…"

You've got email?! The army has got email?!

"And, well, it could all end up being a little awkward, really."

Awkward?!

"The Americans are keen to have us—"

Us?! Who?!

"—but the Russians aren't going to let us go without a fight. They've got the real phage expertise, you see."

Excuse me?!

"Still, you'd hope that under the circumstances, day and age, etc.… I suppose it could be China… How would you feel about China?" he says to me, marching past cages of cute pets.

Ahead of us, there is a glass wall, a laboratory inside. Behind that, there is another glass wall: huge steel tanks inside…that look like…like a brewery. Seen drums like that before at Buckfast Abbey, when me, Mom, and Simon stopped off on a tedious walk…and then Mom had to walk back and get the car and drive us home because Simon sampled too much of the monks' lethal concoction.

Beardy is already keying in a code on a security pad and opening up the glass doors to the lab.

"*RUBY?!*" Darius yells.

"JUST A SEC!" I yell back.

I run into the lab after Beardy, who is rummaging through a mess of papers.

"Do you mean *me?*"

"What?"

"*Us*—who's going where? Do you mean me?"

"Of course I mean you," says Beardy, his brow deeply furrowed like he cannot quite believe I could ask such a stupid question.

"But I don't want to go to any of those places."

"Really?!" says Beardy. "Not even America? We'll be *world famous stars*, I tell you." He whispers to me: "I think they're sending a private jet."

For 0.1 micrometers of a milli-nanosecond I am lost in an image of me and Beardy lounging on that private jet, then climbing down one of those wheel-up stairways onto the tarmac…someplace nice and sunny. People cheering, taking photos, that kind of thing.

"*RUBY!*" I hear the Spratt scream.

"Hey, my friend's in there," I tell him, pointing back at the cells—but Beardy isn't interested.

"Um, now…" he says, picking through papers. Papers that are marked up with notes, blazing with lurid highlighter colors. The guy's a nerd. Total nerd.

"Can you just let my friend out?" I ask him politely. Any second now, I'm going to run out of my very—VERY—limited reserves of politeness.

"Grab that bag," he says.

Now, see, when Hollywood comes back and this whole story gets made into a movie and I get begged to star in it, I want this whole scene rewritten. (Actually, there is quite a lot that I would like rewritten, but it's this scene that troubles me most. It has GOT to go.) What I want in its place is…

So say the whole building is under siege—lots of explosions, gunfire, that kind of thing. Not far away; close up. Probably the Americans bust in at the last second and say, "Ruby Morris?"

"Yeah," I snarl. "Who's asking?"

And out of a cloud of smoke, this figure steps forward.

"Me," he says. (It's the President of the United States of America, obviously.)

I square my chin proudly. "You're a little late, aren't you?"

"Yes, sorry about that," he says.

A colossal explosion happens. I am the only one who does not cower in terror.

"Sometimes…sorry isn't good enough," I say coolly. "But I accept your apology."

I don't even wait for him to respond. "Keys," I bark at Beardy. He chucks them to me and I commando leap through a wall of flame to get to Darius's cell. I unlock it and—uh, this part is going to take

308

some working out, because something has to happen so me and Dar don't just run hand in hand through smoke and flame to freedom. I want to be carried out. I just want to know what that feels like… I know! I get overcome by smoke at the last moment (but it looks worse than it is; I'm going to recover), so Dar (weeping—that'd be good) has to carry me through smoke and flames.

"She was only ever trying to help," he gets to sob at the president as we emerge from the building.

And I get to cough a bit weakly.

All around, people gasp. "That's Ruby Morris! Thank you, Ruby… Thank you!" they cry and I—

Oh, what's the point?! What happens instead is I grab the bag Beardy wants—it's one of those giant "eco-friendly" supermarket shopping bags (they're very useful)—and hold it open so he can dump the papers in.

This is what is technically known as *superficial compliance*, i.e., going along with whatever the parenty/teachery/scientisty-type person wants in order to ease the often complex process of getting what you want. It is a highly risky technique, because you might just end up doing whatever it is they want and still get told no about whatever it is you want. In this case, that's exactly what happens.

"Come on, then!" says Beardy.

"You need to let my friend out," I tell him.

"No, it's OK," says Beardy, "I just need one of you. Backup supply in case I lose the phage samples. Always losing things…"

I dump the bag. "I'm not going anywhere without Darius."

"Is he your boyfriend?" Beardy asks, squinting curiously at me.

"I…I…"

For a moment, I am gripped by a school flashback, imagining I am being asked this question in front of the entire cafeteria. I am being asked whether Darius Spratt, subnerd of subnerds, is my boy-friend. And I answer.

"Yes."

"Oh," mutters Beardy in a mildly interested sort of way as he revisits a pile of papers.

YEE-HAA. "LET HIM GO!" I screech.

Startled, Beardy stops what he is doing…and I follow him back to the cells to release the yelling Spratt.

You will notice, again, that this story is not quite over.

Darius and I kiss passionately in the way that only two **FREAKS** who love each other can do.

Until we are interrupted.

There is a terrible kerfuffle going on outside. So terrible we are forced to break off from the kissing to investigate. As we round the corner, we see how it is: it's the revolution! A bunch of ordinary-looking people—you know, people who just look like people's moms and dads—are trying to bust into the scientists' pet shop.

"Hey," I yell at Beardy, who's back in the lab reading some paper or other. "You gonna let them in?!"

"What?" he says, looking up.

"We're being rescued!"

"Oh, yes," he says, like he has also only just noticed the revolu-tion has arrived. "Just a moment…" And he goes back to what he was reading.

But we are not being rescued.

And there will be no need for Beardy to open the door, because when I look back at it, Ms. TVSOYMMSTTVCOMB is keying in the entrance code. She is shoved out of the way (hurray!) as the good, ordinary folk bust in to poke their way through the pet shop (I only hope they're thinking about rehoming the poor fluffy ones, and not stewing them up for dinner)…but among them I spot not-so-good, not-so-ordinary folk: Xar, Court members… no Grace.

"Dar, this is bad," I blurt and run for the lab.

I don't see what happens behind me. I just thought Darius would be right there. It's only when Beardy slams the lab door shut that I see Darius Spratt is on the other side of it.

"These people. They tried to kill me—twice," I jabber, watching the Court approach the lab…they're armed. Dar just standing there. Why's Dar just standing there?!

Xar tests the door—the fact that it is now locked does not comfort me.

"That guy, he's in charge of them! He's a psycho! He just wants to kill everybody!"

"Ooh," says Beardy.

"Everybody! He thinks the planet would be better off without people!"

"Well…" says Beardy. "Got a point in a way, hasn't he? I mean, environmentally speaking we—"

"He'll kill me!"

Someone hands Xar a gun.

"He'll kill you!" I try; Beardy's weird calmness is sending me into desperation yee-haa overdrive. "He'll destroy the rockety thing!"

"I'm sorry?"

"THE PHAGE!"

"Well, that wouldn't do at all," says Beardy. "But don't worry. That glass is bombproof and—"

A bullet comes shattering through the glass wall. Beardy falls.

He is shot, blood erupting from his shoulder as he crawls for the brewery door.

311

"DO SOMETHING!" I scream at him as another bullet smashes through the glass—and the Court comes smashing their way in after it, using anything they can get their hands on to bust their way through.

"We-must-release-the-phage," Beardy gasps, clawing his way up to standing and frantically keying in a code. "We-must-purge-the-tank."

He slumps in through the brewery door, and I slam it behind us.

"Purge!" moans Beardy, sinking to his knees.

I look at the steel drums; I see a set of buttons on each. On top of a red button, separated from the rest, covered by a plastic flip-top cover, I see:

PURGE

I hardly even know what that word means. I look at Beardy, shaking my head, suddenly unsure about trusting him.

"It-will-go-down-the-drain-and-into-the-sewer-and-into-the-treatment-works-and-into-the-river-and—"

Before I can point out that I do know that stuff, actually (because we did it in geography), he collapses completely. He's bleeding. A lot. Trying to stem the flow of his own blood as he groans, "Where-are-the-✱-Yanks? Where-are-the-✱-Russians? The-✱-Chinese?"

I sure wish someone would come. We are going to die in a hail of bullets in a glass-walled lab filled with giant tanks of nose juice because I look up from the horror of the bleeding, swearing professor to see the Court has assembled in the lab.

King Xar cocks his head at me, like a dog would, trying to understand a most curious thing.

He fires his gun at the phage brewery.

"Ha!" gasps Beardy, so totally pleased that the bullet hardly even dents the glass. It ricochets—and the Court ducks. This place *is* bombproof and bulletproof and soundproof. From in here we can hear next to nothing… It's just unfortunate that we can *see* absolutely everything. That would include Ms. TVSOYMMSTTVCOMB, who strolls on into the room behind the Court.

"Oh no!" I shriek at the sight of her, my eyes widening.

To be honest with you, I have no idea what she was going to do…and I never will know—because Xar sees the look on my face, misunderstands it, and makes his move; in an instant, he has hold of her, gun against her head. He marches her up to the glass.

"Purge!" Beardy pants, gasping horribly with pain.

Xar stares at me. Ms. TVSOYMMSTTVCOMB stares at me. This must be pretty bad for her. In fact, I would say that *I* am now *her* Ms. TVSOYMMSTTVCOMB. I would say that the very sight of me must be making her sick to the very core of her being, and that she must be wishing quite hard that she had been a bit nicer to me. Or not. Her mouth is moving…but it doesn't exactly look like she's pleading for her life. ✹ knows what on Earth she must be saying to Xar, probably offering him halfsies on a few countries or something. I don't think Xar's that interested. It's the whole planet he wants. As he stares too, the tiniest flicker of a smile creeps onto his face. It is for me.

"He'll kill her," I say out loud.

"So?" Beardy gasps, and groans in agony. "Purge!"

Like, really, seems to me that the prof could have spared everyone this hideousness if he'd just quietly purged the phage himself when no one was looking, but I guess he's been up to his own international wheeling and dealing. But this is not the time to go into such matters.

I am *paralyzed*. Can't move. Can't handle this situation. Can't even look at it…so I look away. I see Dar.

A zap, a lightning bolt, of emotion goes through me, but I

grab it and I stop it and I look back at Xar, and I realize I was not quick enough.

Xar grins…and turns his head. Dar just standing there. Why's he just standing there?

His glasses. He's lost his glasses.

SO HERE IT IS, HOLLYWOOD. HERE IT IS. THIS IS THE END.

Xar lets go of Ms. TVSOYMMSTTVCOMB. And maybe she was more panicked than she looked because she crumples on the spot. For a second, it looks like all Xar is doing is leaving the lab—but only for a second. He grabs Darius.

And puts the gun to Darius's head, and as he walks the Spratt toward me, Darius's expression changes. He sees me.

And I see him.

Darius Spratt. We have been on a long journey. We are both tired. So tired.

Dar's free hand creeps up in front of his body. It makes the shape of a dog's head…that slowly points its nose to the sky and howls.

"*I love you,*" I whisper.

I know he cannot hear, but I know he *sees*.

This is what I have to do.

My heart—my small, sad, human heart—it shed one final tear.

Journey's end. I pressed the button.

So that's it. That's how I saved the planet. I pressed the button that launched the rockety thing that saved the earth.

It might seem like a lot of other people were involved, but basically anyone can see that it was all down to me.

The End

D ar is watching me write this part. He's laughing his head off (IT'S QUITE ANNOYING) and he says there is NO WAY he's going to let me get away with that ending.

He also likes to claim that NO WAY was he giving me any kind of signal that it was OK for me to go ahead and do what I did, that it was a simple "I love you" howling dog hand shape and not an "I love you, and yes it's absolutely fine for you to sacrifice me for the good of humanity bye-bye" howling dog hand shape.

But we both know that's not true.

Anyway, Xar held the gun against Darius's head for what felt like an eternity longer, during which time I became vaguely aware that Beardy was making *really* horrible and *slightly* strange, pained, choking noises that seemed appropriately death-ish, considering what was going on.

I stopped looking at Darius and looked at Xar instead. I have no conscious memory of this, but Dar says I smiled. I've got him to show me how I smiled, and I can confirm that it was THE GRIN OF INDIFFERENCE.

What *I* remember is that Xar slowly cocked his head at me again and smiled. I don't know how to describe that smile. "Creepy" just doesn't cut it.

As Xar lowered the gun, he said something. I couldn't hear, of course, but I knew what it was before Darius even told me.

"See you around, Ladybird."

And we all watched him walk out of that lab—which he could do, because it was chaos out there, just chaos.

THE END

Oh, shut your face, Darius—all right, all right…

OK, so something happened.

Turned out that although Beardy was very horribly injured, the *really* horrible and *slightly* strange, pained, choking noises were about something else entirely. As soon as Xar had gone, he let go of his wound, raised up a pointy finger, and—

"Not *that* tank," he screamed, writhing in agony, "*that* one!"

Oh.

I hit PURGE again.

What can you do?

Whatever was in that first tank (even Beardy had no clue), no one I know of has grown three heads or anything. I'm sure it's all fine.

THE END

THE PART AFTER THE END

So here we are.

We?

Me, Dar, and the Princess who is called Priti.

We are in Spain, but where the specific "here" is I am not prepared to say, just in case everything goes horribly wrong all over again. Also, the Lancaster people have basically begged me not to tell anyone.

I went with the professor in the ambulance. I wanted to just go, to leave. But me and Dar went with him.

The prof was not especially grateful about any of it…but before Beardy really did get to fly off on a private jet to a country I am not supposed to name, he told me what he thought:

"Mucus exchange," he called it, his "theory," which means, basically, that the snot out of my nose was enough to save people. If I kissed them. A lot.

A prettier name for it might be "The Kiss of Life."

I told him I had seen a boy I'd kissed die in front of me…and he was really disappointed…but then he perked up, to YIPPEE! levels—that made nurses rush in to check he was OK—when I admitted I hadn't *actually seen* Caspar McCloud die.

So…scientifically, it is possible that Caspar McCloud is still alive. Also…Andrew Difford.

Like, really, hear me now:

If I see either of you again, you are **SO** *gonna wish the rain* had *gotten you.*

The Princess who is called Priti remains a mystery.

I kissed Darling the Chihuahua, and Darling the Chihuahua lickily kissed Priti…but Priti, who does now speak a little on a regular basis, says she has always been this way, from the very first night that—

She walked out of a car wreck in the pouring rain.

Her whole family died.

A mom, a dad…a brother.

A brother she adored.

Thirteen years old.

It is a mystery how she survived, one possibly involving yet another fairy/leper/hope-of-the-hopeless well, but I have yet to ask her about this.

I know what it feels like to be asked questions about a past it hurts to remember.

When Priti does speak, she swears a lot. I tell her off for it, even though everyone swears all the time.

There is no need for it, I tell her.

Obviously, there is.

But.

We've been hanging out on the beach a lot, the three of us. If it wasn't for the postapocalyptic goings-on, you could say that I'm finally on vacation in the sort of place I always wanted to go on vacation to.

This doesn't make me particularly happy.

The Lancaster people are very nice to us, but somehow, we tend to keep ourselves a bit separate. We are still *different*, you see—or we think we are.

Prof Beardy was a bit hazy on exactly how long that tankful of nose juice would take to annihilate the micro-murderer space beast, though he did seem fairly confident that it "would, probably, happen eventually"—especially, if you ask me, since me, Dar, and Priti must have helped it along. I probably dosed up the whole of the Irish Sea by swimming about in that estuary.

I am now working on the Mediterranean, which is a lot more pleasant.

Glaring Barry, who, along with Psycho Catherine, joined the Confusion* at the army base, offers on a daily basis to literally test the water. He says he doesn't mind having a finger or two chopped off.

Everyone (except the keen amateur historian) is still saying no to that, but that day might yet come…because what we need is a proper testing kit, to see if the water's safe—and even though we hear rumors, like the ones about how the phones and the Internet are going to come back, nothing seems to have happened just yet.

Sort of sounds like it could be OK, doesn't it, lazing around on a beach with your true love while the environment—hopefully—sorts itself out?

Sometimes, for minutes at a time, it *is* OK…but I think I have

---

* Annoyingly, that is what people have started calling it. I was not the calm, crucial center of the storm of revolution, I was at the heart of a "confusion." Do not get me started.

yet to get through a whole hour without some awful, sad, or scary thought—and the nightmares? They haven't stopped either. I can't even say that it's getting better day by day, because it doesn't seem to work like that. You can have one day with a lot of really good minutes in it, and the next day…not.

Sometimes I find I can't be with Dar and Princess Priti, and then I just sit with Bridget for a bit. She lets me talk to her. She is not my mother, but it helps.

Bridget says none of us *will* ever forget what has happened. She says some things are so bad, they are remembered by the whole planet for thousands of years.

Yup, it's definitely actually fairly tricky for the world to get back on its feet after an apocalypse. It's hard enough getting back on your own feet. But I am. I will.

Mom, I am still breathing.

…I'd better wrap this up.

Um…what else is there to say?

Hn.

Although Darius can still annoy the ✳ out of me (he says I have to say that it's mutual), we don't fight quite as much now…but the one subject we are guaranteed to snarl about is…going home.

I want to go home.

You'd think the Spratt would be up for that; I mean, what with the prescription glasses and the prescription meds alone, he's got to have a fairly serious interest in rebuilding some kind of society where you can get stuff you need.

I have less of a serious interest since I persuaded Glaring Barry to remove my braces, although I would quite like to get a replacement tooth. Dar says I look cute without it, like a sexy pirate queen.

But he says a lot of things like that, with a goofy smile.

322

OK—OK! With a *sexy*, goofy smile. Now quit pouring sand onto my back, Dar—yes, it does feel nice, but go away and let me finish this.

He has gone. But he says I'll never finish because I don't know when to shut up.

But he said that with a sexy, goofy wink.

We **will** be going back.

I mean, I'm guessing probably the whole of the UK has gone on vacation for the winter, but we'll go back.

I know this in my heart—where I also know Dar really feels the same. I think he is just trying to buy us all time.

But spring is here already, in this place so far from home; in the UK, it'll just be getting going. There will be daffodils flowering on the bank where Zak's mom, Sarah, chewed wheel ruts into the mud trying to get me home—on that night, the very first night when the rain fell…

No, I'm stopping myself. I'm not going to do this. That world has gone.

In the new world that I sort of keep feeling like maybe we should lend a hand with, I'm not sure what I'm up for doing exactly. I'm not even sure that I'd be up for doing much. In some ways I feel, like… So maybe I already did enough?

And also: But what could I do? I'm officially useless, remember?

Where I will start is with what I need to do. I want to put a copy of this story in Dartbridge Library, right next to my earlier epic tale of survival. I want to do this just in case people in the future need to know what happened. No more lies must be told.

I want to do that and then go look for Whitby… He *cannot* be dead. My mind refuses to allow the possibility. And sometimes my mind is right.

And then—is it wrong that this comes last?—go look for my dad.

I have ended up where I started: *Where is my dad?*

And this is where I have the Spratt for sure. He wants to look for his mother.

Together, we'll go and do that.

With the Princess. With Priti.

I will start asking her questions about the rest of her family—about grandmas and grandpas and aunts and uncles and cousins—but I will do it very gently, because I know how much this stuff hurts.

We are the orphaned children of the apocalypse, and we will come home.

Also: ***the British Army has got my cell phone.***

ACKNOWLEDGMENTS

I would like to thank:
My family.
Steve Geck, Kate Prosswimmer, Elizabeth Boyer,
Alex Yeadon, and the team at Sourcebooks.
In the UK, Rachel Petty, Helen Bray, and the
team at Macmillan Children's Books.
My agent, Louise Lamont, at LBA Books.

Dr. Matthew Avison (University of Bristol), for kindly
providing excellent scientific advice. Again, I am very
sorry about the made-up bits. I blame Ruby.

My consultants: Ruby T, Stan, Aidan, Kate, and
Luke…and their Taunton and Totnes families.

The readers…since *H20* was published in 2014, your support
and encouragement has meant everything to me. To the people
who emailed and tweeted, who blogged and vlogged:
thank you so much!

I would also like to thank my lovely friends, big and small. Most
especially: Hilary Hunt, Donovan Hawley, and Jackie Pridham.

The fabulous Hilary Beard.

My friends and neighbors in Hotwells, Bristol.

And:
Alice, Lucy, Benedict, Finn, Héloïse, Isadora, Nathan, and Rosie.

Vx

There are many books about clouds and about survival. The ones I have are the following: *The Cloud Book: How to Understand the Skies* by Richard Hamblyn, and *SAS Survival Guide: How to Survive in the Wild, on Land or at Sea* by John "Lofty" Wiseman.

ABOUT THE AUTHOR

Virginia Bergin grew up in Abingdon, Oxfordshire, and went on to study psychology, but ruined her own career when, while dabbling in fine art at Central Saint Martins, she rediscovered creative writing. Since then she has written poetry, short stories, film and TV scripts, and a play that almost got produced—but didn't. In between and alongside more jobs than you've had hot dinners, she has worked as a writer on TV, eLearning and corporate projects, and has twenty-two broadcast and non-broadcast TV credits. Most recently she has been working in online education, creating interactive courses for The Open University.

She currently lives on a council estate in Bristol and has taken to feeding the birds.

Visit her at virginiabergin.com.